Other Titles By
Giselle Carmichael

I'LL BE YOUR SHELTER

LACE

MAGNOLIA SUNSET

The Politics
of Love

Dedication

To Donna and Varner
May you be blessed with a lifetime of love and happiness.

Acknowledgements

I'd like to thank Parker Publishing, LLC for welcoming me to the team. Deatri, your talents are greatly appreciated.

To my Biloxi family, Terry, David, Mary, Larry, Charles, and Ruth Anne, thanks for your years of friendship and support.

And to the numerous fans who have encouraged me to continue to dream and create, I hope you enjoy.

Chapter One

Fuming with anger, Eden Warner waited in the dark wings of the school's auditorium. Instead of being in class, her third graders stood on stage preparing to play backdrop for mayoral candidate Chase Mathews. One of four men vying for the office, his candidacy announcement was received with a great deal of excitement. However, as time ticked by and her students remained out of the classroom, missing subject after subject, Eden's patience was wearing thin. School children belonged in the classroom, and anyone who valued education would not support pulling them out of class for the purpose of being props to a political campaign.

She looked out into the growing audience and noticed the large campaign poster taped to the back wall. The man was a hottie, which was no doubt the reason for the large number of women sitting out in the audience. The men, on the other hand, were there to see and be near one of the city's power players. Well-bred and educated, Chase Mathews had a reputation for solving problems and making money. Actually, he was exactly what the city of Hilton needed. A neighbor to Atlanta, Hilton possessed many of the same problems as the sprawling city. The current mayor was a nice man, but unfortunately, had made some really poor decisions on behalf of his constituents. Feeling the heat and some recent health problems, he had decided to withdraw from the office, hence the need for a special election. The citizens hoped for a brighter future with the announcement of Chase's candidacy. To be honest, Eden too was hopeful. His announcement speech was well thought out and refreshingly informative. He clearly spelled out his desire for the city, and avoided using tried and true clichés. For those reasons, she didn't understand the need for this press conference at the school. It rang with insincerity.

The Politics of Love

The noise in the auditorium raised several decibels. She peeked from behind the heavy curtain as the throng of print and television reporters crowded around. They were like ants, scurrying for the best location to see and be seen. Today they would be the candidate's best friend, but by the end of the campaign season, they would be picking the flesh from his bones for a better story. Her students didn't need to be a part of such an event. They belonged in class preparing for their futures. But what did these people care? Most were far removed from the lives her students led.

"This really ticks me off," Eden complained to fellow teacher and friend, Angie Thompson, who stood to her right. She continued to watch the well-dressed audience, oozing prosperity.

"What does?"

"How candidates magically appear with the press in tow, at the nearest public school when it's time for election speeches and photographs to be taken. Where was this guy when the library's computers were stolen and we were literally begging the public for replacements? And look at his supporters. How many do you think attended a public school?"

"I don't know, but that doesn't mean people don't care."

"I know that, Angie. But it's disgusting how our children are used as political props during the campaign season, yet ignored the rest of the year."

"Wait a minute. I thought you liked this guy?"

"I do … I did. This staged press conference leaves a bad taste in my mouth," Eden explained. "I don't like politicians pulling our children out of class for the sole purpose of promoting their agendas. It seems phony…like going around kissing babies."

"I believe Mathews is genuine. He really wants to revamp the city's school system," the voluptuous blonde replied.

"They're all genuine about their promises during the campaign season, but once that final ballot is counted, their promises go right out the window."

"You're being a little cynical aren't you?"

"I'm being honest. Mathews doesn't care about our children.

How can he, when he hasn't stepped one foot inside the classroom? Before you can make an agenda, you have to know what the issues are, and he doesn't."

"You don't know that." Angie folded her arms over her ample chest.

Eden gave her *a get real* look. "You know like I do that he hasn't visited any school. If he had, it would have been captured in black and white by the parade of reporters following him. They simply sit down and scribble the usual buzz words across a pad and think people are gullible enough to believe their every word."

"Honey, give the man a chance. He hasn't even stepped on stage yet."

"Okay, I'll give him a chance, but he sure better have something worth listening to."

"And what would that be?" Angie asked, annoyed. She was there to get a glimpse of the handsome mayoral candidate. The fact that he was a bachelor made his appearance there all the more exciting.

Eden picked up on the irritation, but chose to ignore it. "For starters, a sincere candidate would announce he's actually going to spend some time in the classroom, learning and observing before attempting to develop a plan."

"You aren't serious?" Angie glared at her. "Do you actually expect a candidate to do that?"

"Most definitely, if he's interested in improving the state of education, he should first educate himself, either by speaking to a committee of educators, or by getting inside the classroom." She looked over at her friend. "You know as well as I do that education is so much more than the books nowadays. There are real issues to be dealt with before we ever get down to teaching. These guys need to know that if they're going to make improvements," Eden responded passionately. She folded her arms with annoyance.

Angie nodded. "You're right, but it doesn't work like that."

"Well, maybe it should." Eden glanced back out into the growing crowd of reporters and supporters. "If we could drum up just half this enthusiasm for our schools on a daily basis, we could really improve things."

"Keep dreaming."

"Yeah, well, you keep dreaming Chase Mathews is going to sweep you off your feet."

Angie scowled at her friend. "Go ahead and burst my bubble, Eden Warner. I'll have you know that a lady has to utilize every opportunity to search for her true love."

Eden chuckled. "And you believe Chase Mathews is yours?"

"A girl can hope."

"Get real. That man isn't married by choice. He's either a playboy or gay."

"You think?" Angie asked, alarmed.

Eden laughed. "No. I was just running off at the mouth."

"But you're probably right about his being a playboy. However, it doesn't hurt to hope."

"You keep hoping he'll notice you, and I'll keep hoping that he says something worth listening to." Eden waved to her students who were growing more restless by the minute. "This guy had better show before the natives revolt."

"We wouldn't want that, now would we?" a male voice spoke from behind them.

Eden turned quickly, searching through the darkness of the backstage area to make out an emerging figure. As it came forward, she recognized mayoral candidate, Chase Mathews. Her stomach dropped.

Chase greeted the two women with his trademark charismatic smile, while sizing them up. He couldn't miss the fact they both looked guilty. The blonde quickly scurried away, making an excuse, while the African American woman held her ground with her head up, shoulders back, and spine stiff. He liked a woman with a backbone and couldn't help but admire her.

He also liked a woman who knew how to dress. This woman definitely had an eye for fine clothing, as the knit two-piece classic gray suit indicated. The skirt stopped fashionably above her knees, showcasing incredible legs that ran for miles. The black suede boots she wore were sexy and prompted all types of scandalous thoughts.

"Chase Mathews." He stuck out his hand to her.

Eden tried to determine whether or not he had been listening to their conversation as she accepted the offered handshake. "Eden Warner … Ah, it's a pleasure to meet you." Their eyes met and held a beat too long, before Chase thought to withdraw his hand and glance away. Eden followed suit, worried that the man had heard their conversation.

"Is it?" Chase asked, as an afterthought.

"Is it what?" Eden couldn't think past the man's good looks. His handsome face possessed a strong, commanding jaw line.

"Is it a pleasure to meet me?"

Eden met his gaze, and for some foolish reason, believed that her response was important to him. "Of course it's a pleasure to meet you, Mr. Mathews. You're the talk of the town."

"That's Chase, and it's a pleasure meeting you as well." He stood a moment, simply looking at her. "I didn't realize the press conference would cause such a disruption," he stated sincerely. "I thought it would be an in and out operation."

"Afraid not, but I'm interested to hear what you have to say." His earnestness didn't go unnoticed. It caused her to feel better about him. Her eyes wandered over his handsome face. Standing this close to the man, she realized he was far more handsome in person than on television. He was downright gorgeous. Now she understood why the majority of his campaign supporters were women. He was tall, with thick dark hair, stunning blue eyes and a wide, kissable mouth crafted by the devil himself. This man was hot.

Chase admired the woman standing before him. He liked a woman with height. "You might be surprised by what I have to say, Mrs. Warner."

"It's *Miss*," Eden readily supplied. She felt surprisingly feminine standing with him. At six feet tall, she rarely felt dainty in a man's presence, but Chase Mathews had to be at least six-three or four. "I might," she responded politely.

"Do I detect a hint of cynicism?" His eyes looked deeply into hers. The chocolate brown color of them was warm and vibrant with intelligence.

"More like boredom," Eden replied, arching her left brow. The movement drew attention to the intriguing little black mole next to her eye. "You political types tend to say the same old thing. It would be refreshing to hear something new."

Chase laughed with gusto. The richness of the sound was filled with warmth that drew one closer. "I can assure you, *Miss* Warner, you'll never be bored by me." His eyes locked with hers as the words hung in the air between them.

Eden's brows rose in response. She suddenly had the distinct impression that the man was talking about something other than his speech. Liking the sound of his voice, she slowly joined him in laughter. But, uncertain of what she read in his eyes, she glanced away before being pulled in to whatever game Chase Mathews was playing. Her eyes landed on her students as she suddenly remembered she and Chase weren't alone in the universe. But it sure had felt that way when he looked at her.

"It's been a pleasure, but I see my spokesperson waving at me," Chase said, drawing her attention back to him. He secured the button to his blue jacket. "I'm sure you'll have plenty to say after my speech, so I'll see you later." He turned and walked away. Then as an afterthought, he turned back around. "Miss Warner."

"Yes?"

"I'm definitely not gay." Chase winked at her before heading back toward the stage and signaling his spokesperson that he was ready to begin.

Eden gasped with shock as she watched him go. She grinned to herself as she quickly took the steps leading to the auditorium floor, locating a place to stand in the crowded auditorium along the side wall. From this vantage point, she would be able to experience the full impact of the candidate's speech. The man intrigued her. Feeling an atmosphere of anticipation, she glanced around the room. The women waited with bated breath, while the men looked on with admiration. Hoping the man was more than simply a pretty face, Eden stood there.

Angie slid in next to her as Chase finally walked out on stage. "What did he say?" she whispered to Eden.

"Nothing much."

"Are you sure? He was talking with you for quite a while for nothing."

Eden barely listened. She was distracted by the sight of Chase's commanding stride and broad shoulders.

"Did he hear our conversation and threaten to report us to Principal Daniels?"

"Ah, he heard some, but didn't threaten us." She continued to watch Chase.

"Hopefully he won't."

"Yeah, hopefully." Eden watched the man behind the podium. At that very moment, a pair of mesmerizing blue eyes looked down and connected with hers.

"Is he looking at you?" Angie glanced at Eden, but found her friend returning the candidate's gaze. "Now I know something was said."

Chase stood at the podium, looking at the woman he wouldn't soon forget. He waited for the exuberant applause to die down. As it did, he launched into his well-rehearsed speech. Today, he was laying out his blueprint for Hilton's educational system. But as he spoke the familiar words, the hollowness of each one reached his ears. His eyes scanned the room, before once more making contact with the beautiful woman whose words he couldn't ignore. She looked at him with great expectation, and he realized in that very moment he didn't want to disappoint her.

"I'm going to detour from my speech," Chase announced, pausing to look down at Eden.

"Oh no," she whispered under her breath.

"I would instead like to tell you about a conversation I overheard while waiting to come on stage today," he continued.

"Oh, God!" Eden softly cried with alarm. She stared into his smiling face.

"Miss Warner over there," Chase said, pointing her out, "issued a challenge of sorts. She said that if a candidate was sincere about improving the education system, then he should spend time in the classroom, educating himself about the need. I find myself in agreement with her and have therefore decided to spend a week in her classroom, with Principal Daniels' permission of course."

Eden leaned against the wall for support. "Please tell me he didn't just say what I think he did," she spoke low so only Angie could hear.

"He did, and now Principal Daniels knows what we said."

Chase could tell Eden was upset with him, but the thought of spending a week with her in the classroom was worth it. She was passionate about her profession and just the type of person he would love to have on his education committee. And something about the lady, that he wasn't prepared or ready to acknowledge, appealed to him.

The reporters went wild upon his announcement. The flashbulbs were going off one after the other. Principal Daniels, who was always thrilled when Barrett Elementary made the press, beamed for the cameras as he publicly extended the invitation. Then the reporters' attention focused on Eden as they crowded in on her.

"Miss Warner, may we have a picture?"

"Will you be supporting Mr. Mathews?"

Eden pressed herself firmly against the wall. She didn't like being in the spotlight and was looking for a way to make a graceful exit. The reporters wouldn't be denied. They gathered in closer as they fired one question after the other. "What party do you belong to?" a local newspaper reporter inquired.

She skittishly tried to make her way through the circling reporters. She wanted no part of the press. "I'm sorry, but I have to

8

get back to my students." She searched for the quickest exit.

"I'll take care of your students, Miss Warner. Take the picture," Principal Daniels said to her from the left. He was smiling broadly, pleased with the publicity.

Chase, on the other hand, could see Eden was uncomfortable with the attention. He quickly made his way down the stairs, cutting a path through the reporters to reach her side.

Eden watched as he advanced in her direction. Relief flooded her system. However, as Chase reached her, the press crowded in, forcing him in closer. He wrapped a protective arm around her waist to keep her from being trampled. The light touch of his hand on her hip was a surprise, yet not unwelcome. The man possessed the ability to make one feel secure.

"Relax and smile pretty," he whispered against her ear. Soft brown hair stroked his cheek as his warm breath caressed her sensitive flesh.

"I'm going to my students," she replied under her breath.

"Oh, no you don't. You started this, and therefore have to see it through." His arm tightened.

"I didn't start this. *You* were eavesdropping," she reminded him low and intimate.

"I was not eavesdropping. You simply didn't know I was standing there."

Eden scoffed. "Any self-respecting person would have made his presence known. You, Mr. Mathews, were indeed eavesdropping." She glared at him mindful of the press. "But I'll get you back for making me a part of this circus you call a press conference."

"It's not that bad is it?" he asked.

"You have no idea how difficult this is for me."

"Come on, you're a beautiful woman. What harm will a picture do?" Chase chuckled and drew her even closer. His eyes sparkled with humor because this woman had spirit. She stood up to him, and he liked it. He inhaled the enticing fragrance wafting from her beautiful, dark brown skin, and felt the muscles in his stomach knot with unexpected desire.

Eden delighted in the compliment. A dreamy expression quickly spread across her face as she glanced back over her shoulder, trying to gauge his sincerity. Chase flashed a heart-stopping smile meant only for her. At that very moment, the photographers began snapping away, forever capturing the moment.

"Well, it was a pleasure meeting you, Mr. Mathews." Eden turned to face him. The reporters had asked their questions and received answers. Now they were busy packing up their gear and talking amongst themselves. She and Chase were finally left alone. "You know, no one really expects you to show up on Monday."

Chase looked at her intently. "I expect me to be there Monday." He leaned forward. "One thing you should know about me is that I'm a man of my word. I'll see you promptly at eight."

In the privacy of her bedroom, Eden looked at the morning newspaper, captivated by the photograph of her and Chase. She recalled the words spoken between them and the rush of pleasure that she experienced from his compliment. The man was gorgeous, and so not the man for her. But God, she couldn't get him off her mind. The fact that he was from a prominent white family should have been enough to bring her back down to Earth, but it didn't. She was very much attracted to the man and frightened by the fact.

She tossed the newspaper onto the bed as she continued to dress for work. The time had come for her to behave like a sensible woman and not a daydreaming teenager. Chase Mathews was a known playboy and probably flirted without thought. Besides, what would he want with her, when he could have his choice of any woman in the city? Not to mention, he was in the midst of an election, with no time for a relationship. *Whoa. Who mentioned anything about a relationship?*

She quickly pushed thoughts of the man to the back of her mind. Nothing had happened between them outside of a little flirting. She grabbed her purse and satchel, containing papers that she had brought home to grade, and headed for the door. This was her reality. Chase was from the world of expensive restaurants and grand affairs. She felt foolish for giving the man so much thought. He probably hadn't thought of her once.

Chase studied the black and white photograph of himself and Eden with great interest. Their heights complemented each other. The expression captured on their faces hinted of a private moment. He wondered if anyone would notice. He wondered if Eden noticed, and whether she thought they looked good together like he did. The acknowledgement surprised him because he had never thought of himself with an African American woman. However, since their brief meeting yesterday, she was all he had thought about. He counted the hours until he joined her third-grade class Monday morning.

He continued to analyze the photograph. Deep in thought, he ran his index finger over her image. He knew nothing about her except that she was passionate about her students and wasn't intimidated by him. For the latter, he was grateful. The women in his social circle said and did what they thought would please him, each in her own unique way, vying for the title of Mrs. Mathews. He wasn't conceited, just knew it was true. However, he wanted a woman who would challenge him as well as speak her mind, and form her own opinion.

Chase folded the newspaper and placed it beside his plate. He had to get a handle on his attraction before Monday. He couldn't show up with a hard-on for the teacher. But he wanted her. He could at least be honest with himself about that much. The question, however, was whether Eden shared his desire.

"She's a beautiful woman," his grandmother commented, taking a seat. She had noticed him staring at the picture all morning. "You two make a handsome couple."

His eyes came up to meet hers. She was always able to read him so well. "She speaks her mind like someone else I know."

Belle laughed. "Good women are difficult to find. Don't miss out on something special simply because you weren't expecting it." She left him to ponder her words while attending to her paying guests.

Chase watched her work the room, while turning her words over carefully. She was right. He hadn't been expecting Eden Warner to walk into his life. Now that she had, what was he going to do about it?

Chapter Two

White chalk tapped against the blackboard as Eden placed the weekly spelling words on the board. Aware of the time, she peeked at the clock and wondered if Chase would indeed show as he had stated. A part of her hoped he would go back on his word. Then the part of her that couldn't wait to see him again, prayed he was a man of his word. She had just completed the last spelling word when the door to the classroom opened.

She straightened to her full height and returned the chalk to the tray. Her eyes met his as she turned to welcome him. She brushed the chalk from her hands.

"Welcome to third grade," she greeted him, fearful she was broadcasting her happiness to see him.

"Thank you and good morning." Chase tried to tone down his excitement of seeing her. She was dressed casually today in black slacks with low-heeled shoes and a soft pink cashmere sweater that made her skin look radiant. He was pleased he had thought to dress casual as well. This wasn't the place for tailored suits. His blue jeans and white button-down shirt with tie was perfect.

"Come on in. The bell will be ringing any moment. You can sit at my desk while you're here. I rarely use it myself," she rambled with nervousness.

Chase had never wanted to touch a woman more than he did at that very moment, simply to know if her skin was as soft and warm as it looked. Her long hair was pulled back into a ponytail today, exposing her graceful neck. As her hand touched her neck, then fell away, it became obvious to him Eden was as nervous as he was. It confirmed that she, too, had been aware of the strong pull of attraction between them last week. His eyes dropped to her hands. They were fluttering around with no destination in sight. He took the short steps that would bring him face-to-face with her, and captured them.

"I'm a little anxious myself, but I promise not to bite if you don't."

Eden laughed. She shook her head, clearing it. "I'm sorry. I don't know why I'm so scattered today."

"I think you do, but I won't push it." He met her suddenly large eyes. "So, how many students do you have?" He released her hands and walked around the room, reading the construction paper name tags taped to the desks.

"Thirty students…sixteen boys and fourteen girls, all filled with questions and boundless energy." Eden chose to let her hands drop as well.

"Wow. Do you have an aide to assist you?"

"I'm afraid not. Some of the area schools are fortunate enough to have aides, but not all."

"You must be a magician to keep all that youthful energy harnessed and directed."

"It can be a challenge some days, but for the most part, the children are well behaved and eager to learn."

"Forgive me, but I'm not familiar with the inner workings of the classroom as you said, so I hope my questions aren't a nuisance."

"This is what I want you to do. These are the things you should know when you sit down to make an agenda for the school system." She smirked shyly. "There I go again, getting on my soapbox."

Chase looked at her and smiled. "Soapbox or not, you were right to challenge me. My agenda consisted of financial and political issues. I didn't take into consideration the social issues that affect the school day."

"Believe me, we need financial help, but you have to know how and where to spend it." Eden leaned against the wall by the door. She folded her arms across her chest, unaware that the action drew Chase's attention to her breasts.

He forced his eyes away from the delectable sight. The fullness of her breasts caused his mouth to water.

"I get what you're saying. You can't simply throw money at a problem without first knowing what the actual problem *is*."

"Exactly."

The first bell rang, signaling the start of the school day. Eden looked over at Chase. "The natives are coming. Do you think you can handle it?" she teased.

"With you by my side, I can handle anything."

She stared at him, receiving a hidden message. Just as she was about to question him, her first students entered the room.

"Good morning guys," Eden greeted the two best friends. They wore identical sports jackets.

"Who's that?" Thomas Jacob asked, the moment he spotted Chase.

"We'll discuss it when the rest of the class arrives. You boys take your seats," Eden instructed. She glanced shyly at Chase before going to stand in the door of her classroom. She greeted each of her students as they crossed the threshold. Passing students yelled good morning to her as they scurried off to class. The second bell sounded. Finally, every seat was filled. She closed the door and quickly went through the morning rituals.

"Okay, class, I see all the glances in our visitor's direction. I'll introduce him, after everyone has written down the new spelling words on the blackboard. When you're finished writing them down, turn your papers over and put your pencils down. Now get busy," she ordered.

Chase watched Eden in action from the desk in the corner. She was soft-spoken, yet firm. Obviously, the students adored her. They each sought her praises and attention, as she walked up and down the rows of desks checking writing skills. In a non-criticizing manner, she gave instruction, topping it off with praise when the student did better. He could see she was born to teach.

"Is everyone finished?" Eden asked. She glanced around the room, making sure she had everyone's attention.

"Is he a new student?" Thomas, the class comedian, asked and received a series of giggles.

Eden and Chase also laughed.

"He's too big to sit in a desk, stupid," Eric, the class smarty-pants, responded.

"Settle down and no name calling," Eden said, before things got out of hand.

"I know who you are," Tasha, the shy class brain, spoke up. "You're Chase Mathews, and you're running for mayor."

"That's Mr. Mathews to you," Eden reprimanded the little girl with glasses. "But you're right. Mr. Mathews is a candidate in the special election for mayor. He'll be sitting in with us this week to observe. I want everyone to remember their manners and be on their best behavior."

A small hand shot up, waving for attention.

"Yes, Katie?" Eden addressed the class diva.

"My mama said Mr. Mathews was a babe. She said she could get lost in his blue eyes."

The class erupted into childish giggles. Eden and Chase exchanged glances before laughing themselves.

"A person can't get lost in somebody's eyes," Eric, said.

"Thanks for that tidbit of information, Katie," Eden responded, but Katie wasn't quite finished.

"What do you think, Miss Warner?"

"Think about what, Katie?"

"About Mr. Mathews being a *babe*. Could you get lost in his eyes?"

Chase barked with laughter in the corner. He was having a great time. It had been a while since he had been around little ones, and this time with the students reinforced his desire for a family.

Eden's eyes were wide with surprise as she fought the urge to look in Chase's direction. Obviously, she had no way around answering when all eyes were on her. So, she squared her shoulders and responded as best she could. "Your mother is right. Mr. Mathews is a babe and has lovely blue eyes."

"But could you get lost in them?" the little girl pushed.

Chase was anxiously awaiting Eden's answer as well. Katie had definitely put Eden on the spot and wanted a response as badly as he did. "Come on, Miss Warner. Could you get lost in them?" he repeated the question while fluttering his eyes at her.

The children giggled in response to his antics. But they all watched and waited for their teacher to answer the question.

Eden scowled at the little girl, wanting to put an end to the conversation. And for Chase, who stood in the corner laughing, she shot him a withering glare. The man was worse than the children.

"Yes, Katie, I could. They are very beautiful just like yours," she finally said, unable to avoid answering the question. She turned to Chase and stuck out her tongue. The children giggled several minutes more. How unlikely it was for their teacher to break a rule.

Eden was exhausted by the end of the day. The numerous questions about Chase and the children's thoughts about the two of them left her drained. They liked him and had continued firing questions at him. He had been a good sport, answering each one as clearly as he could for their age. But he had been just as stumped as she when they began interrogating him about his marital status. *Was he married? Why wasn't he married? And if he planned on marrying Miss Warner because she wasn't married either?* At that moment, Eden had wanted the ground to open and swallow her whole. Chase had looked at her with a long, penetrating stare, as though actually considering the question.

She could still feel the intensity of his gaze as she exited the side door of the building to the faculty parking lot. Mr. Daniels stood outside the door. On spotting her, he walked over, cutting off her exit.

"How did things go today?"

Eden loved working for Mr. David Daniels. An African American, Mr. Daniels was of average height, which meant shorter than her. He was highly educated, but knew how to speak to everyone. And, Barrett Elementary was his life and love.

"It went well. Of course, the children were curious about Mr. Mathews, but they were on their best behavior." She didn't dare tell him the children had drilled the candidate about his marital status.

"I'm happy to hear it, because Mr. Mathews has been good to us."

She looked at him, confused because she had no idea what he meant. "How so?"

He beckoned her closer and lowered his voice. "Chase doesn't want anyone to know this, but I trust you to keep a secret. You know the new computers in the library?"

"The replacements the board finally gave us?"

Mr. Daniels shook his head. "The board didn't give us those computers. Chase donated the new computers, and made sure they were equipped with the latest educational software available."

Eden's mouth fell open with shock. "Why would he keep something like that a secret?" Realizing she had misjudged the man, she groaned.

"That's the way Chase is. He's well off and doesn't have to be bothered by the rest of us, but he cares and he shares his wealth."

"You keep referring to him as Chase. Are you two friends?"

The man chuckled. "You're a smart one. Chase and I were roommates while at Massachusetts Institute of Technology."

While copying the day's lesson, Eden thought about Chase's superior education at MIT. Without enough money to purchase workbooks for everyone, she had purchased one and copied from it instead. He no doubt knew nothing of stretching a budget. Public education was so far removed from his elite education, and yet no one would know. He interacted casually with her and the other teachers at lunch, and on their break. He listened when one spoke. It would be very easy to fall under his spell. The door to the office opened, allowing a rush of cold air in, breaking her train of thought. She quickly gathered her papers, and made her way back to the classroom.

The students began filing in and placing their jackets on the hooks in back of the classroom. It was the first week of November, and the temperature was already dropping. The weatherman was forecasting temperatures in the low forties for the remainder of the week.

Eden and Chase stood outside the door when Derrick Powell came rushing down the hallway. His arms were folded across his chest while his teeth chattered, and his little body trembled.

"Where is your jacket? You're going to be sick," Eden asked, concerned.

The child didn't respond. He stood silently in front of her, looking toward the floor.

"Derrick, where is your jacket?" Eden asked softly. She tilted his chin up so that he was looking at her. Embarrassment and sadness swam in the dark eyes. "You don't have one do you?"

"No ma'am," his voice was low and trembled from the cold.

"Yes, you do," she told him. "Wait right here." Eden disappeared into the classroom and opened the large wooden cabinet beside her desk. She rummaged in a box on the bottom shelf, removing a red and blue jacket with a hood. She rolled it quickly into a small ball, and then placed it inside a large bag. She closed the cabinet when finished and looked right into Chase's curious eyes.

The woman was amazing. His heart opened wide to receive all that was Eden. He remained in the classroom, giving the child privacy as Eden scurried back into the hallway carrying the bag. The young boy came running in wearing a jacket a short time later. His face was lit with a smile as he joined the other children in hanging up his coat. Chase walked toward the door to corner Eden as she slipped in.

"That was the most loving thing I've ever witnessed. You're a special woman, Miss Warner," he whispered the words with emotion. His eyes traveled over the surface of her pretty face, liking everything about the woman.

"Stop looking at me like that," she whispered back, uncomfortable. He was making promises with his eyes that had nowhere of going.

"I don't know what you mean."

"Liar." Eden walked past him, ignoring his soft chuckle and the warm fuzzy feeling inside of her. "Take your readers out." She focused on her students rather than on her growing attraction to the man.

The morning hours were dedicated to the reading lesson. Most of the children were doing well. A few of the boys were having difficulty, and Eden wanted to work with them one-on-one. She asked Chase to finish reading the story, instructing him on the list of questions to be asked in the rear of the book. The exercise was designed to strengthen the student's listening techniques.

"I'd prefer to work with the boys," he responded to her request. "I think they will respond to me since I've been where they are."

"You had difficulty?" she asked curiously.

"Sure did, but my grandmother worked with me using phonics cards day and night, until it clicked. I'm a voracious reader now."

"You're just full of surprises, aren't you?" She opened the bottom drawer on her desk and removed a deck of phonics cards, waving them at Chase. "My mother believed in them as well." She dropped the cards into his outstretched hand. "Use the back table."

The next day Eden watched Chase, not knowing what to think of him. Every assumption she had formed about him had been swept away by the more she learned. He had arrived early, arranging materials to work with the boys once again. Upon the children's arrival, he had ushered them away to work on their reading. The boys ran eagerly over to the area, their excitement over having Chase work with them imprinted on their faces.

Eden later instructed everyone to return to their seats and pull out their notebooks. "We're going to practice our handwriting," she told them.

"Ah, Miss Warner," Karen Jones said, waving Eden over.

"Yes?" Eden squatted down so that the child could whisper in her ear.

"My mama took my notebook and gave it to my big brother. She said he needed it more," the child told her sadly. "She didn't have any money to buy another one."

Eden rubbed the little girl's back affectionately. "Don't worry, I've got plenty," Eden whispered back. She made a trip to the cabinet once more and returned with a new notebook.

"Karen, I found your notebook on the floor after school yesterday. I put it in the cabinet for safekeeping," Eden said loud enough for the other children to hear.

The little girl beamed with happiness. Miss Warner had made it look like she had a notebook. "Thank you," she whispered, taking possession of her new notebook.

Once again, Chase observed Eden work her magic. He couldn't wait to see what would come out of that cabinet next. At lunchtime, he approached the subject.

"What else do you have in that cabinet of yours?" He bit into his sandwich.

Eden laughed. "I'll never tell," she teased.

"Well, tell me where you get the supplies." He watched her closely. She wore her hair in a ponytail again. He wanted the right to reach across the table and remove the decorative barrette. He bit into his sandwich to prevent himself from following through on the impulse.

"The women's circle at church collects jackets and coats. I pull out a few and keep them on hand at school."

"And the notebooks?"

"Notebooks, pencils, pens, crayons, and several other items are my donations. I catch a sale and stock up. It's not like the items are going to go bad."

"Do all the teachers go the extra mile like you do?" he asked, loving the way the light shining through the window highlighted the red in her hair.

"Most do. There just isn't enough money in the budget for all that is required. And the jackets, gloves, and hats aren't considered educational materials." Eden enjoyed talking like this with Chase.

She felt he really cared and wasn't just going through the motions of appearing interested.

"I now understand what you meant about education being more than simply the books."

"Thanks for being sincere."

"Did you think I wasn't?" His eyes dared her to tell the truth.

Eden blushed sheepishly. "In all honesty, Chase, I didn't know what to think of you." Her eyes danced with mischief.

He noted the moment, because she had actually called him by name. Not Mr. Mathews or Mr. Chase as she had instructed the children to do, just simply Chase. The sound of it rolling off her lips was music to his ears. "And now, what do you think?" His eyes held a far greater meaning than the simple words implied.

She didn't dare tell him she thought entirely too much about him. Or that this morning when he sat on the floor with the boys, practicing with the phonics cards that her heart had responded to him like no man before. "I think you are a kind and generous man."

Analyzing her response, Chase sat back in his chair. His eyes held hers. "I appreciate those words, but don't think for one minute that I believe that's all you think." His mouth curved into a flirtatious smile.

Eden laughed nervously. She glanced around the room and saw the children watching them. They gave her knowing little glances. She rolled her eyes before concentrating back on Chase. "That's your problem, because that's all you're getting." She pushed away from the table, leaving him to watch her exit.

And what an exit it was. The woman possessed the best butt he'd ever seen. In the blue jeans she wore today, it appeared firm, nicely rounded, and just the right size.

"You're going to go blind looking at that," Principal Daniels said, taking a seat.

Chase barked with laughter as he looked at his friend. "A man should be so lucky."

"She's a nice lady, Chase. Don't go after her unless you're serious."

"Why haven't you gone after her? I know you're not a foolish man." Chase observed his friend fidget. "Do you and Eden have something going on?" he asked with a sinking feeling.

David frowned as he tightened his gray and yellow striped tie. He wore the charcoal gray suit often because Eden had told him it was one of her favorites. "The lady works for me. That would be unethical."

"But it doesn't stop you from wanting her."

"If you haven't noticed, the woman is taller than me."

Chase laughed deeply. "You can't be serious? You passed on an incredible woman like that because she's taller than you?"

"Shut up, man. You're taller than most men and don't have the problem of being shorter than a woman. And besides, I don't think you really want me going after the lady." His dark eyes taunted his friend.

Chase sobered as he glanced off in the direction Eden had taken. When he looked back at his friend, his expression was thoughtful. "I have an election to win. A woman that special deserves all of a man's attention."

"Come on. This is me you're talking to. I know how you are when you want something, and the look in your eyes tells me you want Eden."

"Let's walk." Chase rose from his chair. He and David entered the school's courtyard where they leisurely strolled. The cool air helped to focus his thoughts. "I am interested in the lady, but I sense she's fighting the attraction."

"She would. There are some real issues to be addressed." David shoved his hands into his pockets. "Make sure you're prepared for the fallout when you go chasing after that woman. I don't want her hurt."

Chase met his friend's sharp gaze. He understood perfectly what David was telling him and knew he had some serious thinking to do.

He returned to the lunchroom and joined Eden back at their table. As he sat down, Angie strutted over to stand beside his chair.

Her heavy breasts were practically shoved under his nose.

"I hate to interrupt, but I wanted to invite Chase to Mario's. A group of us are getting together on Friday for dinner and drinks, and anything else that comes to mind." She fluttered her lashes like a schoolgirl.

"Thanks for the invitation, but the campaign doesn't allow for much socializing."

Angie turned to Eden for assistance. "Come on Eden; tell him I'm worth it."

Eden couldn't believe Angie was making such a fool of herself. Nor could she believe how angry she was at her. She couldn't believe her friend would assume she would eagerly assist in her campaign for Chase's attention. Not once had she considered that she might be interested in the man for herself.

Chase held his breath, waiting to see what Eden would do. Would she hand him over to another woman? He didn't think so.

"What I'm going to do is remind you that you're at work and not in a bar. The children are watching you," Eden reprimanded.

Chase laughed to himself because he had been right. Eden wasn't handing him over to another woman, although she would never admit to wanting him for herself.

Chapter Three

The week progressed quickly for Chase as he learned the daily routine. He had grown fond of the children and staff. Wednesday, he had sat in on the teacher's staff meeting after school and learned a great deal. Then, Thursday had brought the dark side of reality crashing in. He recalled how Eden had once again handled a difficult situation with grace.

"Gather around everyone. Let's see if this thing will work," Eden said to her bright-eyed students. Their voices were high with excitement as she flipped the switch on their class science project. All eyes watched as one section fell, prompting a response from another, until the ultimate goal was achieved. The bell rang, causing the children to cheer with their success. "Congratulations everyone." She patted the children on their backs, bestowing praise for each of their efforts in constructing the project. As she patted Reed Maxwell's back, the child flinched with visible pain.

Chase noticed and glanced at Eden who also had witnessed the reaction. Suspicion lurked in her eyes as she discreetly ushered the young boy outside the door. Chase followed, but stood in the door, keeping a close eye on the children around the project table.

"Reed, does your back hurt?" Eden asked compassionately. Her whole body was strung tight with fear of what she would discover.

The child only nodded.

"May I look at your back?" She waited for his permission. She didn't want to do anything that would cause the child more discomfort.

There was another nod.

She turned the child slightly sideways, so she could get a good view. She took a deep breath and pulled the shirt up. Dark, angry handprints, along with what looked to be cigarette burns, marred the child's back. She nearly choked on the stifled gasp of shock that struggled to be set free. Her watery eyes searched out Chase.

Anger like he had never experienced before overcame him. He wanted to find the S.O.B who had done this to this defenseless child and beat the hell out of him. He reached out, caressing Eden's hair with reassurance. He probably shouldn't have touched her so intimately, but he couldn't stop himself. She had looked at him with tears in her eyes, and all he had wanted to do was to wrap her in his arms.

"Sweetheart, can you tell me who did this to you?" She had her ideas, but preferred hearing it from the child's lips. She held his tiny hands tenderly. "It's okay."

"He'll be mad," the child answered with a nervous voice. A tear slipped down his freckled cheek.

"Come here," Eden said, taking the boy into her arms. She held him lovingly, yet mindful of his injured back.

"He said real men didn't cry," the boy hiccupped.

Chase tilted the child's chin up. "Good men cry. It's a sign of compassion, and there is nothing shameful about it. But I tell you what real men don't do. They don't hit women and children. Real men protect those they love."

Eden was grateful for his kind words. Her eyes held all that she was growing to feel for him. "I'm going to take Reed to see the nurse. Will you take over the class for me?"

"Sure. We can finish the art projects you began yesterday."

"That's perfect." She took Reed by the hand and led him to the nurse's station.

Today was his last day. He had mixed emotions about it. He was going to miss the smiling little faces and all their antics; then of course, there was Eden. He looked at her dressed in green corduroys and a warm-looking yellow sweater. She sat in her desk chair near the door, keeping a watchful eye over the playground. She looked beautiful with her hair down today, blowing in the breeze. His stomach tightened as he realized this could be his last time seeing her.

"Did you always want to be a teacher?" he heard himself ask. The question had plagued him since the first day in class, but he hadn't planned on asking it. The thought of possibly never seeing her again prompted him to ask.

She glanced at him, thoughtful. "Of sorts, my original plan was to major in mathematics and pursue a position as a university professor."

"So what led to education?"

"During college I participated in an after-school program. I assisted the children with their homework, or tutored them when needed. I realized early education was the key to all the rest. I also saw so many African American kids getting lost in the system. The boys weren't learning, nor were they interested. But I possessed a real talent for reaching them."

Chase was impressed. "Is that what you call it? You're beautiful, and the little boys wanted to impress you."

She laughed. "Well, whatever it was, I knew what I wanted to do. Do you know that statistics show that by the fourth grade, minority males start losing interest in school and begin getting in trouble?"

"No, I didn't. Is there a theory why?"

"Yes there is. It has to do with cultural differences between the teacher and student, and how a teacher perceives the child's behavior."

"Please explain that," Chase asked with great interest.

Eden shook her head. "It's long and complicated. The point is that I wanted to be that teacher who understood the child's behavior and inspired him to learn."

"I'm really impressed and would love to hear more about this theory. Possibly we could…"

"Your turn, Mr. Mathews," one of the boys yelled.

The moment was lost. Chase and Eden stood there looking at each other. It felt like the last time that they would be together like this.

"You'd better go before they come get you."

Eden watched as Chase ran off to take his turn at bat. She had been surreptitiously watching him, watch her. She could only guess what he was thinking; as she was coming to terms with the fact he wouldn't be there Monday. He had proven himself to be a wonderful man. The children loved having him around and the attention he gave them. *She* loved having him around. When he looked at her, and there were quite a few times during the day that he did, she felt it deep inside her soul. But the man was running for mayor. An involvement with her could adversely affect his bid for the office. Of course, she could be getting ahead of herself. But the look in his eyes and that comforting caress in her hair yesterday had spoken volumes.

She shook her head to clear away her thoughts. She had to stop thinking about the man. She watched as Chase stood on second base, encouraging the batter to hit a home run. She laughed as he began taunting the little girl pitching. Then a loud angry voice from her left, drew her attention. She was struck by a powerful blow against the cheekbone that sent her tumbling from the chair. She struggled to stand up, but found her right foot trapped underneath the chair. Another blow made contact, as a large man stood over her yelling. Everything seemed to be happening in slow motion. His words seemed jumbled, and yet they slowly pierced through the fog. He was angry about Reed.

"How dare you send the police to my house," Norman Maxwell bellowed with a drunken slur. He stumbled, trying to reach Eden again. "They took my boy. I'll teach you to stick your nose in my business," he continued to rant while swinging at her.

Chase heard the ruckus as he rounded third base. Eden's frightened scream reached his ears and spurred him to continue running until he reached the brute attacking her. The momentum of his body barreled into the man, knocking him to the ground. He grabbed the drunk by the collar and drew back as Principal Daniels came running over to stop him.

"Not in front of the children," David said. He grabbed his radio and contacted the school's security guard for assistance. Together, he and Chase held the cursing man to the ground until the guard arrived to take charge.

"The police have been called," David informed Chase.

But he wasn't listening. His attention was fully focused on Eden, who was only now managing to stand. She shook like a leaf. Her eyes were wide with shock, and she sported a rapidly swelling left cheek.

"God…Eden, are you okay? How's your vision? We need to get you to a doctor," Chase spoke excitedly.

"Take care of the children. Get them back to the classroom," she instructed, concerned for their well-being.

"The kids are okay. You're the one hurt."

Eden grabbed Chase's hands. She looked anxiously into his eyes. "The children don't need to see this." A tear slipped down her cheek. "Please, I'm embarrassed enough without them seeing me fall apart."

This time Chase understood and did as requested. But before he ran to the frightened children who stood looking on with concern, he settled Eden into the now up-right chair.

❦

"Here you go," Chase said as he passed Eden a cup of steaming tea. He had driven her home after the nurse assured him nothing was broken and all Eden needed was bed rest. "Drink this. It'll help settle your nerves." He helped her to position a pillow behind her back.

"Thank you." Eden sat on the sofa, staring down in her teacup. Embarrassment and fear were choking her. The warmth of the cup felt wonderful against her cold palms.

Chase noticed her trembling and knew the shock of the attack had caused her coldness. "Where's a blanket?"

"There's a quilt across the foot of my bed. Top of the stairs and to the right," Eden responded, not caring that she was sending a man she knew little about into her bedroom.

"Drink your tea. I'll be right back." Chase took the stairs two at a time, and following her directions, found the quilt right where she said. He quickly retraced his steps.

"Let's get this around you," he crooned to her, while wrapping the quilt around her trembling body. He sat down on the sofa beside her.

"How's the ankle?"

"It aches a little."

He reached down, pulling her foot onto his thigh. "Drink your tea before it gets cold." He removed her boot.

"What are you doing?" Eden asked, trying to remove her foot. She moved the teacup to the arm of the leather sofa.

"I'm going to massage your foot, then place an ice pack on it."

"You don't have to do that." Eden was barely holding it together. She was afraid that if Chase continued to touch her she would fall apart. A tear tracked down her cheek.

Chase reached out, swiping it away. It broke his heart to see her in such a fragile state. He removed her sock and stuck it in the boot. Her foot was soft and ice cold in his hand. The red toenail polish surprised him because the lady obviously had another side he had yet to see. "I'm not hurting you, am I?"

Eden shook her head no as she watched his hands stroke her foot. His hands were a surprise against her skin. They were large and gentle with a slight roughness that caught her off guard. She had assumed his hands would be soft from sitting behind a desk. Obviously, she had been wrong about that, too.

"Tell me something, Eden." Chase waited for her eyes to meet his. "You don't like tea, do you?" His lips twitched with humor.

Eden smiled for the first time since the attack. "I can't stand the stuff. I only keep it around for my mother."

"Why didn't you tell me?" he asked, laughing. He took the cup from her and placed it on the coffee table.

"You were being so sweet I didn't have the heart to tell you." Her eyes suddenly filled with tears as the dam on her emotions broke. "I was so frightened, Chase. I didn't see him until it was too late," she cried, bowing her head. Her shoulders shook from the force of her sobs.

Chase drew Eden onto his lap and held her in his arms while she cried. The sound of her anguish tore at his heart. "Cry it out, baby," he whispered and held her tighter. "I was terrified, too. When I saw him standing over you…" His body tensed with rage.

Eden reached out, touching his face. Her eyes held his. "I'm okay, thanks to you."

He caressed her cheek. "You're going to be sporting a bruise for a couple of days." He leaned forward, kissing her forehead.

"I couldn't have gotten through the day without you." Her eyes studied his face.

"I'm glad I was there." He kissed her bruised cheek, tenderly. "Here, rest for a while," he said, drawing her head back to his chest. He lightly stroked her hair as the tension slowly escaped his body. His eyes roamed around the living room while he held her. The open floor plan of Eden's home was warm and inviting. The walls of the three-bedroom brick home were painted in a pale peach and smelled of fresh peaches. The room was neat and orderly, without being cold. The leather sofa and oversize chairs were expensive-looking and comfortable. Her mantle held family photographs he was eager to explore. As he sat there holding her against him, he realized how right the moment felt.

Eden lay against Chase's chest listening to his heartbeat; slow and steady like the hand in her hair. Despite all that had happened today, she suddenly felt happy. He had called her *baby*. She knew the endearment was meant to comfort and probably didn't mean anything, but she couldn't help the way she felt.

"How old are you?" Chase broke the silence.

"Twenty-eight… And you're thirty-three if I remember correctly."

"You remember correctly. Why aren't you married?"

"I could ask you the same thing."

"Like you said, I'm not married by choice."

Eden giggled against his chest. "You didn't miss any part of that conversation."

Chase laughed. "You're a beautiful woman, Eden, both inside and out."

She raised her head to stare at him. "And you're my hero."

Chase placed his fingers into her hair and pulled her face to his. His eyes dropped to her mouth, lush, and alluring as he drew closer. A little more and he would finally know the taste of her. His heart thundered with anticipation.

Eden closed her eyes expectantly. She could already feel the warmth of his breath against her face. She held her breath, waiting for the moment when his lips would lay claim to hers.

"Baby, it's Mama. I came as fast as I could," a female voice called from the foyer as the door was opened.

Eden and Chase snapped to attention. He hurriedly sat her on the sofa as he slid down to the opposite end. By the time Mrs. Warner and her children joined them in the living room, Chase and Eden sat there, the picture of innocence.

Too innocent in Mrs. Warner's estimation, she glanced at her daughter, noticing the brightness to her brown eyes and the guilty expression she knew so well. Her eyes narrowed as she looked across the sofa to the man sitting too far down. She recognized the candidate immediately and grew concerned. The man was handsome and known as somewhat of a playboy. If he hurt her daughter, it would be the very last thing he did.

The rest of the Warner clan swarmed into the room and stopped. They, like their mother, looked from one to the other.

"Everyone, this is Chase Mathews," Eden made introductions while attempting to stand up.

"Sit down and stay off the ankle," Chase ordered as he eased her back to the sofa. All eyes were upon him.

Eden sensed her family's curiosity. "Chase came to my rescue today. He stopped Mr. Maxwell's attack on me." She looked appreciatively over at him.

"Thank you, young man," Eunice Warner said. She walked

over, pulling Chase into her arms. "Thank you for saving my baby from that drunk."

"You're welcome." Chase stared at Mrs. Warner and realized he was getting a glimpse into the future. Eunice Warner was a stunningly beautiful older woman with wrinkle-free skin. Her brown hair was streaked with a scattering of gray, which only enhanced her beauty.

Eunice Warner stepped back, assessing her daughter's bruised face. She sat down beside Eden and drew her into her arms.

Victor Warner stared at the man with suspicious eyes. Tall, like the rest of the Warners, he stuck out his hand to Chase. "Thanks for looking out for our sister."

"I'm glad I was there." Chase accepted the handshake. He nodded at the two young women standing behind Victor. Their striking resemblance to Eden was unmistakable. "She's been battered and bruised pretty badly. The ankle is slightly swollen and should be put up," he said, making his way toward the door. "Now that you all are here, I'll be leaving."

Eden almost groaned with regret. She hated to see him go, but knew he had to.

"I'll check on you in a couple of days," Chase said before taking his leave.

Eden watched his departure with mixed emotions. On one hand she felt extremely safe and in control when she was with Chase. On the other hand, she was treading into very dangerous waters and didn't know whether she was strong enough to go against the current. As the door closed behind him, she realized she wouldn't mind giving it a try.

"If I wasn't involved in a case right now, I'd be all over that," Taylor said bluntly. She stood watching Chase's departure from the large front window. An inch shorter than Eden, her hair was worn in a long braid. "That man is fine."

Mrs. Warner threw her daughter a warning glare. "You're not too old to have your mouth washed out with soap, young lady."

"Oh, Mom."

"No sister of mine better be hooking up with the competition," Victor declared vehemently. He gave Eden a pointed stare because the family was supporting Camden Nelson.

"Boy, give it a rest," Taylor replied, bored. "That's a single man and we're single women. Nobody gives a d ... darn about politics." She glanced at her mother, remembering that she was present.

"Girl, will you get your mind off men? We came here to check on Eden," Skye reminded Taylor. The youngest of the four, she sat in the chair opposite the sofa.

"Your father's in court and will be over later. Now tell me what happened, baby." Eunice stroked her daughter's head tenderly.

The Warner family listened as Eden began recounting the details of the attack. She loved her family dearly, although they didn't always see eye-to-eye. She basked in their attention. Taylor and Skye eventually went into the kitchen to prepare dinner. Victor lit the fireplace while their mother cuddled her.

"I want that man prosecuted for what he did to you," Eunice said angrily.

"How did you all find out about the attack?" Eden asked.

Taylor came over from the kitchen. "I was returning from court when the call came across the radio. I radioed into the station for some down-time and picked Mom up."

"I'm disappointed in you, Taylor. I would have expected you to roll with lights and sirens all the way to the school," Victor teased his sister.

"Don't think that I didn't think about it," Taylor said, waving the knife she was using to dice potatoes. "The only reason I didn't go was because I probably would have shot the guy."

"Now that sounds like my big sis," Victor said, laughing.

The others laughed as well... everyone except Eden. The last thing she wanted to hear or think about was more violence. She'd had enough this week to last her a lifetime.

Mrs. Warner noticed her daughter's solemn expression and signaled for the others to pipe down. "I'm so thankful Mr. Mathews was there to help you." She took her daughter's hand.

"Me, too. I was afraid, Mom. One minute I was in my chair, and the next, someone was punching me." Tears ran down Eden's swollen face again. "Chase brought me home. He even made me a cup of tea." Eden grinned.

Mrs. Warner laughed. "He meant well."

"Yes, he did."

"He could take care of me any day," Taylor commented with a wink in Eden's direction. But her sister wasn't amused. Taylor was just one more in a string of women interested in Chase.

Mrs. Warner looked at her daughter. Something lurked in Eden's eyes. "Honey, is something going on between you and *Chase?*" She stroked Eden's hand affectionately.

"Of course not," Victor answered for his sister. "She wouldn't get involved with Camden's competitor."

"Victor Emanuel Warner, I don't believe I was speaking to you," Mrs. Warner snapped. "I was speaking to Eden."

Eden glanced from one to the other. Was there anything between them? She was forced to analyze her feelings for Chase in a flash. So what if they had shared a couple of laughs, and a little harmless flirting. And not to be forgotten, the almost kiss. But, did that mean anything?

"No, of course not," she heard herself say.

Chapter Four

M s. Warner, this is Chloe Little from Hilton A.M."

"What can I do for you, Ms. Little?" Eden asked as she dropped her purse and school satchel on the sofa. She had rushed into the house on hearing the telephone. Foolishly, she had thought of Chase as she let herself in, kicking the door closed behind her.

"We would like for you to appear on our show Friday morning."

"Friday morning? Why would you want me on the show?" Eden wasn't interested. She leaned over pulling off her boots.

"Ms. Warner, since you challenged the candidate, you and Mr. Mathews have become the darlings of the campaign. People are interested to know what happened during his week in your class-room."

"Will that be all that is discussed?" Eden asked suspiciously.

"If you're referring to the attack, Mr. Mathews told us the subject was off limits."

Eden's heart gave a little flutter. "Mr. Mathews will be on the show with me?" She held her breath waiting for a response.

"Oh, yes ma'am. Can we expect you?" Chloe asked hopeful.

Eden's doorbell chimed. She excused herself while she opened the door. Taylor stood waiting. She waved her sister inside as she focused back on the telephone conversation. "All right, I'll do it."

"Great. I promise you it will be a pleasant experience." Chloe quickly went through all the necessary information for Friday's appearance. "I look forward to meeting you, Ms. Warner."

"Thank you. I look forward to meeting you as well." Eden replaced the telephone and leaned against the kitchen counter. She was already nervous about appearing before the cameras, and with

Chase Mathews at her side, even more so. For a man of his word, he hadn't kept his promise to check on her.

"Is everything okay?" Taylor asked, placing a hand on Eden's shoulder. She stared into her sister's eyes, realizing she was miles away. "Who was on the telephone?" She removed her gold blazer, placing it on the back of a chair. The hip holster, which was camouflaged under her jacket, was removed as well and placed in the chair.

Eden took a calming breath, turning fully to her sister. "That was *Hilton A.M.* I just agreed to be on their show Friday." She ran the palms of her hands down the length of her thighs with nervous energy.

Taylor noticed the old habit. "Are you sure you want to do it? Is the interview about the attack?" She unbraided her hair and combed it with her fingers.

Eden watched her sister go through her daily routine with fascination. Taylor was a beautiful woman in a predominantly male profession. She wanted to be perceived as tough and one of the guys, so she downplayed her looks. It didn't work, but Eden wouldn't be the one to tell a lady carrying a gun.

"No, it's not." Eden pushed away from the counter and opened the refrigerator. She removed salad fixings. "They actually want to interview us about Chase's week in my class." She washed her hands thoroughly before ripping off a paper towel and drying them.

"So Chase will be there?" Taylor washed her hands as well, and then began peeling the carrots for their salad. "How is the candidate?" she asked, watching her sister's response.

Eden ignored the question while she removed a bowl from the cabinet, and took it over to the center island. She quickly began tearing pieces of lettuce into it. She wasn't in the mood to hear another woman drooling over Chase. The last week had been spent listening to Angie and the other teachers doing just that. When they weren't drooling, they were grilling her for details about Chase. A few had even gone so far as to ask for a hook-up.

"How would I know?" she finally answered.

"You haven't heard from him?"

"No, Taylor, I haven't heard from him. Why don't you tell me why you're really here? Do you want me to set you up with Chase?" Eden asked impatiently. She was now throwing lettuce rather than dropping it.

"Time out, Eden. I don't know what your problem is, but if I want the man, believe me; I know how to get him."

The sisters stood facing off. Taylor was the first to speak.

"I know you told Mom nothing is going on between you and Chase—"

"There is no *but*," Eden interrupted. "There is absolutely nothing between us." She grabbed one of the carrots her sister had peeled and began chopping feverishly.

Taylor laughed. "Girl, you would never make it as a cop. Your face gives you away every time."

Eden had had enough. She slammed the knife down onto the countertop. "What are you talking about?" she glared at her sister.

"I'm talking about you and Chase sitting on opposite ends of the sofa like guilty teenagers. You and that man both looked overheated and in need of a bed."

"You're disgusting."

"I'm honest, unlike someone I know." Taylor looked at her sister.

Eden walked out of the kitchen and into the living room. She collapsed onto the overstuffed chair by the bookcase. "All week long I have listened to women talking about Chase. They have gone as far as asking me to introduce them."

"And no one has taken into consideration that you might be interested in the man yourself," Taylor surmised. She sat on the sofa.

"Of course not. Chase is white, a power player, and gorgeous. And like Angie, they all believe he's looking for a blue-eyed blonde."

Taylor chuckled. "Well, I for one can tell them the man isn't interested in a blonde. Unless you're planning on dying your hair."

Eden laughed. "Not a chance."

Taylor leaned forward, resting her elbows on her thighs. "So what's going on with you two?"

"Nothing is going on." Eden rolled her eyes heavenward. "We've talked, laughed a little, and flirted some."

"You flirted? I'm proud of you, sis," Taylor teased. Eden was fierce when it came to her students and people she cared about, but for herself, she could be timid and reserved. Considering the past, Taylor guessed her response was reasonable.

"Stop it. This is potentially serious." Eden pulled her legs up into the chair with her. She massaged her scalp in thought. "The day of the attack, Chase was wonderful. He was protective and tender. And just before you all arrived, he was about to kiss me."

"Oh, Eden." Taylor, suddenly, stood up. "This *could* be potentially serious."

"Maybe not, considering he hasn't called or come by like he said he would."

"In Chase's defense, he does have a campaign to win."

"I know, and that's why we shouldn't be attracted to each other." Eden draped both legs over the arm of the sofa. "But from our first meeting, there has been chemistry between us."

"This chemistry you speak of, are you sure it isn't curiosity?"

Offended, Eden glared at Taylor. She leaped from the chair to face her sister. "That's just great, Taylor, of course the man couldn't be interested in me as a woman."

"Whoa, you know I don't believe that. I just don't want you making more out of this than what's to it. Do you think he's changed his mind?"

The air went out of Eden's sails. She plopped into the other chair. "It crossed my mind."

"Did it cross your mind that you may be interested in Chase out of curiosity? You've never dated a white guy, have you?"

Eden laughed. "No."

"So why Chase?"

Eden still didn't have a response to her sister's question as she entered the studio of *Hilton A.M.* She had resigned herself to the fact that whatever had happened between them was a mistake. She was also thinking that agreeing to this interview was a mistake. A security guard located her name on his clipboard and pointed her in the direction of the makeup room. There, she was met by a flamboyant bleached blond male artist who touched up her makeup.

"You have beautiful skin, love." He dusted her face with powder. "And that mole is *so sexy*." He waved his hands while talking. "Speaking of sexy, your pal Chase Mathews is yummy."

Eden laughed heartily. This guy was just what she needed to forget her problems.

"All done." He turned her toward the lighted mirror.

She rose from his chair and checked her appearance. The red Donna Karan suit was a recent purchase and worth every penny. She had chosen to wear a pair of heels today since she would be paired with Chase. As the thought entered her mind, she realized she had dressed for the man as well; a man who had no interest in her.

"Girl, red is definitely your color." The makeup artist touched her shoulder.

"Miss Warner, I'm Chloe Little. It's a pleasure to finally meet you." A petite brunette entered the room greeting her. She was all energy with her wide, bright eyes and toothpaste-white smile.

"Nice to meet you," Eden replied, thinking the woman was too perky. She reminded her of all the cheerleader types in high school that had made her feel like a giraffe.

"Wow, you look incredible in that suit. The camera is going to love you."

"A compliment twice in a matter of minutes," Eden said, smiling. "This might not be so bad after all."

All three laughed. Eden thanked the artist as Chloe led her to the sound technician. She was quickly outfitted with a microphone. "There is no reason to raise your voice. Simply speak normally, and don't stare into the camera. Look at Crystal Sherman and carry on a normal conversation."

"That's easy enough." Eden glanced around the studio, wondering where Chase was. She started to ask Chloe when the woman supplied the answer.

"Mr. Matthews has just arrived from the airport and will be joining us in a moment. We'll have the candidate sitting between you and Crystal because it will make a better shot. And because rumor has it that the two are involved," Chloe whispered in a conspiratorial voice. She led Eden onto the morning show set with the view of the sprawling city on display behind them. Three tall wooden stools were being used as seating. Eden was ushered to hers and a sound check on her microphone was conducted. When Chloe was satisfied everything was in order, she excused herself to check on Chase.

Eden sat in the studio with activity all around her and felt completely alone. So that explained Chase's absence. He hadn't scored with her, so he had moved on to his next conquest. She should have known that the stories about his womanizing ways had some foundation in truth. Better to know now where she stood with the man. The feelings she was starting to have weren't so deep that they couldn't be overcome. She and Chase were acquaintances and that was okay. She would be polite, and when the show was over, they would part ways, never to meet again.

Activity in the studio increased as airtime neared. Chase was escorted onto the set. He quickly spotted Eden, and his heart kicked into overdrive. The woman was a knockout in the sexy red suit, and her brown legs looked incredible. The thought of them wrapped around his waist entered his mind so fast it caused him to stop short. All the reasons he had analyzed over the past week, as to why pursuing Eden was all wrong, flew right out of his head. There were no reasons. This was the woman he wanted, and he intended to move heaven and earth to have her. At that very moment, Eden looked in his direction and smiled.

The response had come naturally to her on spotting Chase standing at the technician's station. So what, she had smiled at the man. It didn't mean anything. *If that's true, then why is your heart thumping so hard?* She told herself it had nothing to do with the fact that the man looked *yummy* in a black suit and red tie. Or the fact that his blue eyes were staring at her with intensity that set her pulse racing. She was merely being friendly. She wasn't a teenage girl who didn't know her way around men. *You've had one serious relationship in your life. You don't know your way around men. Especially men like Chase Mathews.* She quickly looked away, pretending to be interested in what was going on around her.

Chase noticed the sudden change in her mood and knew he was responsible. He stepped onto the set, greeting her with a quick kiss on the cheek. "Hi. You look great," he whispered low and intimate. He took his seat and adjusted his jacket and tie before looking over at her.

"Thank you. Nice tie." She was cool and reserved.

"Eden, look we need to talk."

She looked directly at him. "We are talking."

"About the—"

"Don't forget you're wearing a microphone, candidate," Eden stopped his next words.

Chase glanced down at the black apparatus clipped to his lapel. "Right, but this isn't over."

"There, you're wrong," she said with smugness.

Morning show diva, Crystal Sherman, strutted onto the stage, halting their discussion. All the men in the area took notice of her cat-like walk and the itty-bitty black skirt she wore. She approached Chase with a flirtatious once-over.

"Welcome home, handsome. How was Savannah?" she greeted him, loud enough for everyone to hear. She pressed a kiss onto Chase's lips. Now, with all eyes definitely focused on her, she took her seat, confident she would be the talk of the studio. She tossed her dark red hair over her shoulder as she waited for countdown.

Eden sat next to Chase, feeling as though she had been kicked in the stomach. Foolishly, she had taken time this morning to dress to impress, not knowing the man had moved on. She was pathetic.

She could feel Chase watching her, but didn't dare look in his direction.

Chase cursed Crystal and her games as he saw Eden flinch. She obviously thought something was going on between them. The woman was her own best publicity agent. She was known for creating more scenes and rumors than the local tabloid newspaper. But she had gone too far today.

"Eden," Chase said, leaning in her direction. He placed his thumb discreetly over his microphone. "It's not what you think."

"Quiet on the set," someone yelled as the countdown to airtime began. The morning show's music began as the red light on the camera came on.

"Good morning and welcome to *Hilton A.M.*," Crystal opened the show. "Today we have the hottest couple in Hilton on our show. Well that's political couple." She smirked, running her hand down Chase's arm flirtatiously. "Chase Mathews and Eden Warner are with us. So Chase, what did you think when a teacher challenged your political agenda?"

Chase glanced to his right at Eden. "I thought, finally a woman who speaks her mind. Then as I listened to her comments, I realized that she was correct. So I decided to join her classroom. See, I hadn't taken the time to enter the classroom and learn firsthand what teachers have to deal with each day." His eyes swept over Eden's face. "This lady is no shrinking violet. When she believes in something, she stands up and voices her opinion. I admire that."

"The way I heard this story told was that Eden opened mouth and inserted foot," Crystal replied sarcastically. She had watched Chase and the woman from the technician's station. She could see that Chase was interested, but Eden had other plans. She looked at Eden with a sneer on her face. "Tell us about it."

"If you're referring to Mr. Mathews eavesdropping on a private conversation, then yes that part is true." Eden was angry. No doubt Crystal and Chase had shared a little pillow talk. "But I meant every word. I'm not the type of woman who tells a man what he wants to hear. I don't have time for stroking egos. I speak my mind and have independent opinions."

Crystal bristled.

"Chase, I know you're a MIT graduate. No doubt you'll be putting that *higher* education to work if elected mayor."

"That's the plan if the citizens of Hilton elect me into office."

"Eden, where did you obtain your degree?" Crystal asked, trying to showcase that they had nothing in common.

"That would be degrees, Crystal, Mathematics and English majors with a Masters in Education, all from Harvard." Eden saw the woman's eyes widen with surprise. She sat proudly, knowing she hadn't been prepared for the response.

Chase hadn't known either and looked over at Eden, impressed. He glanced back at Crystal and chuckled. The woman had officially been put in her place.

The attractive host quickly realized she had underestimated her guest. "Please tell us about Chase's week in your classroom." She decided to back off for the moment. The situation called for a new approach.

"Out. That's a show," the same man who had yelled earlier, announced. Technicians scurried around tending to details. A woman rushed over to Eden and removed her microphone, then moved over to Chase.

Eden was out of her seat the moment the woman freed her from the apparatus. She didn't stick around for the phony thank-you or chitchat. She quickly retraced her steps and pushed through the metal door leading to the parking lot.

"Eden wait," Chase called from behind her. He rushed to catch up. "We need to talk."

She stopped short and turned around to face him. In a calm voice she said, "There's nothing to talk about. I want to thank you again for coming to my rescue." She turned to walk away, but Chase grabbed her arm, stopping her.

"Don't act like there's nothing going on here. I don't want to ignore it." He looked deeply into her eyes.

Eden glanced around the parking lot. "I like you, Chase." Her eyes swung back to his face. "And I respect your vision for the city. I'll definitely vote for you. But outside of friendship, there's nothing."

"You're in denial. Where the hell is that woman who called me on my politics?" Chase asked angrily. Reaching for control before speaking again, he lowered his voice. "I'm attracted to you, and you're attracted to me. But the middle of the parking lot isn't the place to have this conversation. Have you had breakfast?"

The morning show was at five o'clock in the morning. Their appearance had been at five-thirty. The time currently was five minutes to six.

"No I haven't, but…"

"No buts. Where's your coat? It's freezing out here." He rubbed her arms in a warming fashion.

Eden pointed in the direction of her vehicle. "I left it in the car. I didn't know what the setup here would be, so I just ran in. The wool suit I have on is warm."

"It's beautiful and you look great, but you really need a coat." His eyes swept down the lines of her body.

Eden refused to be suckered in. "Are you going to feed me or stand there ogling my body?"

Chase laughed. "I can ogle while I feed you. Come on." But the one thing he refused to do was ignore his feelings for her, or allow Eden to ignore hers for him.

Chapter Five

Thirty minutes later, Chase led Eden into Madame Belle's. The popular restaurant was a favorite of the downtown business crowd. Serving all three meals, Madame Belle's was known for wonderful food and a relaxing atmosphere. As they approached the hostess station, the room suddenly erupted into applause. They were quickly met by a tall, slender older woman with piercing blue eyes. Her arms opened wide as she approached Chase and drew him into her arms for a long embrace. Releasing him, she turned her full attention onto Eden.

"Madame Belle, I'd like for you to meet Eden Warner," Chase said, making introductions. He stood back, watching both women.

"Son, I know who this is," Belle said excitedly. "This is the beautiful woman you couldn't con with your good looks and charm." She winked at Eden. "Hi, darling, I'm Belle Gautier, Chase's grandmother."

Eden was surprised. "It's a pleasure to meet you, Mrs. Gautier."

"Belle, sweetheart." She smiled, taking their coats and passing them over to the hostess. "We had the television on in here this morning and watched the morning show. Once you shut up that snobby Crystal Sherman, the interview was good." She laughed as she slipped her arm through Eden's. "Always did like a woman who stood up for herself." She escorted Eden to a private table off the kitchen marked 'reserved.' "This is Chase's table. He usually drops in here to see me at least once a week."

"How sweet," Eden teased Chase, who walked behind them greeting supporters. She liked his grandmother immediately. She was obviously a free spirit who lived life on her own terms. Her personality was reflected in the short, spiky cut of her silver-gray hair and her Bohemian style of dress. The décor of the restaurant also reflected this style.

"Eden, are you related to Adam Warner?" She stopped at their table dressed in a deep purple tablecloth with sari like material draped across it.

"Yes. He's my father."

"Adam comes in here all the time. He's a damn good attorney as well. He straightened out a little issue for me a year ago," she told them.

"Why didn't you use Benjamin Tate?" Chase asked, getting back into the conversation. He assisted Eden with her chair.

Belle waved a dismissive hand. "I didn't need the family in my business." She bent to kiss Chase's cheek. "I'd like to keep it that way."

"Yes, ma'am."

"Good boy, now go get your breakfast. I'll bring over some coffee."

"She's pretty wonderful. I love coming here. It's one of the few places where I get to simply be Chase."

"You mean no demands and preconceived notions about who you are or should be?"

"Exactly. My grandmother allows me to be who I want and loves me just the same."

Eden nodded, knowing how precious that was. "So what about your parents? Do they have different ideas about what you should be doing?"

"They did until they realized I was more like my grandmother." He laughed and looked deeply into Eden's eyes. "She likes you almost as much as I do."

"We've had this conversation. You're supposed to be feeding me."

"And ogling your body. Let's not forget that," he teased her with a wink.

Eden laughed as she shook her head. She looked at him and felt her resolve weakening. Belle arrived with their coffee, giving her a moment to regroup. She glanced around the room, noticing that her companion was the subject of several female conversations.

"Two coffees," Belle said, placing their cups before them. She deposited glasses of orange juice and water as well. "Go on back to the kitchen," she told him, then excused herself to see to arriving diners.

Chase stuck out his hand for her to join him. "Come on. Let's get breakfast." Eden took his hand and followed him through the swinging door. The kitchen staff greeted them warmly.

"Hey, Chase, what are you whipping up today?" the chef asked.

"You're cooking?" Eden asked, turning to the man beside her.

"Don't look so shocked. Donovan over there taught me everything I know." He motioned in the direction of the aging cook.

"More surprises from you?" she said teasingly.

"You have no idea, but I'd love to show you," Chase crooned close to her ear. He pulled back, looking into her eyes for a meaningful moment.

Eden ran her palms down her skirt. She glanced around the professional kitchen with interest. There were seven people working, all moving in different directions but working toward the same goal. They quickly made room for Chase as he washed his hands, and then removed an apron from the coat tree.

"Everyone, this is Eden," he said, wrapping the ties to the apron around his waist to secure it in front.

Eden waved shyly.

"Sit here," Chase indicated a stool by the pantry. "Now what would you like to eat?" His eyes were bright and playful. "I'm going to have an omelet with waffles and a fruit bowl."

Eden couldn't resist smiling at him. He was so not what she had initially thought. "Waffles are my favorite, so make it two." She sat there watching as he moved around the kitchen preparing their meal. Conversation between the staff was a constant stream as they worked. Eden and Chase were included in each topic and joke. When he announced their meal ready, Eden was having a wonderful time and feeling more relaxed. She held the door open for him as he carried a tray with their meal out to their table. He efficiently placed each item on the table, before dashing back into the kitchen to deposit the tray. He lowered himself into the chair across from her. Together, they said grace.

"This is wonderful." Eden was impressed with the fluffiness of the omelet. The waffle was golden brown and delicious.

"Thank you." They ate for several minutes, talking off and on about an assortment of topics. "Can we get back to discussing us?" Chase asked when it seemed Eden would continue to avoid the real reason for their breakfast.

"There is no us," she whispered across the table. "As I heard it, you and snobby Crystal are an item." Just saying the words left a bad taste in her mouth.

Chase shook his head. "You bought into her act. Crystal creates her own publicity. I've been completely focused on my campaign until you entered my life." He looked at her intensely.

"Why do you persist in trying to make there be more between us?"

"I persist because I refuse to give up on something or someone I want." He covered her hand.

"Want. So that's what this is about?" Eden scoffed, removing her hand. "The playboy in you can't take no for an answer."

Chase was immediately offended. He leaned forward, stabbing the table with a finger. "Don't you dare reduce this conversation to sex. When I said *want*, I meant all of you. But if you think I'm going to lie and say I don't want to take you to bed, you'd be mistaken, because I do. You want that as well." He looked at her long and hard, daring her to deny it.

"We're virtually strangers," she fired back.

"Then get to know me."

Eden couldn't allow herself to be drawn in. She shook her head with disbelief. "You don't have the time. You're in the middle of an election."

"Why don't you let me worry about the campaign?" Chase covered her hand with his.

"Do you realize the consequence of getting involved with me?

Why risk it?"

Chase sat back thoughtful. "This is also about the campaign."

"Yes, it's about the campaign." Eden looked at him as though he were an alien. "What world do you live in, Chase? I'm an African American woman, and you're a white male. Correction, the number-one white male bachelor in the city, and women all over town are vying for your attention."

"I know one who isn't."

"You're being ridiculous."

"You're being stubborn and chicken. But you know what? I don't have time for this."

Eden was suddenly alarmed. "So it's your way or no way? We can't be friends instead?" Her eyes were wide with worry.

Chase was pleased with her response. He had noticed the flare of concern at his surrender. Eden definitely wanted more out of their relationship than friendship. He appreciated her looking out for his campaign, but he didn't live his life worried about what others thought. In time, she would realize that and come around to his way of thinking.

"Of course we can." He reached across the table, covering her hand. "Now that I've met you, I couldn't imagine my life without you."

"I feel the same way." Her eyes strayed to his hand covering hers. The contrast in color wasn't as alarming as she would have thought.

Chase followed her gaze. He wondered what she was thinking. "Do you have to go into work today?" he asked, removing his hand.

"No, I have the entire day off," Eden said, placing her hand into her lap. She missed the warmth of his touch.

"Good, let's get out of here."

Chase took Eden to campaign headquarters. A banner with his name written in bold, red letters hung over the doorway. Posters were taped in the large storefront windows. Two vehicles parked out front along the curb were fitted with magnetic campaign signs on the doors. He escorted her inside. "This is it. So what do you think?"

People were everywhere. Several worked the telephones while others stuffed envelopes. A group was returning from the local mall where they had passed out buttons. It appeared to be a well-oiled machine, with plenty of adoring female supporters.

"I didn't realize you had so many people working down here. It's quite busy, isn't it?" she commented. She walked over to check out a table of mailers. She quickly read through the information. "These are very good. Your message is clear and concise."

"I'm glad you approve," Chase replied, pleased. He took her around, making introductions.

The petite, dark haired spokesperson she remembered from the press conference walked over to meet her. "Ms. Warner, I'm Alison Sanders. I can't tell you how indebted we are to you. That challenge you made has garnered us great publicity."

"That wasn't the plan, but I'm glad to be of assistance." She appreciated the woman's friendliness. "I don't know if you need the help, but I would love to come by on my days off and help out."

Alison laughed. "Honey, we could always use the help. I look forward to seeing you here." She excused herself to see to another matter.

Chase slipped his hand into Eden's and took her over to his office. He looked around at the battered desk and second-hand chair. Then, there were the old metal file cabinets from another era. The sofa was another thrift store find. The only new item in the room was the television. From the beginning of his campaign, he had dedicated the majority of his funds to promote the issues and cover campaign expenses.

Eden collapsed onto the comfortable-looking sofa. She crossed her legs, taking in the shabby chic décor, knowing that Chase could do better. However, his lack of concern for comfort and style, opting to focus his funds on the campaign instead, emphasized his dedication to the cause.

"I think it's clean and functional." Eden watched him walk over to sit on the edge of his desk. "Why did you bring me here?"

Chase dropped his head. He slowly brought it up to look at her. "I wanted you to be a part of something that's important to me. This is where my dream begins, and I couldn't think of anyone else that I wanted to share it with more."

"Thank you." She was humbled. "Why do you want to be mayor? The responsibility is so great. It's almost like putting your life on hold."

"See, that's where you're wrong. This is my life. For as long as I can remember, I've wanted to be mayor. My grandfather served as mayor several years ago."

"I read that. So is that your reason for wanting the office?"

"No." He shook his head in thought. "I've traveled all over the world. First as a child with my parents, then as an adult, and you know what?" He was looking right at her.

"What?" Eden was held captive by this insight into the man that she was falling for.

"There's no place like home." He smiled wistfully. "This is where I want to plant roots, get married, raise a family. Right here in Hilton. This city has so much to offer, and I believe I have the ability to make it even better. What good is my elite education if I don't put it to good use?"

When he spoke like this, he was intriguing and a threat to her conviction, not to mention her heart. The man was far more fascinating than she had expected, and that's what made him so dangerous. "Most people would consider making as much money as possible with their elite education, putting it to good use. Why not you?" She looked at him closely, searching for a flaw. Something, anything, to douse the feelings that were rapidly growing.

"I'm disappointed, Eden." He looked at her sadly. "You're like everyone else who believes privilege and money equate to selfishness. I wasn't reared that way, and I won't be bringing up my children that way either." He pushed from the desk to join her on the slip-covered sofa. "I don't have to share this with you, but because I'm being completely honest about what I want from you, I'm going to tell you. I'll inherit a fortune. But everything I have now, I worked for. Sure, I obtained loans, both public and private, easily enough, but it's my complete responsibility to turn a profit and pay the money back. Yet if it succeeds, I succeed, and if it should go under, so do I." He picked up her left hand and squeezed it with his. "This campaign is about what I can give to my hometown and nothing else."

She didn't know what to say. The man had laid his private business out on the table for her to see. She covered the hand that still held hers. "That's why you have to put these feelings for me aside. This campaign is too important to you and the citizens of Hilton."

"I said that I would, but I don't have to like it," Chase said, standing up. He ran his hand over his hair. "Don't you understand that I want to get to know you?"

Eden rose from the sofa, going over to him. "We can do that as friends."

He studied her face for a moment, before reaching out, pinching her nose. "We'll try it your way, but you might as well know up front that I intend to change your mind. I want the right to touch you, kiss your smiling lips." His eyes dropped to her mouth.

"Chase."

"Don't 'Chase' me. I'm agreeing to what you want." His eyes rose to meet hers.

"No you're not. You're pacifying me."

"True. But since you won't allow me the opportunity to date you, pacifying you is the next best thing." He grinned at her. Movement outside the door of his office caught his attention. Stanley Elliot, his campaign manager, stood watching them. Chase waved the man inside.

"I didn't mean to disturb you," Stanley said as he entered the office. His steely gray eyes swung to Eden, assessing what he had interrupted. He absolutely despised having to look up to a woman. He pushed his glasses up on his nose as he forced a smile. "Consorting with the enemy, Ms. Warner?"

Eden gasped with shock. She looked at the older gentleman with interest. His tone of voice indicated he wasn't happy to see her. She glanced at Chase to see whether he noticed, but the friendly manner that he greeted the man indicated that he hadn't. Maybe she had misread the remark. Chase knew the man far better than she did. "I didn't realize that Chase and I were enemies."

Stanley noted the ease with which she used Chase's name. They would definitely have to have a little discussion about his latest conquest.

"This is Stanley Elliot, my campaign manager, Eden. Don't take him seriously. The man possesses the driest sense of humor," Chase explained.

Very dry. "Glad to hear it," Eden said, pleasantly. "I was feeling unwelcome."

"Any friend of Chase's is a friend of this campaign," Stanley spouted casually.

"I'm hoping that she'll become more than a friend," Chase said, drawing both their anxious attention. "I was going to ask Eden to join the educational committee," he said to Stanley.

"I thought you had already assembled the committee." Stanley didn't like the idea one bit. This woman had already caused a setback in his campaign agenda with her foolish challenge.

"Not quite. I want to bring Hal Yates on board, as well as Eden." He looked over at her.

Eden was focused on the manager. She got the distinct impression that Stanley wasn't too pleased with Chase's request. To be honest, she wasn't either. She felt the man had ulterior motives for including her on his committee; however, she was curious as to why he would ask Hal Yates to join. The man was his biggest business competitor. Just last month, the newspaper had reported how Yates had won a multimillion-dollar contract over Chase's company.

"Why would you ask Yates to join your committee?" she

couldn't resist asking. She could sense Stanley's resentment, but chose to ignore him.

Chase laughed because he could see that his decision made no sense to her. "Yates Industries is my competition in the business community, but in the city of Hilton we're all citizens. A quality educational system benefits both companies. And although I hate to admit it, Hal is intelligent and creative. His input of ideas would be a real value to the city."

"You're incredible," Eden told him, with no thought to Stanley being in the room. "The citizens of Hilton will be extremely lucky to have you for their mayor." Her eyes held admiration and a little something that caught both Chase's and Stanley's attention.

"I'll go place the call to Yates," Stanley added. He looked up at Eden. "Will you also be joining the committee?"

She knew that he wanted her to say no. And she wanted to say no, because to be around Chase any more than an occasional weekend stuffing envelopes was asking for trouble. But she looked into his expectant eyes and answered *yes*. She heard Stanley scurry out. She knew without looking at the man that he disapproved.

"Thank you for agreeing to be a part of my dream. David, I mean, Principal Daniels," Chase corrected himself, "is heading the committee for me."

Eden laughed. "I know who *David* is, and I also know that the two of you were roommates." She sat on the edge of the desk facing him.

Chase went to the door and closed it. The mini-blinds were already down and secure.

"What are you doing?" Eden asked, alarmed. She watched as Chase stalked back toward her. What was going on behind those baby blues?

He placed both hands on the desk, trapping her in place. "I'm about to steal a kiss from the most beautiful woman in the room."

"I'm the only woman in the room." She leaned back out of reach. A smile danced on her lips.

Chase grinned as he leaned with her. "Yes you are, and you've asked that we remain friends."

"You agreed."

"Correct again, but before I settle for chaste pecks on the cheek, I want to know what you taste like." His eyes dropped to her mouth. He touched her red, painted lips with a thumb.

"Chase, don't." Eden held on to his hand. Her heart was beating with excitement.

"Tell me that you don't want this, and I'll stop." He looked deeply into her eyes. He could hear her excited breath belying her request.

"Chase."

"That's what I thought." He wasted no time in covering her mouth with his. He pressed lightly, learning the shape and feel of her lips.

Eden closed her eyes and gave herself up to the moment. She framed his face with her hands as he kissed her sweetly. God, she had never been kissed like this before. The man nibbled her lips as though he had all the time in the world.

He wanted this moment to last forever. He placed his arms around her waist and pulled her more firmly against him. He swept his tongue along the seam of her mouth before sliding it between her trembling lips. She was everything that he expected. Sweet, warm, a little shy, yet filled with a passion that was just waiting to be unleashed.

Eden wrapped her arms around his neck. She wanted more of what he was offering. Her heart thumped wildly in her chest as his mouth took complete possession of hers. If she didn't stop now, she wouldn't be able to later. She pushed against Chase's chest to get his attention, tore her mouth away and turned her head to avoid his lips.

"We should stop."

"No, we shouldn't." He kissed her ear, then turned her face back around so that he could kiss her lips once more.

"Yes, we should," she managed to say while dodging another kiss. "You have an election to win. There's nowhere for this to go."

"We could always take it over to the sofa."

"Chase."

"Just kidding." He pushed away from the desk. They both needed space to cool down. He watched Eden closely, delighting in her shaken state. The sight of her smudged lipstick served as evidence that she wanted him as much as he wanted her.

Chapter Six

Adam Warner arrived at home, surprised to see all the children gathered around the dining room table. Rarely did they share a Friday dinner together. One or all usually had plans. He sat down at the table and immediately turned to Eden. "I saw your interview this morning."

"You did?" Eden sat up straight. Her father seldom acknowledged the events in her life. Tall and extremely handsome, he had been her first love. When she was a child, he had made time for her and been impressed with her intellect. She had gone with him everywhere; the office, the courtroom. People had expected big things from her, and with one decision, it had all come to a screeching halt.

"The entire office did to be specific. People still can't believe that you attended Harvard to become a schoolteacher. You could have done something great and rewarding with your life."

"Adam! Eden is doing something great and rewarding. What could be more important than shaping the minds of children who will one day become the doctors and lawyers of the world?"

"Of course, you're right, Eunice. I didn't mean anything. I'm sorry, baby. I know you went through a lot of trouble preparing this meal, and I'm not going to ruin it."

Eden cringed every time he brought up the old battered subject, and she didn't care to revisit it again.

"I couldn't believe the nerve of that Crystal," Eunice added. She hated the way Adam dismissed Eden's accomplishments. "You handled yourself with class and dignity, baby. I was so proud of you."

"Me too, Eden, because I would have walked off the set," Taylor commented.

Eden nodded politely, but withdrew from the conversation. She allowed her mind to wander and was eventually lost in thought. Well, not really lost. She was replaying the kiss in Chase's office for the millionth time. She hadn't wanted it to end, but with his campaign before him, their relationship had nowhere to go. But like he'd said, they could have taken it to the sofa.

"So what or who has put that smile on your face?" Taylor leaned over, whispering in her sister's ear.

Eden snapped out of her daydream. She had been unaware of smiling. She looked guiltily at her older sister.

"I need to ..."

"What are you two talking about down there?" Adam Warner asked, interrupting his daughters' conversation. "Taylor, I know there's always something exciting going on in your life."

"Criminals no doubt," Victor answered for his sister. "What else does Taylor talk about?" He delighted in bugging his sister. Being second in line and the only son in the family, his responsibility was to taunt his sisters.

"Guns and bullets," Skye chimed in.

"Don't you have a woman to chase?" Taylor shot back at Victor.

"Later. And what will you be curling up to tonight?" he taunted.

"Her revolver," Skye added, laughing.

The usual wisecracks and talking over one another began. Eden listened and watched as her parents were eventually drawn into the mix. She quietly excused herself from the table. She grabbed her purse from the entryway table and slipped out the front door. Her thoughts were in a jumble this evening and she simply couldn't deal with the noise.

She drove home at a leisurely speed. The local jazz station played low in the background, not competing with her thoughts. She slowed at the red light and waited for it to change. A couple strolling hand-in-hand walked in front of her car. They looked happy and in a world of their own. She wanted that with someone. The light changed and she proceeded on. Would she ever have that type of relationship? Now that was the real question. She turned right at the next corner and pulled over into a parking space.

Downtown was virtually empty, with the exception of campaign headquarters. There were lights on and people milling around inside. She stared at the building, knowing that what or rather who she wanted was right inside.

As she continued to watch the building, she spotted Chase and Crystal coming out of his private office. They were an attractive couple. No doubt they would make a powerful couple in the city. She checked her mirrors then quickly drove off. The sight of the two of them together only added to her depressed mood. She kept driving until she reached the sanctuary of her home.

A hot shower was just the thing she needed to feel better. Her resolve was firmly in place and with no regrets. Chase had a dream. A dream that would benefit the citizens of Hilton, and she wouldn't be responsible for derailing it. She finally settled in the living room on the sofa. Locating the remote to the television, she turned it on and began channel surfing. Nothing appealed to her, until she switched the channel and a campaign ad for Chase was playing.

His blue eyes seemed to be looking right at her. His voice was familiar and commanding, but his mouth held the greatest of attention for her having awakened something inside of her long ignored. She quickly hit the off button and went to bed, but sleep wouldn't come. Then the telephone rang, giving her a reprieve from her thoughts.

"Hello." Eden pushed up against the headboard.

"I hope that I didn't wake you," Chase crooned on the other end.

"No, you didn't." Her pulse quickened. "Are you okay?"

"Yes, I'm fine. I saw you this evening."

Silence.

"Eden?"

"I was leaving my parents' home."

"Why didn't you come in?"

"Why was Crystal there?" Eden could have swallowed her tongue. She hadn't planned on asking that question.

Chase stared into the dark. He was sitting in his recliner at home. He had arrived only minutes before. "Why does it matter? You aren't interested in a relationship, remember?"

Silence.

"She's doing a piece on each candidate and wanted to ask me a couple of questions. You know, this is never going to work."

"You can't afford a relationship with me right now."

"Why don't you let me worry about the campaign?"

"I would, if I felt you were taking the matter seriously." She drew up her legs under the quilt. "Racism is an ugly thing."

"I am and I know that. But, I'm also taking what I feel for you seriously. I want to spend time with you, getting to know you better." Chase was now pacing the floor of his den.

"Is that why you asked me to join the committee, because you want to see me?"

He released a heavy sigh. "Yes, I want to see you. Everyday if you must know, but I'll respect your decision, even though I don't agree with it."

"I'm doing what's best for your campaign," Eden tried to make him understand. She left the bed to pace across the floor.

"Try doing what's best for my *heart*." Chase could have kicked himself. He hadn't planned on mentioning his growing feelings. "Look, I want you on that committee because I value your intelligence and opinion. Please don't change your mind about joining."

"I haven't changed my mind about the committee, or our getting involved."

"We're already involved, Eden. Just because we don't act upon it, doesn't change the fact that we want to. You're only prolonging the inevitable because you can't harness emotions."

Silence.

"Talk to me." Chase sat back in his chair.

Eden climbed back into bed. "I don't want to be responsible for you losing your dream."

"Are you ashamed of being attracted to me, Eden?"

"No!"

"Do you believe that I'll hurt you?"

"No."

"Well then, I don't see what's stopping us from being together."

Eden was frustrated and so incredibly lonely. She believed her reasons were clear and the best decision to be made. As she continued to listen to Chase chip away at her resolve, she'd had enough. "Damn it, Chase, leave it alone. I'll be on your committee and I'll be your friend, but I will not fall under your spell." She slammed the phone down and groaned. Who was she kidding? She was already under the man's spell.

Chase lay in bed, thinking about Eden. She was all a man could want; smart, compassionate and stunningly beautiful. Yet, she didn't realize that having her in his life was of more value to him than winning the campaign. He laughed into the dark. If someone had told him that he would one day say that about a woman, he wouldn't have believed them. But then, Eden wasn't just any woman.

Her declaration about not falling under his spell was hilarious because he was under hers. She was a mystery of sorts. The more he peeled away the layers, the more was revealed. Well, he wanted to know it all. He wanted to know what made her happy and sad. He wanted to know if she preferred a bath or a shower, which side of the bed she liked to sleep on. Did she sleep on her back, or her stomach? Damn it, he wanted to know everything he could learn about Eden Warner.

He continued to lie there, wide-awake for another hour. He turned over Eden's words in his mind. She was right about losing supporters. There would inevitably be people who opposed a relationship between them. And it *could* cause him to lose the election. However, he believed in the citizens of Hilton to focus on the issues.

As he continued to ponder the situation, he recalled reading about an African American mayor who was married to a Caucasian woman. The relationship hadn't cost him the election. Ex-Secretary of Defense, William Cohen's wife was a beautiful African American woman, and their marriage hadn't prevented his climb up the political ladder. Many more politicians were in interracial marriages with successful careers. He too would succeed in his quest for the mayor's office, and in winning Eden's heart.

The insistent ringing of the doorbell awakened Eden from a restless night of sleep. She pushed her hair away from her face as she lay there orienting herself. Tossing the covers aside, she dragged her heavy body out of bed. She was exhausted. Hours of laying awake thinking of Chase had left her worn out. She came awake fully. Was it Chase at her door? The ringing continued. She snagged her robe and hit the floor running. At the door, she whipped it open expecting to see him.

"Oh."

"Expecting someone?" Taylor asked.

"No. What's the matter? Who's hurt?" She stepped back, allowing her sister to enter.

"Calm down, no one's hurt," Taylor rushed to assure her.

"No one's hurt?"

"No." Taylor headed to the kitchen in search of coffee.

Eden closed the door, and then followed her sister into the kitchen. "If no one's hurt or sick, then why are you here at ... five thirty in the morning?" Eden demanded, reading the clock in the kitchen. She removed coffee cups from the cabinet and placed them on the counter. She sluggishly made her way to the table, where she collapsed into a chair.

"Sorry about the time, but I was headed into work and wanted to talk to you." Taylor leaned against the counter, waiting for the coffee. She looked at her sister, noticing how listless she appeared.

"What did you do last night?"

"Nothing."

"So, why did you leave without saying goodbye?"

Eden placed both elbows on the table, threading her fingers under her chin. She closed her eyes briefly unable to face so much conflict so early in the morning.

"I wasn't in the mood to do battle with Dad," she answered, opening her eyes.

Taylor hated the way their father treated Eden. It left her sister feeling like an outsider. She wanted to mend the divide.

"I'm sorry about Dad. He loves you."

"I know, and there's no reason for you to be sorry."

Taylor filled both cups with coffee and carried them over to the table. She slid into the chair next to Eden. Adding sugar and cream to her coffee, she turned to her sister.

"Tell me what's going on. You were distracted over dinner."

"All right, but please keep this between us." Eden's eyes sparkled with excitement.

"You have my word."

Eden squirmed in her chair while trying to decide how much to reveal. "After the interview on *Hilton* A.M., Chase and I spent part of the day together."

"About the interview, once you got Crystal off your back, you did good. Have any idea why she was in such a snit?"

"Sure I do, but it doesn't matter."

"That's code for Chase, right?" Taylor laughed.

"Something like that." Eden sipped her coffee.

"And ..." Taylor could see that Eden really wanted to talk about whatever was on her mind, but hesitated.

"He took me to his grandmother's restaurant for breakfast."

Taylor leaned back in her chair, getting comfortable. This was going to be good. She could tell by that little faraway glint in her sister's eyes. "What's the name of it?"

"Madame Belle's."

"You're kidding? Every chance my partner and I get, we go by that place for breakfast, lunch, and dinner."

"Like the place do you?"

The sisters laughed. Taylor reached across the table, taking her sister's hand. "You like this man, don't you?"

"Yes." Eden looked at Taylor. She smiled, remembering the moment. "He kissed me."

"Was it good?" Taylor wiggled her brows.

Eden laughed like a schoolgirl. "Better than good. I've never been kissed with so much tenderness and passion before. I didn't feel like I was being mauled."

Taylor laughed. "I know what you mean. I dated this guy once who thought it romantic to pull on my hair while trying to choke me with his tongue."

Eden spewed coffee as she coughed with laughter. "Oh, my god, Taylor, what did you do?" She continued to laugh.

"I reached down and grabbed something of his and pulled."

Eden doubled over with laughter as tears rolled down her cheeks.

"Needless to say, we didn't go out again." Taylor giggled as she looked at her sister. This felt good. It had been a while since the two of them had hung out like this.

Eden wiped tears as she slowly sobered. "Well thank goodness Chase isn't like that. In all honesty, I was the one clinging like a vine. That is, until I came to my senses."

"So now that you've had a big helping of white sugar, what do you think?" Taylor taunted wickedly. "You know too much will give you diabetes."

Eden rolled her eyes while suppressing a smile. "Will you stop it?"

"You stop glowing over there. Damn, girl, what did that man put on you?"

Eden howled with laughter. She couldn't remember the last time that she and Taylor had had so much fun together. "Taylor, that man makes me feel dainty and feminine. I feel desirable and wanted."

Taylor sighed with envy. "Now you have me depressed."

Eden dismissed Taylor with a wave. "What am I going to do?" She suddenly stood to pace the room.

"What does your heart tell you to do?" Taylor watched her sister walk the floor.

"My heart tells me to go with what I'm feeling, but there's the election to consider."

"What does Chase have to say about the two of you?"

"He wants us to date and get better acquainted like most couples." She came back to the table and sat down. "But this could blow up in our faces."

Taylor covered her sister's hand. "Or you could discover something wonderful."

"Chase told me to let him worry about the campaign."

"He's right. Listen, Eden, if this man is willing to risk an election to be with you, he's a keeper."

Eden chewed on her bottom lip thoughtfully. "I don't want him to look at me one day and blame me for losing."

Taylor released a heavy sigh. "I give you credit, dear sister, for being extremely intelligent, but predict the future you can't. You have to live each moment the same as the rest of us."

Eden smirked. "You know he asked me last night whether I was ashamed of my feelings for him. That really hurt, because the issue with race that I have isn't about our being together, but the effect it will have on his bid for the mayor's office."

"Are you sure of that, or are you using the election as an excuse?"

Outraged, Eden slapped the table with her hand. "I am not ashamed of my feelings for Chase. God, I haven't felt this alive in years. The man looks at me and my heart starts to race."

Taylor listened with longing. "Good. Then stop worrying about things you can't control and give this relationship a chance." She quickly checked her watch and realized she was out of time. "Hey, I've got to go, but think about what I've said. And call me if you want to talk."

"I will." Eden walked her to the door. "Taylor, you won't say anything—"

"Not a word," Taylor said interrupting the request. "Love you."

"I love you, too."

Eden arrived at the first committee meeting steadfast in her decision to keep their relationship casual. What Chase could do for the citizens of Hilton was too important to risk. If what they felt for each other was meant to be, then they could wait until after the election to explore their feelings. She exited her vehicle, right behind Principal Daniels who would be heading the committee. With him present in the room, she was guaranteed Chase would be on his best behavior. She quickly caught up to the principal, and together they entered campaign headquarters.

Chase stood inside his office door, waiting for Eden to arrive. With any luck, she would arrive before the others and he would be given an opportunity to chip away at her resolve. It had been a long two days since their late-night conversation, and he was more determined than ever to make her see things his way. But as the door opened and David walked in, followed by Eden, he knew he had been outmaneuvered. Well, he would simply change tactics and appeal to her senses rather than her intellect.

He stood there admiring her sexy body visible through her open coat. She wore tan suede boots today, with a camel-colored skirt and sweater. Her hair was curled and bounced with each step she took. His groin tightened at the sight of her. He stepped from his office, making his presence known. Their eyes connected immediately. Deliberately, he gave her a long, smoldering head-to-toe once-over. By the time his eyes connected with hers again, a little heat simmered in their brown depth. He smiled to himself, proud that he could warm the lady's blood with one admiring stare. She didn't stand a chance of resisting him much longer.

The Politics of Love

Eden swallowed hard on spotting Chase. He was dressed in blue slacks and a white shirt. His tie had been removed and the cuffs of his shirt folded back, exposing his strong forearms. He wore a gold watch on his left wrist. His dark hair was freshly cut and begging to be caressed. The man got better looking every time she saw him. And with each time, her will to resist diminished. *All I have to do is stay away from him. And not let him touch me.*

"David, Eden, this way." Chase led them both back to the appointed conference room. "The others should be arriving any moment." He watched as Eden took the chair in the rear of the room and deposited her notepad. *As far away from me as possible. Well, sweetheart, you're about to realize there's no getting away from the inevitable.* "May I offer either of you something to drink?"

"Coffee would be good," David responded.

"A table is set up right outside my door. Sorry, I guess I should have made the offer when you arrived." He watched as David made the walk back toward his office. He turned back to Eden once they were alone.

"Sorry my foot. You did that on purpose," Eden said, rising from the chair. She didn't want to be cornered by Chase.

He possessed a satisfied expression as he slowly advanced in her direction. "Guilty as charged. I wanted a moment alone with you."

Eden took two steps to his every one. She was now standing midway between the long wooden table. "You and I don't need to be alone."

"I beg to differ. I rather enjoyed kissing you in my office." He continued to stalk her.

"Be quiet, before someone hears you." She took two more steps, all the while keeping an eye on the door.

"You can't run from what we feel for each other." He kept walking.

"I'm not running from what I feel. I'm trying to make sure you get elected and avoid making a mistake." She stepped back and caught the heel of her boot on the wheel of a chair. Losing her balance, she went toppling backward, while reaching for the nearest thing to hang on to. Just as she expected to feel the floor and her backside connect, a pair of strong hands circled her waist.

Chase hauled Eden in against his chest as he straightened. With the boots on, she was almost eye-to-eye with him. Their bodies lined up perfectly as though they were beneath silk sheets. His body responded instantly to the feel of her pressed intimately against him. He flashed a satisfied smile when she gasped in response. He hadn't planned on getting her attention this way, but seduction sure seemed to work.

Eyes wide with the knowledge of his current condition, Eden struggled to get free. She quickly placed space between them by walking clear across the room. This time, however, she was very careful of where she stepped.

David returned carrying a cup of coffee, followed by several more members of the committee. Eden delighted in watching Chase slide into the nearest chair to hide his condition. That is, until she realized as the last member arrived and began easing around the table, she had deposited her notepad in the chair to his right. She took the vacant seat with a sense of dread. As the meeting began, however, she relaxed and became involved in the discussion. It was obvious that the people sitting around the table were knowledgeable and quite dedicated to the cause.

The meeting ended an hour later with many great ideas being put forward. Some research would need to be done before the next meeting. Eden gathered her notepad and said her goodbyes. She rushed for the door in an attempt to avoid Chase. She wouldn't survive another assault on her senses. She wanted to be with him, wanted the right to walk into a room and snuggle next to him. But to give in and act on their attraction could cost him an election and a dream. As she approached the front door, she felt him watching her, and turned around. She searched him out. Her eyes locked with his, and in them, he hid nothing. She watched sadly as he returned to his office.

Chase's heart kicked into overdrive when Eden appeared in his doorway. He anxiously waited to see what she would do. An odd look in her brown eyes led him to believe she was conducting a battle within herself. And just when he thought she would turn and leave, she moved further into the room and closed the door. He watched as she tossed her notepad and purse onto the sofa, followed by her coat. Then she did something he hadn't been expecting.

Eden didn't want to think about it. She didn't ask 'what if.' She simply marched across the room and around the desk where Chase stood and covered his lips with hers. A tiny sigh of pleasure escaped her lips as she took what she craved.

Chase enfolded her into his arms while returning the kiss. He savored the moment, yet understood she wasn't surrendering. But she definitely showed signs of weakening. And when she deepened the kiss, he made sure to convey all the reasons for her coming around to his way of thinking.

Just as suddenly, the kiss ended. They stood returning gazes while their breathing slowly returned to normal. Eden caressed his cheek, and felt his evening beard under her fingertips. "I can't be around you any longer. It's becoming too difficult to resist being with you."

"Stop resisting, and let's just go with what we feel." He covered her hand on his cheek.

"Don't you get it? I feel too much for you already. And because I do, your dream of becoming mayor is important to me. I want to see you win and turn this city around. But most importantly, I want you to always look at me the way you are now." She dropped her hand and pulled free of his arms. Grabbing her things, she turned and ran from the office before she could change her mind.

Stanley observed Eden's dramatic departure from Chase's office while standing in the doorway of his own. She was supposed to have been gone, but here she was leaving once again. He didn't like what he was beginning to suspect. He needed Chase clear and focused on the election, not on a woman. Grabbing his briefcase and jacket, he turned out the lights in his office. His dinner date awaited him. He quickly decided on how to approach the subject as he crossed the room. Chase was sitting on the edge of his desk, deep in thought. No doubt he was thinking about that woman and not his campaign.

"Am I interrupting?" Stanley asked, walking in.

Chase hadn't heard him enter. He quickly pulled himself together as he rose to meet him. "No, come on in."

"I saw Ms. Warner leaving your office. Is there something I should know about?" Stanley looked at Chase pointedly.

Chase scratched his chin. He returned to his desk and sat behind it. "Miss Warner is thinking about resigning from the committee."

"Oh really," Stanley responded, pleased. But when Chase looked at him sharply, he realized that his joy must have been reflected in his tone.

"You don't have to sound so happy about it."

"Listen, Chase, you and I have known each other for years, and I'm not about to start lying to you now. The election is becoming about the two of you as a team, rather than about you the candidate. People around here are already gossiping about the closed-door sessions. They're beginning to question your commitment to winning this election. Don't disappoint those people out there." He pointed to the campaign volunteers.

With that parting shot, he left. He would allow his young political star to think on that. He knew Chase had harbored the dream of being mayor of Hilton for years now. Stanley guessed Chase would approach this election as he did most things in his life; focused, determined, and full speed ahead. He wouldn't be blind-sided by other issues. He would keep his eyes on the prize, and remove all distracting obstacles from sight. Stanley hit the sidewalk, feeling confident his preemptive strike had succeeded.

Eden sat in her car watching Stanley drive away. No way was she asking him for help. She turned the key in the ignition once more and received nothing. Her cell phone was also dead after trying to reach her brother with no success, and then roadside service. It had gone completely dead while she had been placed on hold. From the sound, or rather the lack of sound, when she turned the key, she felt something was seriously wrong. Well, she couldn't sit there all night in the dark parking lot. She grabbed her things, and headed back inside campaign headquarters, ruining a perfect exit.

Chase looked up to find Eden standing in his doorway. He grew concerned because she should have been well on her way home by now. "What are you doing back here? I thought you had left."

"I did, but …" Eden rolled her eyes with embarrassment. "My car and cell phone died in the parking lot. Can I use your phone to call someone to pick me up?" She toyed with the shoulder strap of her satchel.

"*Call someone?* And just who in the hell would you call? A boyfriend, ex-boyfriend, or possibly a lover?" he demanded, angrily. He was fast coming to the end of his rope with her. He wanted to grab her by both arms and shake some sense into her.

Eden sensed Chase's growing frustration. He had every right to be upset with her, but his remarks were absurd. "More like my Dad or brother."

"What about me, or am I not good enough for you?" Chase realized his thinking was ridiculously clouded by disappointment, but he was angry and looking for a fight.

Eden didn't give it to him. Instead, she walked over and gave him a long, thorough kiss. In that moment, she simply wanted to be held by him.

This was what he needed. Chase drew Eden down to sit in his lap while he made love to her mouth. The woman was driving him crazy with her martyr routine. But tonight he had finally realized her refusal to see him romantically was an expression of deeper feelings. His dream of becoming mayor was now her dream as well and more important than what they felt for each other.

The two remained that way for several minutes, exchanging kisses and touches, and all with the door to his office stretched wide open.

Chapter Seven

Chase followed Eden into her home. This time he took the opportunity to really look around. He deposited their take-out meal from Belle's on the countertop of the center island in the kitchen. Beautiful earth-toned granite counters with black specks highlighted the black appliances in the kitchen. Double ovens caught his attention. According to Belle, they were a sign of a good cook.

"Do you cook a lot, or is this place for show?" He watched Eden gather plates and utensils.

"I'll have you know you aren't the only one with skills in the kitchen." She returned to the island and began filling their plates.

Chase liked this side of her. Since the kiss in the office, she had relaxed and simply enjoyed being with him. He hoped the debate about the campaign and the public's response to them as a couple was behind them.

"Where are your wine glasses?"

"Right behind you, second shelf," Eden answered as she carried their plates into the dining room. The lighting from the chandelier cast the room in a romantic setting. For tonight, she was tossing caution to the wind, and enjoying being with a man she found fascinating.

Chase joined her at the table and placed a glass of wine beside her plate. He took his chair and reached for her hand as he bowed his head and said grace.

"Amen." Eden had never felt this comfortable with a man before. She found herself smiling more when she was around him.

"I hope I'm responsible for putting that smile on your face," Chase said, drawing her attention.

She dipped her head with embarrassment. "How do you do it?

You make people around you feel at ease."

"That's a good thing, isn't it?" He returned her contented expression, still holding her hand.

"Of course it is, but how do you do it? This is rare for me to be completely comfortable with someone."

Chase looked at her in surprise. "The woman I met backstage was confident and fearless. Where is this coming from?"

Eden realized she had said too much. She removed her hand from his and began eating. "This really is good," she said, to encourage him to eat.

He reached over, taking her hand once more. He waited for her to look at him before speaking. "Don't hide who you are from me."

She hesitated before saying, "I'm confident when it comes to my intelligence and my abilities as an educator. I'll fight to the bitter end for what I believe in."

"But?" He watched her struggle for words. He could tell this was something she had been grappling with for some time, but had never put her feelings into words.

"But all my life I've stood out for one reason or another. First, I was smart and became labeled a nerd. Then I outgrew everyone in my class and was called a giraffe. Experiences and decisions I've made have all led me to be a little defensive and uncomfortable sometimes."

Chase knew there was a great deal she wasn't saying. "I guess being a girl and being taller than the boys in your class would be a little embarrassing."

"Try a major embarrassment." Eden tucked her hair behind her left ear.

"You don't have that problem with me." He too began to eat.

"No, I don't and I like it. You make me feel dainty and feminine."

"You are both those things. You're beautifully tall, but you don't weigh much."

"I should keep you around to boost my confidence level."

"Don't worry, I'm not going anywhere." He looked deeply into her eyes as the silence stretched between them.

"So what's it like having Adam Warner for a father? I observed him in court one day and was blown away by his skill. He must be so proud of his Harvard-educated daughter."

"Harvard is a school just like any other university."

"True, but it's also prestigious, and a man like Adam Warner …"

"Was completely disappointed when his daughter chose to teach instead of being a great attorney," Eden finished his sentence. "I don't want to talk about my father."

This was big and completely unexpected. He didn't know exactly what to say, but knew it couldn't be ignored. "Don't shut me out. I want to share the good with the bad."

Eden's gaze narrowed on him. She continued to watch him for several minutes, gauging his sincerity. "I promise you we'll discuss it at another time. Tonight I'm feeling too good to ruin it with family matters."

Chase caressed her cheek. "Okay, so tell me why you aren't married."

"That again?" She scrunched her nose up, not liking that topic either. "I'm not married because the right man hasn't come along."

"Ever been in love?"

"Once."

For some strange reason, he was hoping she would have said *no*. "What happened? Is he still around?" Chase wanted to know if her resistance to their openly dating had more to do with this man, than the election.

"He's around. He's my father's hotshot young partner." Eden waited for Chase to piece everything together. It didn't take long as he grabbed his wine glass and drained it empty. He placed it back on the table and looked at her.

"Owen Nelson is the man you were in love with?"

"Once."

"The same Owen Nelson whose father is my strongest opponent in the election?"

"Camden Nelson is Owen's father."

Chase pushed back his chair in anger. He stormed across the room and back, stopping beside Eden's chair. "So all this time you've been giving me the runaround about not seeing me because of the election; it had to do with Owen?"

"What?!" Eden pushed her own chair back as she stood. "My concern is for you and the public rejecting you as a candidate because of me."

"Like hell it is! This is about you not wanting your ex-lover to think you're sleeping with the enemy. And of course, your father would probably be disappointed as well."

"You are so off-base here," Eden yelled back, jabbing him in the shoulder with a finger. "I want to see the best man elected into office, and that would be you. And I never said Owen and I were lovers."

"I'm not a fool, honey. Any man would be damn stupid not to take you to bed," Chase said, giving her a lecherous once over.

"Whoa, don't I have some say about who I sleep with?"

"Well, let me put it this way. Any guy, who calls himself a man, would make damn sure you agreed. Me included, if you were wondering."

"I wasn't."

"Liar."

Eden glared at Chase. This conversation had gone off into a completely different direction than she had intended. She took a deep breath to regain a sense of calm. "Can we talk about this civilly?"

"I don't feel like being civil. And I don't feel like creeping around in the shadows to be with a woman I care about."

"I don't want that either. Not any more."

"You don't?" Chase slowly calmed down. He ran a hand over his hair and collapsed back into his chair. He locked gazes with her. "Tell me this. Do you still have feelings for Owen?"

"No. That was over a long time ago. Owen and my brother shared my father's love of the law. They wanted to be lawyers, so they worked in my father's office during high school and summer breaks from college. They soaked up every word of wisdom he passed on. We were constantly thrown together at social gatherings and eventually began dating. He was two years older, with big dreams of the three of us joining my father's practice."

"I didn't realize you were interested in law."

Eden looked at him, sharply. "I wasn't. No one asked me what I wanted to do. Everyone simply assumed because I was attending *Harvard* that I would study law."

"But you didn't."

She shook her head, *no*. "I always wanted to teach. I thought originally on the university level."

"But that changed after the program you told me about."

"Yes it did, and so did everything else. You see, I'm the only child in my family who isn't in the legal field. Victor is an attorney, and Skye, the youngest, is studying law, and Taylor, the oldest, is a police detective."

"Wow!"

"Wow is right. I chose another path, and my father was furious. Owen begged me to reconsider and told me to stop being stubborn. When I told him I could live my life as I chose, he told me I no longer fit into his plans."

"What?" Chase never suspected Owen of being a fool.

"Don't stress about it because it's over. I just want you to know there are no romantic feelings between us." Eden returned to her chair and took Chase's large, strong hand into hers. She traced the veins visible beneath the skin with a finger. "I want you to be sure of your decision to be with me. I couldn't bear to be told I no longer fit into your plans, as well."

Chase ached for her. He rose from his chair and pulled her into his arms. "You'll never hear those words from me. I definitely want you in my life, Eden Warner." He caressed her mouth with his thumb before claiming her lips with an intensity that shook him to the core. She felt good in his arms; like she belonged there. He left her mouth to trace kisses along her jaw line, then he came back to claim her lips once more.

Eden returned Chase's kiss with eagerness. She matched his desire as she relaxed in his arms and enjoyed the moment. She was releasing her fear and going with her heart. She wrapped her arms around his neck and happily received what he was offering. Her fingers stroked his hair as she shared her own passion for him.

He couldn't believe they were finally past the fear and enjoying each other as he wanted. He backed Eden toward the living room while nibbling at her lips and neck. She smelled good. The fragrance she was wearing was different from the one before, but equally as enticing. At the sofa, he pulled her down on top of him. His hands found their way to the hem of her skirt, and began inching it higher. She was soft there and warm. He shifted their positions, placing her beneath him. Her hair was sprawled beautifully around her. He sat back, admiring the image.

"What are you looking at?" she whispered, feeling self-conscious.

Chase only smiled as he caressed her face with a single finger, trailing it down her neck and into the vee of her blouse. He slipped the tiny pearl buttons open to reveal the swells of her lush brown breasts. He placed a kiss on each one. Reclaiming her mouth, he aligned his hard body with her softness, getting a glimpse at what they would share one day in the future.

Eden moaned at the feel of him pressed between her thighs. The man was like a drug, and she was fast becoming addicted.

"Chase, we have to stop," she said extracting her mouth from his. She breathed heavily from her excitement. "I have work tomorrow."

"I know, honey." He kissed her lightly once more, and then heaved himself up. "I didn't mean for this ..."

She silenced him with a kiss. "I know, but I'm glad it did." She smiled at him while buttoning her blouse. "I've been fighting my feelings for you, but no more."

Chase gave her a burning stare. "God, you're a beautiful woman."

"I feel that way when I'm with you." She dropped her hands down to her side. She suddenly began laughing.

"What's so funny?" he asked righting his own clothing.

"I was wearing my boots while we were rolling around on the sofa. Really romantic, huh?"

"Baby, obviously you have no idea what turns a man on." His voice dropped low as he slid his arms around her waist. "Most men fantasize about a woman wearing either heels or boots and nothing else. I got two out of three tonight and am damn happy I did." He kissed her once more, before leading her to the front door. "Lock up tight and I'll call you tomorrow."

"Good night. Drive carefully." Eden stood in the door until he drove away. She closed it behind him and did as he instructed, returning to the dining room to take care of the dishes. A visit to the shower and right to bed, she lay in the dark replaying the evening. She hadn't planned on giving in to her desires, but she couldn't continue to deny her feelings any longer, especially when the man was so attentive and patient. Heck, he thought she was beautifully tall and admired her intelligence. She just prayed their relationship wouldn't negatively affect the election.

Chase too thought about their evening. He had learned a great deal about Eden tonight. She was strong and determined, but also wounded. She had given him plenty to think about. Not only could there be fallout from the public in response to their relationship, but also downright hostility from Owen and Camden Nelson. Eden could become a target of both her father and the Nelsons. His responsibility was to protect her, but one thing was for sure, he didn't intend for anyone to come between them.

The Warner house was a hub of activity on Thanksgiving Day. Family and friends stopped by to exchange holiday greetings. The sisters were in the kitchen with their mother. The conversation was continuous and lively. Eunice Warner stood back observing her daughters with a proud heart. She studied Eden a little more closely, noticing something different in her daughter. She and Taylor had been with their heads together all day. They giggled and whispered like schoolgirls. Then, Eden had blushed shyly in response to something her sister said, and Eunice immediately recognized the signs of a woman falling in love. But with who was the question?

"How's work going?" Eunice asked Eden as she sat beside her at the table.

"It's great. The kids are wonderful and eager to learn." Eden beamed.

Eunice understood her daughter's pleasure in working with children. As a stay-at-home mother, she had enjoyed every moment watching her children learn and grow. "So what's going on with you these days? You haven't been around much."

Eden suddenly sensed she was being interrogated. Eunice Warner was skilled in her method of extracting information. "I've been keeping busy with school and Chase Mathews' committee."

"Oh, I forgot you were doing that. Are you enjoying working with him?" She watched her daughter try not to squirm. She smiled with suspicion.

"Sure. You know Principal Daniels is on the committee as well, and several business leaders from the community. It's rewarding and hopefully after Chase wins, a worthwhile tool for improving the school system."

"Why are you associating with the Mathews camp?" Adam asked his daughter from the doorway. He entered the kitchen where the women were sitting. "Camden is like family and you should be supporting him."

Eden rolled her eyes, because she didn't want to get into this with her father. "Let's not talk about this today."

"Answer the question, Eden. Why are you supporting that man?" he bellowed.

"I'm supporting Chase because I care about him and believe in his campaign," she yelled angrily. "And I wouldn't cast a vote for Mr. Nelson to save my life."

"You watch your mouth, young lady. What's gotten in to you these days?" He stormed over to the table where she sat. "You're a disappointment, Eden."

"So are you." The words shot out of her mouth before she could stop them.

The room grew completely silent as father and daughter faced-off. Eden slowly rose from her chair. "I'm sorry. I didn't mean to say that."

"Not another word from either of you," Eunice hissed, getting everyone's attention. She rarely raised her voice. However, when she did, everyone took notice, including her husband. "Everyone out, except Eden and your father." She gave her children the eye they all knew from childhood.

"It's Thanksgiving, and we have plenty to be thankful for. Adam, your daughter is a good woman and a wonderful teacher. She's quite capable of deciding who she wants to support and date. You should be proud of her accomplishments. She's an individual and has the right to live her own life. And just for the record, Camden is not family, neither is *his* son. Now you can persist in this behavior and lose your daughter, or come around and accept who she is."

Tears blurred Eden's vision. Her mother had finally come to her defense.

"Eden," her mother continued, "it's about time you stood up for yourself. I have watched you disappear into the woodwork for years. I'm proud of you and I love you, but the next time you speak to your father in that tone, you'll answer to me."

"Yes, ma'am."

"Now, everybody smile and pretend to be enjoying yourselves."

Chapter Eight

The Christmas holiday was upon them. Chase and Eden saw each other as much as their schedules allowed. She participated on his committee and worked at headquarters on the weekend. And away from the politics, they got to know each other better. They found they shared similar views on many topics, and when they didn't, they enjoyed debating the issues.

Chase unlocked the door and waved Eden inside. "Welcome to my home." He closed the door behind her. "Here, let me take your coat." He hung it in the closet by the front door. Taking her hand, he showed her around.

"This place is huge. I can't believe you live here by yourself." Eden followed behind him while getting the tour. "How many square feet?"

"Fifty-five hundred, and you can always move in with me." He tried to see the place through her eyes. "My grandfather left me this house when he died."

"It's fabulous," Eden remarked with awe. She stood in the towering foyer. The grand staircase was like something out of the movies. The hardwood floors shone in the light provided by the enormous chandelier.

"Come on, this is where I hang out." Chase led her to the spacious family area.

The room was decorated casually in burgundy, green, and black. She laughed when she saw the black leather recliner. "You are such a typical man. Where's the remote?"

He fished around in the chair, locating the device. "Got to have it, baby."

"Had to have the plasma television, too?"

"You know it." He smiled like a child with a new toy.

Eden continued to look around and had to admit the room looked homey and inviting. A huge fireplace with a stone mantle added an old world charm to the room. "I like it. I especially love these large windows." She walked over in front of them. "I bet this room is flooded with light during the day."

"Why don't you stick around and find out?" Chase suggested, slipping his arms around her. He loved the brown suede pants she wore. They felt soft under his fingertips and clung to her hips perfectly.

Eden smiled up at him. "One day I will." She kissed him. "Now show me the rest of this house."

Chase took Eden from room to room. He shared childhood stories of visiting his grandfather's home. When they came to his bedroom, he stopped. "I'm not sure if it's safe for you to go in there." His smile was devilishly wicked.

"I'm a big girl. I'm sure I can handle it."

"Don't say I didn't warn you." Chase opened the door to his suite. "This was the room I stayed in as a boy when I visited my grandparents."

"My goodness, it's too big for a child." She walked through the suite, containing a sofa, chair, and television. The bedroom area was decorated in dark cherry wood furnishings. The bed was a king-size sleigh bed with two nightstands flanking it. The other piece in the room was a beautiful carved dresser with a mirror.

The bedroom was painted in a steely gray with the bedding a darker shade of gray, yellow, and white. The room was masculine, yet beautiful. "This is quite nice."

"Thank you. The bed's comfortable, want to try it out?" he teased, making love to her with his eyes.

Eden grinned while backing up to the foot of the bed. She ran her hand across the fine bedding. When he looked at her like that, she was almost ready to throw caution to the wind. But what they shared was too important to her to go falling into bed too soon. "I'll take your word for it." She cut a quick path to the door. "Didn't you invite me for dinner?"

Chase followed her out the room and back down the hallway. "And dessert," he reminded, catching up to her.

Eden laughed all the way to kitchen. Standing in the doorway, she thought she had died and gone to heaven. "This is my dream kitchen." She stepped into the contemporary-styled kitchen with awe. She went directly to the Viking six-burner gas stove. "You even have water here."

"Hey, if I'd known I'd get this type of excitement out of you, I would have shown you the kitchen instead of the bedroom." He checked his lasagna.

"Oh, be quiet. Let me enjoy myself." Eden trailed her fingers over the black granite countertop, while admiring the lighted cabinets. She spotted the double dishwashers. "This was a long time coming to the home."

"You know you're welcome to use my kitchen any time you want."

She looked at him. "Thanks. I may take you up on that. I like to bake for the children during the holidays."

"You'll do it here this year."

Chase sorted through the mail while Eden continued to explore his kitchen. An envelope from the current mayor's office caught his attention. He ripped the side and removed the red glittered invitation. He laughed, walking over to join her at the sink.

"This is like a surgical sink. It's wonderful." She kicked the pad at the base of the cabinet. Water flowed freely from the faucet.

"As you know, I like to cook. The hands get dirty and this way, I never have to touch the faucet to wash them." He waved the invitation at her.

"What's this?" She took it and began reading. Her eyes connected with his.

"Obviously you have one at home just like it."

"Yeah, and it informs me you're to be my escort for the evening. I think the mayor is looking to stir things up by having us come together. He knows my family's connection to the Nelsons."

"You're probably right." Chase pulled Eden into his arms. "So will you be my date for the Christmas gala?"

"I don't see how I can refuse, when he has specifically instructed you to escort me." She leaned into him. "But, I'd love to accompany you."

He caressed her cheek. "You know Owen and his father are likely to be there?"

"I know. My parents will be there as well."

"Are you sure …"

Eden covered his mouth with her hand. "I'm sure." She sealed their date with a kiss. "Now, is that lasagna about ready?"

"Coming up." Chase removed the spinach salad from the refrigerator. He measured oil and vinegar, and then tore open a seasoning package, creating the dressing. Garlic bread was popped into the oven and the timer set. "Ten minutes and dinner's served. Now while we wait.…" He reached for her. "I want dessert first."

He captured Eden's mouth with his, and thrust his tongue between her parted lips. Her taste was a sweet addiction that he craved more and more of each day. His hands slid into the back pockets of her slacks. They caressed and cupped her bottom intimately. Still kissing her, he backed Eden against the cabinet as he caressed his length against the juncture of her thighs. The grinding friction of their bodies had him hard and aroused. Catching her by surprise, he picked her up and deposited her on the granite countertop. He kissed her with a series of drugging kisses, before trailing more kisses down her neck. He released the side button on her white silk wrap blouse, pulling it free of her pants and open for his viewing pleasure. The sight of her full breasts encased in white lace made his erection painfully stiffer. He had to touch her, taste her. He met Eden's eyes, expecting to be stopped. Instead, she reached for the front clasp of her bra and released it.

Eden had never felt so daring. But when she was with Chase, she wanted to experience life to the fullest. She watched him as he slowly peeled the cups from her breasts, and stood there looking at her. When his hand covered her left breast, she thought she had never felt anything better. That is, until his tongue snaked around

85

her protruding nipple, making circles. The feel of his warm breath mingled with the cool wetness of his mouth was incredible. And when he actually blew on her wet nipple causing it to tighten further, she thought she would fly apart in his arms.

Chase couldn't stop touching her. She was so unbelievably responsive to his touch that he wanted to touch her everywhere. He lapped between her breasts and bending his knees, continued down to her navel. He released the button on her slacks at the very moment the timer on the stove went off.

He straightened to his full height, sucking in a deep breath as he reached for control. He pressed a lingering kiss into the bend of her neck before stepping away.

Eden slid from the counter like a rag doll. She couldn't believe what they'd done and in the kitchen, no less. She blushed shyly as she quickly righted her clothing.

After dinner, the couple cleaned the kitchen together and retired in the family room. Chase built a fire, and drew Eden down onto the sofa beside him. They lay curled together, enjoying the dancing flames. Soft music played in the background.

"I had a wonderful time tonight and your home is lovely."

"I hope you become a regular around here." He kissed her ear.

"Thank you."

"What are we going to do about the gala? People will take one look at us and know we're a couple."

"We are a couple. And I'm too happy to care what people think any more. As long as you're sure."

"Baby, people are going to vote for me or they're not. Besides, I've already won the best prize."

"What are you after, Mr. Mathews?" Eden asked smiling.

"I already have it right here in my arms."

Chase and his traveling entourage entered Belle's place a little after one. The crowd was thinning, making it the perfect place to grab a bite and talk over the morning visit with the police union. Stanley and Alison joined him at the back table. They had just taken their seats when his grandmother came from the kitchen spotting him.

"Hi, handsome," Belle greeted Chase with a kiss. Today she wore another one of her skirts, with boots. Large, chunky earrings dangled from her ears.

Stanley looked at the woman with a disapproving glance. Her style of dress was all wrong. Didn't she know her appearance was a reflection on Chase? The citizens wanted to know their candidate came from a traditional family with down-to-earth values. This Bohemian he called a grandmother would never do on the campaign trail.

"Hi, Grandmother," Chase greeted. "May we have a pot of coffee and some sandwiches brought over to the table?"

"I take this is a working lunch?"

"Yes, it is. We're coming from a meeting with the police union. I think they're going to endorse my campaign." His eyes shined with excitement.

"You are the best candidate." She patted his cheek. "Ah, by the way, I've been hearing about this Christmas gala. Will you be attending?" Her eyes danced with mischief.

Chase leaned in toward her. "If you're asking whether I'll be escorting a certain beautiful lady, the answer would be *yes*."

Stanley half-listened to Alison ramble on about their meeting. He was trying to make out the conversation between Chase and Belle.

"I knew you were a smart man," Belle said, pinching Chase's cheek. "So does my daughter know about you two?" Belle noticed Stanley paying more attention to their conversation than to his own. She grabbed Chase's arm and drew him back into the kitchen with her. She quickly placed his order, and then returned to their conversation.

87

"Mom knows I'm seeing someone, but no, she doesn't know who. You know how she is," Chase said, throwing his hands up helplessly.

"Yes, I do. She half-listens while people talk."

Chase laughed. "I love her dearly, but she has never been a doting mother. Not like you." His eyes softened, returning her gaze. "I love you." He kissed her cheek once more.

"And I love you." She cupped his cheeks like she did when he was a child. "Edward is your father, but you are the spitting image of my Ruben."

Chase smiled, remembering his late grandfather. "He would like Eden. She possesses his compassionate nature. The things she does for her students to help them, while going out of her way to save them embarrassment, is amazing."

Belle touched his hand. "Sounds like your feelings for this woman are getting serious."

He nodded, thoughtfully. "They are. What we have is really good."

"Then treasure it because it can be taken away so quickly."

"I do."

Belle hesitated before she spoke her next words. "Protect her Chase, because once people learn that you two are a couple, things can get ugly."

"You sound like Eden."

"My sweet boy, you have never been ostracized. The world has been yours for the taking, but if you choose to be with Eden, things will change. You'll discover who your real friends are." She thought about Stanley out there. "All I'm trying to say is be sure of your feelings and commitment to her."

"Sandwiches up," Donovan called to Chase.

"Go on and take the sandwiches out. I'll bring coffee and my famous apple turnovers."

Chase returned to the dining room with platter in hand. He deposited the sandwiches on the table and sat down to join the conversation. However, his mind kept straying to his grandmother's remarks. He knew she loved him and wanted to see him happy, but he also knew she'd experienced a prejudice of sorts in their social circle for her freestyle living. He had watched her be hurt over the years. Even her own daughter looked down upon her. He wouldn't allow Eden to become a target of such narrow-mindedness.

"Earth to Chase," Alison called.

"I'm sorry, Alison, my mind was elsewhere."

"Yes, we noticed," Stanley remarked dryly. "We were discussing the Christmas gala. It's the perfect opportunity for you to appear mayoral. At every opportunity, work in the campaign issues," he instructed. "Remember you're not there to enjoy the evening, but to work the room."

Chase nodded, but had every intention of enjoying the evening with Eden on his arm.

"Try this one," Taylor said as she passed yet another gown through the dressing room door. She and Eden had been to two department stores and were now visiting local boutiques in search of the perfect dress.

"They're beautiful, but they don't have that wow factor I'm looking for."

"I get it. You want to knock the man flat on his butt." Taylor laughed.

"Something like that." The door to the dressing room suddenly opened.

"Get dressed. I know just the place," Taylor told her, excited. "Now the place is pricey, but I guarantee you'll find something that leaves Chase speechless."

"Speechless is good." Eden pulled her sweater over her head, and tugged on her jeans. "Where is this place?" She zipped up her boots and reached for her coat.

Taylor pulled on her gloves. "I responded to a break-in there about two months ago while assisting the robbery unit. The woman who owns the shop happens to do a great deal of the designs herself."

"Sounds good, but what's the name of the boutique?"

"Allure."

"I like it." Eden used the keyless entry to unlock the doors to her car.

"Girl, I couldn't inspect the crime scene without checking out the clothes. They were fabulous."

Eden backed out the parking space. "I can't wait to see them. Lead away."

Twenty minutes later, Eden pulled into the small parking lot of Allure. The old converted house was located on the outskirts of town. The parking lot was almost completely occupied. Eden took it as a good sign. She entered the boutique, immediately liking what she saw. The styles, colors, and fabrics were fabulous.

"What did I tell you?" Taylor whispered, following behind her.

Eden was too busy staring at the stunning creations to respond. Curved, stainless clothes stands held one-of-a-kind designs. "You were right. Let's locate the evening wear."

"Detective Warner, I thought that was you," the owner of the boutique greeted Taylor. "What can I assist you ladies with?"

Taylor pointed to the right. "This is my sister, Eden. She's looking for a gown that will leave a man speechless."

"Or flat on his butt," Eden added.

The woman laughed. "Forget speechless and flat on his butt, honey. I have just the thing to leave your man begging."

Chapter Nine

Eden stood in the closet admiring her reflection in the floor-length mirror. She liked what she saw. The gown was beautiful and sexy without being tasteless. It was exactly what she had been looking for. Her blood pulsed with excitement. She couldn't wait to see Chase's reaction. She returned to the bedroom and dabbed on her favorite fragrance; a little behind each ear, both wrists, and last but not least, between her breasts. The evening was too important to miss a beat. If Chase was willing to place his campaign on the line to be with her, then she would make him proud to have her on his arm.

The doorbell chimed, signaling Chase's arrival. She grabbed the wrap to the gown and her purse, and headed downstairs. She took a moment to compose herself before opening the door.

Chase turned toward the door and at the sight of Eden, lost the ability to speak. She looked indescribable. To use words like pretty and beautiful were understatements. Breathtaking was more appropriate as she returned his stare.

"Are you coming in?" Eden asked with a smile.

"I'm not sure if that's a wise move. I don't think I'll be able to keep my hands off you if I come in." His body stirred with a hunger that wouldn't be ignored.

Eden was overjoyed by his response. She felt beautiful and sexy. Her smile was bright and flirtatious. "I assure you I'm touchable." To prove her point, she drew him across the threshold, and into a kiss that left him wanting more—much more. They were both in need of air as they parted. She finally closed the door. Turning around, she took a moment to assess his appearance. "You look quite handsome, Candidate Mathews." She ran a hand down the lapel of his black tuxedo.

Chase licked his lips, tasting her, as he slowly walked around her. He admired the gown while feeling his heart beat with excitement. She was truly lovely. He breathed deeply to cool his boiling blood, and inhaled the familiar fragrance, mixed with a splash of Eden. His gut tightened even more.

"But you, Miss Warner, are a vision in holiday red."

He couldn't take his eyes off her. The long-sleeved red velvet gown was sexy, yet classy. The bodice showcased the lushness of her breasts, by displaying just the right amount of cleavage to leave a man wanting more. And when she moved, the fabric moved with her, silhouetting her tall, womanly physique to perfection. But the thigh-high split, set off-center to the left, gave the most mouthwatering sight of her long leg. The woman was making tonight a test of his strength, because all he really wanted to do was peel the gown from her body to discover the hidden treasure beneath it.

"You realize I'm not letting you out of my sight tonight?" Chase informed her.

Eden laughed flirtatiously as she used her thumb to wipe away her lipstick from his mouth. "That's good, considering I'll be keeping an eye on you as well. I don't want some woman hitting on you tonight."

Chase laughed deeply. He enjoyed her little flashes of jealousy. "There's only one woman I want."

"Make sure you keep it that way." She caressed his cheek.

Chase covered her hand with his. He felt himself grinning like a schoolboy and didn't care. The woman fascinated him. Each day he peeled away another layer and fell more in love with her. "I can't wait to show you off tonight."

Eden searched Chase's eyes for a sign of doubt and found none. All she saw reflected back at her was *love*. She quickly dropped her hand to retrieve her wrap. Her heart was beating so rapidly with excitement, she felt faint. She took a couple of quick breaths to clear her head. By the time she returned to him, still waiting by the door, she was in better control.

"Let me help you with that." Chase took the black velvet wrap.

and draped it around her shoulders. He pressed a lingering kiss behind her ear. "Shall we?" He held out his arm for her.

"We shall." Eden draped her arm through his.

The couple arrived at the downtown civic center thirty minutes later. A steady stream of people headed inside. They were all dressed formally and in search of a good time. Chase assisted Eden out of the car, and giving her his arm once more, escorted her to the door. Members of the press were circling outside the entrance. Chase felt Eden tense beside him as they were spotted and quickly set upon by the reporters. He covered her hand, offering comfort while steadily propelling them forward. Questions about the election were thrown at him while flashbulbs went off. Like the mayoral candidate he was, Chase skillfully answered each one.

"Are you all right?" he asked Eden as they entered the building. He removed her wrap and gave it to the woman checking coats for the evening. He placed his arm around her waist, and then turned to look at her.

Eden smiled, reassuringly. "I'm fine. I'm just not used to the press. That's your thing, future mayor of Hilton."

"From your lips to God's ears, baby," Chase whispered close to her ear.

They fell in step behind another couple. The mayor and his wife stood inside the doorway, greeting each guest as they arrived. Jazzy holiday music played in the background during the social hour.

"Welcome and Happy Holidays," the mayor greeted them. He smiled up at Chase while giving him a firm handshake. "I know there are four of you vying for my office, but let's be honest. This election is between you and Camden."

"You never know," Chase replied cautiously.

"Yes we do, and I don't envy you, Chase. Camden Nelson makes a formidable opponent, but my money is on you."

"So is mine," Eden interjected. She exchanged pleasantries with the mayor's wife, before formally greeting him.

"I'm delighted you joined us, Ms. Warner," the Mayor said, placing a kiss on the back of her hand. "People are discussing you everywhere I go. The mayoral election hasn't experienced this much interest in years. I had to make sure you were in attendance."

"Thank you for the invitation, but tonight, I'm Chase's date and nothing else," Eden said, taking Chase's arm once more. She smiled over at him.

"You both will be sitting with us tonight," the mayor informed them. "The waiter will show you to our table. Please enjoy yourselves." He studied the couple with great interest as they trailed behind the waiter. He had a feeling the night was going to be quite interesting.

Eden leaned in close to Chase as they followed the waiter. "If you're sitting at his table, where do you think the other candidates are sitting?"

"My thoughts exactly. The Nelsons will be sharing the same table. Are you comfortable with this?" he asked, worried.

Her eyes softened in response to the concern she heard in his voice. "We can face anything as long as we're together."

"You're right, baby."

The grand ballroom was decorated for the holidays. Red and white poinsettias were bountiful throughout the room. Helium-filled balloons in the traditional Christmas hues danced along the ceiling. Red and green streamers were suspended from them to create a forest of holiday colors. Glittered snowflakes also shimmered overhead, casting the room in a winter wonderland. White linen-draped tables were arranged in a semi-circle around the dance floor. Hors d'ouvres lined a table to the right, while the bar was to the left.

Their progress was hampered by people stopping to greet the candidate and offer their support. Eden realized that although she was met with smiling faces and well wishes for the holiday, she was also being looked upon as a campaign prop. Chase went out of his way to introduce her as his date, to no avail. But she was determined not to allow anyone to spoil this evening for them, so she shook off the negative feelings. That determination also included Owen and her father. But as she and Chase approached their table, she heard her father call her name from one of the neighboring tables. Spotting her mother, she smiled. However, when she looked at her father, he was wearing his best courtroom face. She and Chase quickly thanked the waiter, before heading over to greet her parents.

Chase could feel Adam Warner's eyes on him. He wrapped an arm around Eden's waist, staking his claim.

"Mom, you look beautiful," Eden said in greeting. "Daddy, you're looking handsome as always."

Adam looked at his daughter, seeing a younger version of his wife. She was a beautiful young woman, and Chase Mathews knew it and was obviously announcing his intentions. His first inclination was to tell the man to remove his hand from his daughter's waist, but Eunice had made a few things clear to him. He could accept who his daughter was and embrace the fine woman she had become, or he could lose her. As he looked into her brown eyes, he was reminded of the stubborn little girl that would challenge him at every turn. He had loved her tenaciousness as a child, but for some reason had mistaken it for rebelliousness as an adult. Well, he loved his daughter and wasn't about to lose her to this man. He needed to start behaving like a father. If Chase Mathews was the man she had chosen, then he had every intention of making sure the man was worthy of his daughter.

"You look more like your mother each day," Adam said, meaning each word. "You look beautiful, baby."

Eden was speechless. She beamed with happiness. "Thank you. I'd like to introduce you to Chase Mathews."

The men greeted each other with firm handshakes. They stood toe-to-toe, sizing each other up. "It's a pleasure to meet you, Mr. Warner. Your legal skills are legendary and rightly so. I had the pleasure of sitting in on the McDonald case. You were brilliant."

Eden could have kissed Chase right there. He was making every effort to win her father over.

"Your reputation precedes you as well, Mr. Mathews," Adam stated bluntly, every bit the protective father. "Your grandmother speaks highly of you, and since I consider Belle a friend, I'll trust her opinion."

Chase nodded, understanding the man clearly.

Eunice smiled at Adam, seeing the man that she fell in love with years ago. Proud to be with him, she took his arm. She glanced at her daughter and winked. "You two have a good time tonight."

"Thank you and we will," Chase said with a nod. He escorted Eden through the milling crowd in search of his friend. "That went surprisingly well."

"Yeah, I know. Who was that man with my mother?" Eden asked, laughing.

Chase also laughed. Maybe they were worried for nothing.

"Are your parents here tonight?" she asked, waving at a couple she knew.

"Dad is out of town, and Mom doesn't go out socially without him."

Relieved, she nodded. She followed Chase over to a couple by the bar. The man greeted her with a bright, friendly smile. His green eyes seem to almost glow in his golden brown face as he studied her closely. His jet-black hair was cut neatly in a professional style that highlighted his chiseled features and knockout good looks.

"Eden, this is Special Agent Stone Patrick and his date."

"Janice Beverly," Stone made introductions. "Janice is my partner," he made a point of saying.

Eden smiled at the woman, despite being annoyed by Stone's rudeness. But the woman barely noticed her, as her attention was focused on Chase.

"You're more handsome in person, Mr. Mathews," Janice purred. Her blue eyes caressed his body from head-to-toe. "My partner tells me you're old friends."

Stone didn't hear his partner's flirtatious remarks. His attention was on the woman with his friend. He couldn't get over the striking resemblance; however, the visible height difference easily distinguished the two women. "You look like Taylor," he said with amazement.

The statement caught Eden off guard. She looked at the man more closely, now with curiosity blazing in her eyes. "Not quite, she's the oldest. Although, she'll probably kill me if you tell her I told you that," she said with a smile.

"I promise not to tell her." Humor twinkled in his eyes.

"How do you know my sister?" Eden only half-listened to his explanation. Her concentration was on his partner, snuggling up to Chase. The woman was batting her baby blues up at him like Eden wasn't standing there.

"We're working on a case together," Stone informed her, and then realized she was watching Chase and Janice. *Now if I could get this type of response from your sister.*

"I read that you're a wonderful dancer," Janice was saying, while trailing her fingers down his lapel. "Maybe we could—"

"Thank you for the offer," Chase said, cutting her off. He politely removed her hand. "But I have a date for the evening." He reached for Eden's hand, while looking over at Stone. "We'll catch up to you both later." He maneuvered them back toward their table.

Eden's blood was boiling. "The nerve of some people. Can you believe she was flirting with you right in front of me?"

"Do I detect a hint of the green-eyed monster?" He whispered in her ear.

"I am not jealous of that woman."

"Doesn't look like that to me," he teased.

"You're going to get it." Eden shot him a warning glare.

Chase howled with laughter as he slipped his hand into hers. "Well, give it to me, baby." He brought her hand to his lips and kissed the back of it. But as they approached the mayor's table, they noticed the other guests had arrived.

Dinner would have been an enjoyable affair, if it hadn't been for the Nelsons. Camden and Owen Nelson had glared across the table during the entire meal. Although the mayor maintained a steady stream of lively conversation, there had been an air of tension hanging over the table. When one of the candidate's wives engaged Eden in the conversation, Mrs. Nelson, whom Eden had known for years and thought was one of the nicest people, had publicly snubbed her. Eden had shaken it off and pressed on. Chase, on the other hand, was fast approaching the 'don't give a damn' point when he felt Eden's hand on his thigh. She gave it a gentle pat, reassuring him that she was all right. He placed his hand over hers, and instantly felt calmer. The band suddenly struck up a tune, announcing the dinner hour was over. The mayor escorted his wife to the dance floor and requested the candidates and their significant others join them.

Chase looked over at Eden. Her features were strained, but her spine was straight and defiance blazed in her eyes. He whispered so only she could hear. "I say let's ignore them and have a good time." He rose from his chair.

Eden grinned at him. With a look at Owen, she slipped her hand into Chase's. As they took up position on the dance floor, she whispered, "Let's see some of those dance moves."

The couple danced smoothly together. With their complementing heights and good looks, they made for a stunning couple. Chase held Eden tenderly as they danced. Delighted she followed his lead so beautifully, he stared into her eyes.

"You've taken dance, too," he whispered against her ear.

"Mom insisted. She was making ladies out of us." Eden laughed. She would have to thank her mother for insisting.

"I resisted. Real men didn't do sissy dances." He laughed at the memory.

Eden giggled, enjoying herself as he executed a series of spins, followed by a dip. When she was back to vertical, she admired his good looks. She loved it when he laughed and was playful like this. His eyes took on an almost translucent shade of blue.

"I for one know you're no sissy, Mr. Mathews."

"Damn straight, and I intend to prove it to you," he said with a promising wink. He felt a tremor race through Eden's body as she snuggled closer. They had forgotten the others in the room and were all alone in their happiness.

But across the room, the press snapped away, realizing they had stumbled upon something newsworthy. While Stanley knocked back another drink and cursed the day Eden walked into Chase's life, Owen observed, realizing she had never looked at him the way she was looking at Chase. And Adam Warner kept watch with a divided heart. His baby was in love with the man and didn't realize it, nor did she realize the pain that could come because of it.

The tune melted into another as people poured onto the dance floor. Chase and Eden danced several more songs before Chase spotted Stanley who was waving frantically in his direction. "I hate to cut this short, but Stanley is trying to get my attention."

Eden glanced in the direction Chase was looking. The man looked like he'd had one too many drinks. "I'm going to the ladies room. I'll join you in a minute." She headed in the opposite direction.

Owen was waiting for her as she left the restroom. Considerably shorter, he had no choice but to look up at her. His eyes were like hard marbles as he glared at her. They looked as though they would literally pop right out of his head, he was so angry.

"Do you have no pride?"

"Let's not do this." Eden tried to walk around him, but was blocked.

"How could you betray my family like this?"

"Oh, please. What I do is none of your business," Eden responded, angrily.

"I get it. You're sleeping with him to get back at me." He jabbed his finger into her shoulder.

Eden shook her head with disbelief. "You would think that." She started to walk away, but turned back around. "What Chase and I share has absolutely nothing to do with you, or your family. Now get a life for yourself before it's too late."

"For someone who's supposed to be so damn smart, can't you see that the man is using you? You're a way to steal the African American vote from my father and nothing else. Hell, I was with you only to score points with your father," Owen hurled the insult, scoring big when he saw Eden flinch.

"You poor excuse for a man," Chase charged as he came to Eden's defense. "This has nothing to do with the election. You realized too late you were a fool for breaking up with her, and instead of being a man and apologizing, you're hurling insults." Chase wrapped his arm around Eden's waist, protectively. He prayed she wasn't buying what Owen was selling. But he looked into her eyes at the very moment Owen's words turned into a possibility. "Let's go." Anxiously, he led Eden to a quiet corner. He held her face between his hands, while looking deeply into her eyes.

"Please tell me you didn't believe him."

"Of course not," she lied, shaking her head. But she couldn't stop asking herself if Owen's words contained some truth.

Despite her response, Chase felt on shaky ground. Eden doubted his feelings for her, and that unnerved him. What they shared was new and untried. They were only now exploring those feelings, and he didn't want that ruined by a lie. As they stood there looking at each other with an expanding chasm of distrust, he felt hopeless, and did the only thing he could think of to reconnect with her. He drew her into his arms and kissed her with all the passion and desperation he felt.

Eden gave herself up to the kiss because she needed reassurance. It felt right and so natural as Chase tried to wipe away her doubt, but then she remembered where they were and pulled back.

"We should go back inside. It wouldn't look good for the candidate to be caught making out in the hallway." Afraid someone might have seen them, she looked around quickly. She retrieved a tissue from her evening bag and wiped at Chase's mouth. Taking a deep breath, she turned to leave.

"Eden, wait," Chase said, stopping her. He waited until she was looking directly at him. "You are everything to me, and what we have is precious."

"Thank you. I feel the same way."

But as they drove home later, Chase wasn't convinced Eden believed him. She had gone through the remainder of the evening seemingly having a good time. However, he knew her well enough to know she was faking it. He was angry with Owen for putting the idea into her head. However, he was also angry with Eden for believing a man who obviously didn't give a damn about her. He stole a glance at her. She hadn't moved a muscle since taking her seat. She rode looking out of the window, not making a sound. He pulled into his garage and turned off the ignition.

"What are we doing here?" She turned looking at him.

"We need to talk."

"We could have done that at my place."

"I prefer my own."

Eden was out of the car in a flash. She marched to the door that led into the kitchen.

"Damn it!" Chase slammed his hand against the steering wheel. He opened the car door and went after her. Trapping her between the kitchen door with his bigger body, he inserted the key, and followed her inside.

Eden didn't want to have this conversation with Chase. She just wanted a moment alone to think. Her heart was telling her to believe in him, but her head was telling her she couldn't ignore the possibility. Hadn't the press been hooked by the challenge? A relationship would definitely garner more interest for his campaign. She had been used once and wouldn't allow that to happen again. She walked through his home and into the family room. She tossed her purse onto the sofa and turned facing him. "Is the black vote your reason for wanting to be with me? I mean, you were so gung-ho about our going public with our relationship."

Chase swore under his breath. His eyes darkened with anger as he glared at her. His hands hung loosely from his pockets, fighting the urge to shake some sense into her. "Did you agree to go with me tonight just so you could stick it to Owen?" he charged, angrily.

"Don't you dare lay that on me!"

"And don't you dare accuse me of being with you for a damn vote!"

The room suddenly grew quiet as they both tried to calm down. Chase cursed as he turned and collapsed onto the sofa. "Eden, please don't let a malicious lie come between us. We are great together. You have to know how much you mean to me. I've shared my heart and home with you, and introduced you to the only other special lady in my life, my grandmother. I haven't done that with any other woman I've dated." He looked at her, hiding nothing. She saw his anguish and his fear. His shoulders were slumped with defeat. In that moment, she was a goner. She knew as she moved toward him, her heart belonged to Chase.

"Show me how much I mean to you," she whispered.

He stared into her wide, frightened eyes as she held out her hand to him. She was trusting him with her heart and body, and he wouldn't violate either one.

Chapter Ten

C hase's mouth and hands were everywhere as he moved deep inside her. He was gentle, yet demanding, and she had never been loved so thoroughly. His groans of pleasure were like music to her ears. They were good together, and she never wanted the moment to end.

She kissed his chin while her hands palmed his hips. His muscles were warm and firm under her fingers, as she felt them flex with each thrust inside of her. She had asked him to express his feelings, and he was. In every touch, every kiss, every stroke, and every sigh of pleasure, he was demonstrating the depth of his feelings for her, and she would do no less.

She opened wider to receive him, her hips rising to meet his. She applied a little pressure to his chest, indicating her turn to lead. With him beneath her, she covered his lips and proceeded to make love to his mouth to the same slow rhythm she was setting. She heard him swear with frustration as the tempo slowed even more.

Chase wanted to make the night last forever. Grabbing her hips with his hands, the sight of Eden's beautiful brown body straddling his hips took center stage. Her body was fantastic. Firm, high, C-cup breasts with dark sweet nipples, bounced with each slide into her. The sight alone was enough to make a man stand up and take notice. But the biggest turn on were her long, gorgeous legs, wrapped around him. He ran his hand down the length of them as Eden rose, then eased down the length of him. They were smooth, blemish-free, and spread, offering him a view of the paradise they'd found together.

Eden knew he watched her and wanted to convey the depth of her feelings for him. She closed her eyes and threw her head back, giving herself up to the moment. She smiled as she felt Chase's hands cover her breasts, then trail down her body to rest on her hips. She yelped as she suddenly found herself back beneath him. His lips pulled at a nipple while his hips sat a demanding pace that soon had her moaning with pleasure.

"That's it, baby, don't fight it," Chase crooned as he stroked inside of her. She was close, and to guarantee a place inside her heart he wanted her complete surrender.

He raised her hips and pressed forward, ravaging her mouth until neither of them could breathe. Stroke after delicious stroke, he rode her until she began to shake from head to toe. Eyes wide open, she held his gaze as the world suddenly tilted and then exploded around them.

Chase lay on top of Eden for several minutes after the last tremor left her body. He didn't want to move. He was at peace and the moment was too perfect. He had never felt completely content in his life as he did right at that moment. He looked into Eden's smiling face and his heart was forever gone. She owned it and he couldn't be happier.

"You seem pretty pleased with yourself," he whispered, then pressed a kiss to her lips.

"I'm very pleased," she responded with a wiggle beneath him.

"I see you're trying to start something." His eyes were heavy with arousal.

"I think I have," Eden giggled, as she rolled to be on top again. She removed the condom, and then rolled on another one. She sat up looking at him. He was gorgeous and privileged, but also kind, generous, and *loving*. Neither had said the words yet, but they were there. Two people didn't make love the way they just had, and not be in love. But for right now, the words weren't required. The message was being received loud and clear. She grasped his wrists and placed his hands over her breasts.

"I like it when you touch me."

"I like touching you." His voice was lazy with desire.

"Then touch me. I want to feel your hands everywhere."

Chase proceeded to do just that. He brought her to the peak of desire repeatedly with only his touch, be it his hands or his mouth. He touched her everywhere. By the time he entered her body once more, they were both primed and ready to go up in flames. He captured her hands with his and raised them beside her head. With her legs locked around his hips, he pistoned back and forth inside of her until perspiration bathed both their bodies. A final stroke and their cries of ecstasy bounced off the walls in the room.

They lay beside each other, whispering into the night. Eden secure in Chase's arms, and he secure in her feelings for him.

"Why aren't you married?" Eden asked the question this time.

"Just like you, I've been used. Power and money are very seductive, and people sometimes fall in love with them and not the person."

Eden listened to his response, but also heard the pain. "She didn't deserve you."

He snuggled closer. "You're right, but it doesn't mean that it doesn't hurt."

"I know."

"I've learned to protect my heart," he confessed into the dark.

"How?" Eden didn't believe that was the case with her.

"I never allowed myself to get emotionally invested. A date here and there, then I moved on."

"Hence, the womanizing reputation."

"Yeah. I'm not proud of that."

"I know you aren't, but I do understand." She stroked his hand that rested on her abdomen.

"I hope you also know that what we shared tonight wasn't sex."

Eden grinned with happiness as she wiggled closer. "I know that, too."

Chase pressed a kiss into her hair. He was relieved by her response. "I don't know what we'll face from here on out, but as long as we believe in each other, we can overcome it."

"I agree, but politics is an ugly game."

"You're right. But let me tell you about the politics of love."

"I'm all ears," Eden whispered as her stomach fluttered with joy.

"The politics of love is about promoting yourself to a woman until she can't refuse. It's about promising to be there when it seems the entire world has gone crazy. It's about supporting her every dream and desire. It's about rallying her spirits when life gives her a hard knock. It's about campaigning relentlessly for a place in her heart. So this is my announcement speech, Eden Warner. I'm tossing my hat in the ring for a permanent place in your heart."

Eden turned in Chase's arms to face him. Tears ran down her cheeks as she kissed him. "You already have that."

Chase turned and reached into the nightstand behind him. "I know you're spending Christmas with your family, so I'll give this to you now."

Eden looked at the black velvet box before finally taking it. "Aren't you? I just assumed you would be spending Christmas with your family as well."

"Mom and Dad decided to take a cruise, and grandmother has been invited to friends."

"Come with me to my parents' home." Her eyes begged him to say yes.

Chase laughed. "I don't know if your father is ready for that."

"He has to be, because you're a part of my life, and that isn't going to change."

He kissed her. "Check with your mother first. Now open your gift." He watched her face for a reaction.

"Oh, Chase, it's beautiful," Eden gushed. The diamond tennis bracelet was exquisite. "Put it on me." She sat all the way up so that he could assist her. When the bracelet was finally secured on her wrist, she held it up for his inspection. "What do you think?"

Chase chuckled because the bracelet didn't compare to the sight of her nude body. "Breathtaking."

Eden rolled her eyes when she realized he wasn't looking at the bracelet, but her breasts. "Your gift is at home."

"You've already given me your most precious gift, and nothing else could ever mean more to me than that."

"Man, you say the right things." Eden tossed the box onto the nightstand, and then pulled Chase into her arms as they once again made love.

Her cell phone was barking. As the memory of last night came rushing back, Eden opened her eyes. She glanced over at Chase who was now watching her. The phone barked again.

"You need a new ringer," he said.

"I like it because it's different."

"Annoying is more like it. Your purse is in the chair." He wiggled his brows, knowing she would have to walk nude into the sitting room.

"You could be a gentleman and get it for me." She smiled, not caring that the phone rang for a third time.

"I could, but I won't."

Eden threw the covers back. "Be that way. You want to look, take your fill." She proudly strutted across the room over to the chair, and then bent seductively forward while retrieving her phone.

"It would serve you right if I came over there and accepted that invitation," Chase warned her. He wore a roguish smile.

She giggled as she said, "Hello?"

"It's about time you answered this phone."

"Taylor? What's wrong?" Eden sobered.

"Calm down, it's not life and death, but you and Chase are splashed across the front page of the newspaper this morning."

Eden looked at Chase. "What?" And in that instant, she knew their private moment had been captured on film. "What are we doing?" she murmured the words.

"The tonsil tango as the guys at the station would call it."

"Leave it to that bunch to come up with something so crude." The phone on the nightstand rang. Eden listened to Taylor while watching Chase. He had just been told the news. She watched as he pulled on his pants and left the room. "Have you heard from the folks?" she thought to ask.

"No, but since you're not at home, I'd be expecting a call on the cell."

As though she had conjured up a spell, the phone beeped, signaling another call. "That's probably Mom calling now. I'll let you know how it goes."

"What do you mean let me know? Girl, I'm headed over to the house now. See ya."

"Hello?"

"I'm making waffles. I'll expect you within the hour," Eunice Warner informed her daughter.

"Yes, ma'am." Eden turned off her phone. She quickly rushed around the room, picking up her clothing. Chase returned to the bedroom, and held up the front page of the newspaper for her to see. In living color, there they were doing the *tonsil tango*.

"Where are you going?" he asked on noticing the clothes in her hand.

"My mother is making waffles."

Chase looked thoughtful. "She's making your favorite breakfast food because …"

"She wants to have a talk with me."

"Oh." He smiled. "By the way, that was Stanley. He wants to see me as well."

"I don't have to ask what about. I'm going to grab a shower." Eden walked away, headed for the bathroom.

"Hey, you're not taking a shower without me," Chase shouted. He tossed the newspaper onto the bed as he followed behind her. Under the warm spray of the shower, they forgot about everything and everyone except what they had found together.

Eden pulled up to her parents' home barely within the hour. Chase had taken her home where she had dressed quickly and jumped into her car. As she parked in the driveway, she noticed Taylor wasn't there. That could only mean her mother had sent her sister home, which spelled a serious conversation was in store for her. The smell of waffles drew her into the kitchen. Her mother sat at the table with a cup of tea waiting for her.

"Morning," Eden said, entering the kitchen. She moved further into the room, trying to gauge her mother's mood.

"Come on in and make a plate," Eunice replied from the table. She watched and waited for her daughter to join her.

Eden slid into a chair and reached for the syrup. She loaded her fork and took a bite. She was famished this morning. Taking a sip of milk, she swallowed, and then focused on her mother's pensive expression. "I guess you want to talk about the photograph in the newspaper."

"And about where you spent the night." She looked directly into her daughter's surprised brown eyes. "I hope you were careful."

"Mom!" Eden blushed.

"Don't Mom, me. I'm the one who had *the talk* with you. I didn't pull any punches then, and I'm not going to now. You're in love with Chase, and sometimes when we're in love, we get careless." She sipped her tea while patiently waiting for her daughter to respond.

"I wasn't. But how did you know how I felt? I only came to the realization of my feelings for him last night." She took another bite of her food.

"I observed you and Chase together. He couldn't take his eyes off you, as if you were the only woman in that room. And when the two of you danced, he held you like a precious jewel. I believe he's in love with you as well."

Eden smiled, recalling his politics of love. "We haven't spoken the words yet, but I believe the feelings are there. But, you probably think it's too soon."

Eunice laughed deeply. "Oh, sweetheart, I fell in love with your father on the first date, and married him two months later. I thought you knew that."

"No, I didn't." Eden chuckled. "I can't believe sensible Adam Warner popped the question so quickly."

"Haven't you heard Adam Warner is a brilliant man?" Eunice smiled.

Eden rolled her eyes, playfully. "Thanks for talking to Daddy."

"I've been waiting years for you to stand up for yourself."

"If it had been anyone else, I would have, but with Daddy, I found avoiding the subject to be easier," Eden confessed. She stabbed a square of waffle.

"Just like pretending you and Chase were only friends?" Eunice looked at her. "I knew the day of the attack; something was going on between you two."

Eden laughed. "I guess we didn't fool you with the opposite end of the sofa thing?"

"Not for a minute."

"I tried to remain friends with him because I feared our involvement could cost him the election."

"What did Chase have to say about it?"

"He was frustrated and a little angry with me. He said he understood, but he kept chipping away at my defenses."

"A determined man. I like that." Eunice drained her cup, and then slid it out of the way. "You and Chase can't live your lives worried about what people will think. If this man loves you enough to risk the election, then let him, because he's a man worthy of your love."

Eden nodded her head in agreement. "But he's dreamed of being mayor for years."

"Well, then that should tell you about the depth of his feelings for you." Eunice caressed Eden's hand.

"Owen confronted me last night. He said Chase was with me to take African American votes from his father."

Eunice knew her daughter well enough to know she had considered the accusation. "What do you think?"

Eden stood and walked over to the sink. She rinsed her dish and placed it in the dishwasher. "You know me. I analyze everything. I eventually put the question to Chase."

"Oh, Eden, you didn't? You know that was Owen being spiteful."

"I know, but I couldn't ignore the question."

"Well considering where you spent the night, I would say Chase did some fast talking." Eunice laughed.

"Actually, he opened his heart wide and I couldn't deny how I felt about him."

Eunice rose from her chair to join Eden. "I love you, and I want you to be happy. But if Chase is going to be a part of your life, I think the family should get to know him."

"I invited him for Christmas."

"That's good. Now, I just have to inform your father."

Eden left her parents' home feeling much better. Her mother was an amazing woman. She had supported their relationship and encouraged her to follow her heart. She turned into her driveway and spotted Angie's vehicle. Opening the garage door, she pulled in and parked, then walked back to greet her friend. The relationship had been a little strained since that day in the lunchroom. She could only imagine what Angie wanted.

"Hi. What brings you by?" Eden asked when Angie stepped from the car. She waved the woman on into the house. She stepped over to the kitchen while Angie went in the living room.

"I owe you an apology," Angie said, facing her. She hadn't bothered to sit down as she was filled with nervousness. "Things have been awkward between us since I made a fool of myself."

Eden smiled as she turned on the coffeemaker. She joined Angie in the living room and took a seat. "I've missed our closeness as well."

Angie sat in the chair opposite the sofa. "I feel so stupid because I never considered that something was going on between you two."

"That's what hurt so much. None of you gave one thought to me." Eden pulled her feet under her.

Angie nodded. "Stupidly, we saw race, not a man and a woman. However, when I saw that picture of the two of you this morning, it became clear. There was no black or white, only a man and woman falling in love."

Eden heard the sincerity in her friend's voice. She was genuinely touched. "He's really a nice man."

"Girl, please. That wasn't nice passing between you two. That was passion," Angie said dramatically.

The women broke into laughter as they once again began behaving like the close friends they were.

"Are you deliberately trying to lose this election?" Stanley practically shouted. He was furious with Chase and that woman. "You're throwing away everything we've worked for."

"I have done no such thing. It's a picture of me kissing my date."

"Are you that naive?"

"Actually, I'm not. I know where you're going with this conversation." Chase tapped an ink pen against the desk.

"Then you know a segment of the population will be turned off by your involvement with this woman."

"The woman has a name." Chase shot him a look. "And I'm quite aware there might be people opposed to our relationship. But you have to understand I'm willing to take the risk to be with her."

"People want to know you're sincere and focused on the issues. This picture," Stanley waved the newspaper violently, "says otherwise."

Chase leaned back in his chair. "I'm very focused on the issues. And I intend to win this election, with Eden by my side."

"I think your brain has gone south."

"Watch your damn mouth," Chase warned, standing from his chair. His eyes were narrowed with anger. "Don't reduce my feelings for Eden to sex because you'd be wrong."

Stanley stared at Chase in shock. He stumbled back and collapsed onto the sofa. "You're in love with the woman."

Chase glared at his campaign manager but didn't respond. "All you need to know is that Eden is in my life because I want her there."

"Look, do what you want with *Eden,* just keep it out of the papers."

"I'm not ashamed to be with Eden, and I'm sure as hell not going to sneak around town to be with her. People need to know Eden is the woman in my life." He looked at Stanley. "Would you be behaving like this if Eden wasn't African American?"

"Any woman who interferes with your being elected mayor would be a problem." Stanley sat there thinking. "Well, she can go places we can't. If we work this just right, she could help us gain some votes from Camden."

Chase glared across the room to where Stanley sat. He practically shook with rage. "You *will not* turn my relationship with Eden into a campaign ploy. If you're having trouble understanding my position, then maybe we need to sever our relationship."

The campaign manager couldn't believe it had come to this. This woman was becoming more important to Chase than the election, and he couldn't have that. He had a plan for Chase and he wasn't going to let anyone stand in the way of it."

"Calm down. You're right and I apologize. I only want to make sure the best man wins the election."

"I want that as well. And we will," Chase assured him. He laid out some new ideas for the campaign as the conversation was laid to rest.

He entered his parents' home a little after the noon hour. His mother had placed a call requesting to see him. As usual, he felt as though he was visiting a museum rather than his family home. Everything seemed fragile and untouchable. He found her in the living room with the newspaper neatly folded beside her. "Hello, Mother."

Joyce Mathews looked up from the novel she had been reading

to greet her son. "Hello, darling, how are you?"

"Busy as usual. What did you want to see me about?" He admired his mother's ageless beauty. Her hair, dark like his, was freshly styled, no doubt straight from the salon. Her blue eyes focused on the newspaper.

"I knew you were involved with someone, but you never said who." She picked up the newspaper. "Are you serious about this Eden Warner?"

"I'm in love with her."

Joyce nodded. She hadn't been expecting that. Chase hadn't been serious about a woman in years. "When can your father and I expect to meet her?"

"I was thinking the annual New Years Eve Party."

"Good. Will you be sharing Christmas with her?" Joyce wanted to see how serious this relationship had become.

"Eden has invited me to share Christmas with her family."

"And have you met her parents yet?"

"Yes, I have. She's also met grandmother."

"Well, you are serious about her. I don't recall you ever introducing a woman to your grandmother." She sat for a moment, thinking. She finally reached over, taking his hand. "Are you happy?"

Chase smiled. He knew his mother loved him, but this much attention was unusual for her. "I'm very happy."

"And what about the campaign?"

"It's going quite well. I have some major endorsements. I'm feeling pretty confident."

"Good. I know I'm not the best mother, but I do love you." Her blue eyes held his for a long moment.

"I do know and I love you as well."

Joyce rose from the sofa, signaling an end to their conversation. "I look forward to you both joining us."

Chase stared in amazement as she reverted back to being the distant woman he knew. He often wondered who or what was responsible for her detachment. He dismissed her behavior because he didn't understand it. All that really mattered was that she loved him.

Chapter Eleven

The Warner house was alive with the spirit of Christmas as Eden and Chase arrived bearing gifts. Eunice and Taylor greeted the couple with hugs and kisses. The smell of turkey roasting filled the air. The rest of the family could be heard in various areas of the two-storey house. They were directed to deposit their gifts under the tree and head into the kitchen. Mrs. Warner was making her traditional Christmas breakfast.

Chase followed Eden in and arranged their packages. He sat back in wonder. He had never seen so many gifts under a tree before. They were literally spilling out onto the living room floor. As he stood and took in his surroundings, he was overwhelmed. The house was decorated in holiday décor from top to bottom by a family who obviously enjoyed the season. The decorations showed the signs of repeated use, unlike his parents' professionally decorated home. One could feel the love and tradition in the Warner household, and he liked the feeling.

Four stockings with each of the Warner children's names written in glue and glitter, hung over the fireplace. He and his siblings had never had Christmas stockings. He walked over and traced the lettering of Eden's name.

"I don't know why Mom continues to put those things up each year," Eden said from behind him.

"I think it's wonderful." He turned to face her. "The room is wonderful. You can feel the love and joy of the holiday in here." His eyes shined like a child's.

Eden smiled as she listened and watched Chase move around the room examining the decorations. "You made this star in second grade."

"I sure did, and you'll find others on the tree from Taylor, Skye, and Victor." She laughed, shyly.

Chase turned looking at her. "You don't realize how lucky you are. My mother paid someone each year to decorate our house. The tree always had a theme. We weren't allowed to display our school decorations. I remember one time I placed a wooden cut-out shaped like a bell on the tree. My mother had a fit when she discovered it. I found it in the trash later that evening." He looked away, not sure why he remembered that day or why he was telling her about it.

"Did you remove it from the trash?" Eden asked, taking his hands. She couldn't imagine a mother doing such a thing.

"Yeah, I did. Crazy thing is I still have it packed away." He smiled a little sad.

"I tell you what. Next year we'll add your ornament to this tree," Eden told him.

Chase laughed. "You're planning on being with me next year?" His eyes twinkled with surprise.

Eden smiled at him. "I'm thinking possibly yes."

"I like that idea."

Eunice stood in the doorway watching and listening to Eden and Chase. She was reminded of the old adage about money not buying happiness. She cleared her throat dramatically, getting the lovebirds attention.

"Oh, I'm sorry, Mama. We were just talking."

"Or something like that," Eunice teased. "Actually, I was looking for Chase."

Eden's expression grew concerned.

"My daughter tells me you make a mean omelet. How about giving me a hand in the kitchen?"

"I'll help you," Eden stepped in.

"I don't want your help." Eunice gave her daughter the look. "The others are in the sunroom."

Chase glanced from one woman to the other. Obviously Eden's mother had something to say to him in private. He kissed Eden on the cheek, and then turned to her mother. "I'd be happy to assist you." He fell into step behind both women and followed them into the kitchen. He watched Eden go out the back door and into the sunroom where the rest of the family gathered. He focused back on Mrs. Warner. "Let me wash my hands, and then tell me what you need me to do."

Together, Eunice and Chase whipped up breakfast while they got better acquainted. Chase was enjoying the time with Eden's mother. She was gracious, funny, and a straight-shooter. Eden didn't realize the prize she had in her.

"Now you know there are going to be people who will be opposed to your relationship with Eden solely because of race," Eunice approached the subject of his election.

He glanced at her while chopping ingredients for the omelets. "I know, but I don't allow others to dictate how I live my life."

"My daughter will fight and defend anyone she feels has been wronged; however, when it comes to herself, she doesn't always fight back."

"I don't mind a good fight, especially when it's for someone I care about." He looked at the woman directly. He knew she would be able to read more into the statement than what was said.

Eunice nodded. "I'm going to say this straight, Chase. Eden has been hurt, and I don't want to see her hurt again. You're saying all the right things, and I believe you mean them, but understand me clearly when I say *you better* mean them."

"You have my word as a man."

Eunice smiled, liking the man. She switched subjects and began asking questions about his campaign. By the time breakfast was ready, the two were like old friends.

Chase laughed as he sat around the Warner table, listening to the siblings tease each other. He was having the greatest time. He looked at Mrs. Warner watching over her family with a smile on her face and love in her eyes. He knew now she was the one to be feared when it came to Eden. Mr. Warner was tough and intimidating, but Mrs. Warner was a loving mother who would protect her young to the end.

Adam Warner hadn't said very much. He had sat back observing his daughter and Chase. They appeared to be happy and compatible. Chase had actually fit right in with the rest of the bunch. He could tell Eunice really liked the young man. And to be completely honest, he had enjoyed their conversation about the future of the city. He understood the link between education, employment, and crime. He had demonstrated that he wasn't wearing blinders to the reality of city life, but had a plan to improve it.

The young man had further impressed him when he broached the subject of Eden and Owen.

"What I feel for your daughter is as real as it gets, and that's why I'm about to say what I am."

"Go ahead," Adam had nodded. He respected a man who spoke his mind.

"Very well. You and Victor need to find a new partner. Owen used Eden to get close to you. He didn't give a damn about her."

"You're wrong. Eden broke his heart when she broke up with him," Adam defended the man he thought of as a son.

"Is that what he told you? Did you ask your daughter what happened?"

"No," Adam admitted. "I wasn't talking much to my daughter at the time." Adam rubbed his forehead in memory. "I had this idea of building a legal dynasty. Eden was my bright child. Now don't get me wrong, all of my children are intelligent, but Eden was the star. I saw great things for her. Then she announced she wanted to be a teacher, and I saw the dream evaporate."

"It was your dream."

Adam nodded once more. "Yes, my dream and Eden is entitled to hers. I realize that now."

"You should see her in action in the classroom. She's terrific. The children adore her, and she manages to take care of their personal needs without embarrassment."

Adam listened and watched Chase's expression while he spoke of his daughter. The man was definitely smitten. "I presume Eden told you about Owen?"

"No, sir. Owen boldly told Eden the night of the gala all of this. He was attempting to make the point that I was with her for other than honorable intentions, like the African American vote."

"Are you?" Adam inquired with an edge to his tone. He held Chase's gaze.

"No. I'm with your daughter because of who she is and how I feel when I'm with her. This election means more to her than it does to me, because all I want at the end of the day is her."

That had earned the young man some major points. Now that he'd gotten to know Chase personally, he was beginning to see what his daughter saw. Well, he would have to do some serious thinking about Owen remaining on at the firm. Eden was his child, and nobody used her without facing his wrath.

"Thank you for inviting me to share the day with you and your family." Chase held Eden on his lap.

"You're welcome. I think it went quite well." She played with the hair at the nape of his neck. "You and Dad seemed to get along."

"We did. Look, I know the two of you have had problems, but don't doubt his love for you."

"I know he loves me." Eden wrapped her arms around his neck, snuggling closer.

"I wish my family was as close as yours. All the teasing and laughing you and your siblings share, I envy it. My sisters are scattered on opposite coasts. The last time we saw each other was at a family member's funeral."

"Do you all at least call each other?" Eden sat up looking at him. This was a new area of discussion for them.

"On birthdays I can expect a call. I used to call them all the time, but they seldom reciprocated, so I stopped."

"That's sad. As loud and obnoxious as they can get at times, I wouldn't know what to do without my brother and sisters."

"We love each other, Eden, but my mother is a little self-centered and aloof. Unfortunately, my sisters have patterned their lives after her." He kissed her neck.

"And what about your father? Was he aloof as well?"

"No. Dad wasn't aloof. He just suffered from tunnel vision. His focus was strictly on his business."

"So why are you so warm and outgoing?" She stroked his face with loving fingers.

"My grandparents. Belle and Ruben Gautier were the most loving people I know. They loved each other right to the moment of my grandfather's death. I want that type of love." He caressed her lips with his thumb. "If they were across the room, they would seek each other out through the crowd, and exchange the most passionate of gazes. You felt like you were intruding on a private moment by noticing."

Eden smiled broadly. She enjoyed learning about Chase's family. The more he shared with her, the closer she felt to him. "That's beautiful. My parents are the same way. I actually walked in on them in the kitchen making out once." She giggled just thinking about that night. "I showed up to the house unannounced and found them together. Daddy was singing a Barry White tune while chasing Mom around. I don't know who was more embarrassed."

Chase was laughing so hard he almost spilled Eden from his lap. "I'll never be able to observe your father in court again without this image coming to mind."

"Well, you better not let him know I told you about that night."

"I wouldn't dare." He kissed her sweetly. "I liked being a part of your family today."

Eden was delighted thinking how strange others valued things other people took for granted. She was indeed fortunate to have her family with warts and all. She snuggled closer to Chase, making sure to caress his chest with her breasts. "So what did you and my mother talk about?"

Chase chuckled. "You're trying to weasel information out of me?"

"Maybe."

"Well if you want to know what your mother and I discussed, you're going to have to do more than snuggle, sweetheart."

Eden giggled as Chase threw her over his shoulder and headed for the stairs.

Chase covered Eden's hand with his as they sat in the backseat of the chauffeured vehicle. With the champagne flowing tonight, he had decided to hire a car service for the evening of toasts and celebration. They were leaving the last party thrown by a supporter and were now headed to his parents' annual bash. Eden sat quietly looking out of the window. She looked beautiful in a sassy gold dress with shoes to match. Her hair was up, exposing the chandelier earrings dancing in her ears. He smiled with pride as his eyes traced her delicate features.

"Hey, are you all right over there?"

Eden turned to him and forced a smile. "I'm a little nervous. Your parents may not like me."

"What's not to like? You're smart, beautiful, and kind-hearted." His eyes conveyed his seriousness.

"I'm also African American."

He chuckled. "You are? Listen, that's the last thing you have to worry about from my parents. As unique as they are, race was never an issue in our home. Now, the fact you don't belong to the Hilton Country Club or the Restoration Committee might pose a problem."

Eden swatted his thigh. "You make your mother sound shallow."

"I love her, but the lady is all about image."

"She can't be all bad because she reared a wonderful son." Her eyes held admiration.

Chase grinned. Eden had a point. He and his sisters were

decent people with successful lives. "I hadn't looked at it that way," he confessed.

The driver stopped in front of a sprawling estate in the Beaumont Hills community. The exclusive zip code announced money and privilege. Eden couldn't believe the turn her life had taken since that day in the auditorium. She used to drive by these expensive homes, wondering how they were decorated inside, and tonight, she would find out firsthand. She accepted Chase's hand and eased from the back seat. Smiling up at him, she took his arm and followed him to the double doors. She glanced back at the number of foreign and expensive vehicles lining the driveway. This was everyday normal for Chase, and yet, he had garnered great pleasure from spending Christmas with her family.

Entering the home, Eden thought she had stepped into a museum. She couldn't imagine children running around in a place like this. The foyer was towering. The black and white tiled floor shined to a high gloss. Portraits and precious collectables decorated all of the hard surfaces. Festive music seemed to be coming at her from all angles as they made their way through the milling bodies. Chase was greeted every step of the way into the main living area. He proudly introduced Eden around. They had just cleared the living room entrance when they spotted Belle.

"There you two are," she greeted them with hugs and kisses. "I was afraid you would miss the arrival of the new year."

"Not a chance," Chase told her.

"You look beautiful, Belle," Eden complimented the woman's multi-print gown. Bold in color and not your typical style for one of age, Belle carried it off supremely. Eden really admired the woman's attitude toward life.

"Thank you, dear, but you are a beauty tonight," Belle said. "I saw my grandson hanging on to you as he escorted you past those young men." She winked at her grandson. "Oh, here come your parents."

Eden turned in the direction Belle glanced and spotted a distinguished looking couple coming in their direction. The man was about the same height as Chase, but there the resemblance ended. Edward Mathews was extremely fair in complexion with thinning whitish blond hair. He carried a little weight around the middle and wore rather thick glasses. Where his son was captivating and gorgeous, Edward was rather a plain man who seemed completely uncomfortable in the party environment.

Joyce Mathews, on the other hand, was definitely a social butterfly. Every step she took in their direction, she stopped and chatted. She was refinement personified. Her dark hair was swept up for the evening. Her designer gown was in an ice-blue hue that highlighted the blueness of her eyes. She wore minimum makeup and possessed a dentist-enhanced smile that must have cost a fortune. As she stood next to her, Eden caught a whiff of her delicate perfume.

"Welcome, you must be Eden," Joyce said, warm and welcoming. She brushed her cheek against Eden's. "This is my husband, Edward."

"Hello. It's a pleasure to finally meet you both." Eden wasn't prepared for the bear hug bestowed by Mr. Mathews.

"My son was right, you are stunning."

Eden smiled. "Now I know where Chase gets his charm." Her nervousness vanished.

Chase snagged two glasses of champagne from a passing waiter, handing one to Eden. "How was the cruise?" he asked his parents.

"Wonderful," Joyce chimed. She went on for several minutes, giving them the highlights of their trip. "You two should definitely take a cruise."

"Maybe when the election is over we'll be able to get away," Chase commented. He slipped his arm around Eden's waist.

"How is the election going, son?" Edward inquired.

"Early polls indicate the race is between Nelson and me. Rodgers, however, is a close third. The election could definitely prove interesting."

Edward's brown eyes landed on Eden. He noticed the way his son looked at the woman. The two were in love. He looked at the love of his life and smiled. Joyce was still a beautiful woman. He knew people didn't see what he saw in her, but what they shared was priceless, and that was the way his son looked at Eden. "How are you handling all of the publicity? I guess it's not your usual relationship?"

"I think I'm handling things well. The press makes me a little nervous with all their questions and picture taking, but other than that, I'm okay."

"The press can be a brutal bunch," Belle added. "One minute they're your best ally, then the next your enemy."

Eden's eyes connected with Belle's. She knew the woman spoke the truth, but prayed Chase wouldn't find himself on the receiving end of their viciousness.

Stanley Elliot spotted the Mathews' huddled by the fireplace. He cut a path in their direction. He frowned when he spotted Eden laughing with Joyce and Edward. The woman was a problem that had to be dealt with, and soon. The polling numbers were okay, but they could be better, if he had all of Chase's attention. There had to be a way to remove the woman from the picture.

"Good evening, everyone," Stanley greeted the Mathews'. He didn't look in Eden's direction, an act that wasn't missed by her or Belle. "Did you see the polling numbers?" he directed the question to Chase.

"Yes. We were just discussing them."

"We'll have to get out there and work hard to pull them up. Sacrifices will have to be made if you want to win this election. Nelson is going to be tough to beat; especially now with his latest accusation spreading like wildfire."

"What accusations?" Edward asked. He looked at his son for answers.

"I'm afraid I don't know what you're talking about, Stanley," Chase informed his manager.

"Oh, you must have missed the news this evening."

"Stanley, please," Chase said, trying to get to the point.

"Nelson is accusing you of using Eden to gain the African

American vote."

Eden groaned as she reached out and took Chase's arm. "I'm sorry about this. I never expected Mr. Nelson of exposing Owen's accusation."

Stanley watched Chase for a response. He could tell he was angry. Maybe now he would realize being with Eden was damaging to his campaign.

"You have nothing to apologize for," Edward told Eden. "Anyone who looks at you two can tell you're in love."

Eden and Chase looked at each other. They hadn't placed a label on their feelings, but neither denied his statement.

"Dad's right. This isn't your doing, sweetheart, and we'll weather this storm together. The voters are smart enough to ignore the accusations and study the facts for themselves. Now, tonight is a celebration and I suggest we get back to celebrating."

Stanley swore under his breath. What did it take to get rid of this woman? He excused himself in search of a waiter with a drink. He spotted Crystal chatting up one of the campaign contributors and headed in her direction.

The countdown to the new year was upon them. The waiters made sure everyone possessed champagne and party favors. At the stroke of midnight, *Happy New Year* rang throughout the estate. Couples kissed in the new year while streamers and confetti rained down. Chase pulled Eden into his arms and released a handful of confetti over their heads as he claimed her lips for the traditional kiss. When they parted, both were ready to do a little private celebrating. They managed to smile and carry on chitchat for another hour before making their goodbyes.

Chapter Twelve

Eden and Chase fell through the door of her home reaching for each other. Their mouths connected the moment the door closed behind them. Chase devoured Eden's lips while stripping off her coat. The garment fell to the floor as he swept her into his arms and carried her into the kitchen. He deposited his lovely bundle on the center island. He waved the bottle of champagne his parents had given them in his hand. His smile was of the devil's making, and Eden quivered with anticipation.

"What do you plan on doing with that?" Her eyes challenged him to be creative.

"I intend to have a toast." He licked his lips suggestively.

Eden's eyes were dreamy. Her lips spread into a sexy smile, tempting him with their lushness. "Glasses are behind you," she pointed to the appropriate cabinet while holding his gaze.

"I don't need a glass."

"No?"

"No." Chase grabbed Eden's hips and pulled her forward on the island. He covered her mouth once more, as he took his time kissing her. His tongue slid between her welcoming lips to frolic in the sweetness of her mouth. When her tongue engaged him in the mating ritual, he groaned with a burning desire to taste every inch of her. His hands found the zipper on her dress and eased it down. He peeled the dress from her shoulders and down her torso, allowing it to pool around her waist. The strapless bra was next. He dipped his head to capture a dark nipple between his teeth while he worked the dress lower onto her hips. He groaned when he had to free the nipple to assist her in getting rid of the dress.

Eden shivered with need as Chase removed the dress from her hips. She sat in black lace panties and nothing else.

He leaned against the opposite counter, looking his fill. The sight of her long legs was enough to make him hard as a rock. "God, you're sexy." He licked his lips while skillfully popping the champagne cork. White froth spilled over his hands before he turned the bottle up to his mouth and drank from it. "Would you like some?" he asked, wiping his mouth with the back of his hand.

"I'd love some," Eden purred, wantonly. Her pulse escalated as Chase slowly pushed from the cabinet to take the few steps to the island. He held the bottle to her lips and poured. Champagne flowed into her mouth, spilling from the corners to run down her chin and neck, to finally pool on her nipples. She moaned as Chase began to lap at the trail of wine with his tongue. The feel of the liquid coolness, coupled with his warm, wet mouth was more than she could endure. As his tongue tormented her right nipple, she shuddered under the assault.

Chase raised his head to reclaim her mouth in a passionate exchange. While doing so, he reached for the black lace and muttered between kisses, "Up."

Eden complied without question. She tore at Chase's jacket, and then quickly discarded his shirt to expose his solid chest and washboard abs. The man was perfection. Locking him within the circle of her legs, she trailed kisses across his chest before suckling a male nipple into a hard nub. But as she went for the other nipple, Chase pulled away.

"My turn, baby."

Chilled champagne splashed across her breasts and ran south, followed by Chase's lapping tongue. And when his head disappeared between her sprawled thighs, Eden convulsed, nearly falling from the countertop.

"I got you, sweetheart," Chase crooned as he scooped her into his arms and headed for the stairs. In the bedroom, he carried Eden into the bathroom and turned on the shower. He removed the remainder of his clothing, retrieving condoms from his wallet before stepping into the glass enclosure, and pulling her behind him. His mouth covered hers as his tongue imitated the act he was preparing for. And when he was sure Eden was ready to receive him, he raised her against the shower wall and slowly entered her body. The feel of her opening to him took his breath away. She felt so good around him. "Look at me," he ordered, soft and filled with emotion. "I want you to see what loving you is like."

Eden gasped as he began to move inside of her, and his eyes turned a dark blue. They soon clouded over with a haze that could only be described as sheer bliss. And as the pace increased, his moan of pleasure told of his enjoyment. Then the pressure began to build as his face contorted with each stroke into her body, and in the depths of now near-black eyes, love stared back at her. Then the world tilted as release came and euphoria shrouded them in the steam and mist of the shower.

The couple made love throughout the night. Each time was better than the last. Then sometime before dawn, Chase snuggled against Eden, kissing her neck. A smile spread across her face as she rolled onto her back and reached for him. But Chase remained hovered above her. His eyes were soft and moody as they moved over her face. He brushed away a strand of hair clinging to her lashes.

"I can't seem to get enough of you," he whispered. The fireplace burned low, casting the room in a warm glow.

"That makes two of us." Eden ran a hand down his chest.

"This is no casual affair for me. I hope you know that."

Eden laid a hand over his heart. "I do, and I feel the same way."

Chase removed her hand from his chest, bringing it to his lips. "I don't want to jinx what we have, but it feels so right."

"I know what you mean. God, I'm so happy," Eden confessed right before covering his mouth with hers. She slipped her arms around his neck and eased him down on her. This time as they came together, it was slow and tender, an expression of love. When they finally descended from the heavens, they slept soundly in each other's arms.

Late in the morning when Eden awakened, she looked at Chase beside her asleep and smiled. Last night had been beautiful and a night she wouldn't forget. She rolled over onto her back, stealing a glimpse at the clock on her nightstand.

"Oh, my God, it's eleven o'clock!" Eden shouted as she threw the covers back. She bolted to the bathroom and turned on the shower before returning to the bedroom to awaken Chase. "Get up; my family will be here in an hour."

Chase was wide-awake now. He sat up, meeting her frantic expression. "What's going on?"

"I'm hosting the New Year's Day get-together. Each year, the Warners start the new year off by spending the day together watching football. This is my year to host. Everyone will be here in an hour. Now, get into the shower." She shoved him from the bed.

"I should go."

"You'll do no such thing."

"I need clothes."

"In the closet to the right. I picked up your cleaning the other day, and you left a sports bag here when we loaded the Christmas presents into your car," Eden told him from inside the bathroom.

"Perfect, now stop hogging the water." Chase snapped the stall door closed behind him.

In the kitchen, they gave it a thorough cleaning, removing all traces of their activities last night. Eden blushed every time she looked at the center island.

"If you do that while your family is here, everyone is going to know what we did last night."

She looked at him and smiled. "I can't believe what we did."

"Are you really happy?" He caressed her cheek.

Eden came from around the island and covered his mouth with hers. The kiss was sweet and loving. "I'm very happy."

"Me too." His expression was boyish and goofy.

Eden went to the refrigerator and removed the vegetable and fruit platters she'd had the foresight to make the day before. A cheese-and-cracker platter was assembled by Chase. They worked well together.

"Would you mind if I invited David and Stone over? They were to come over to my place for the games."

"Sure. Here, give them a call." Eden handed him the phone.

She had everything under control by the time the first Warner arrived. Before long the house was bustling with people, and the sound of football on the television filled the air. Her parents had chosen to sit in the oversized chairs, while her brother tossed a pillow on the floor. Her sisters were in the kitchen with her. Chase passed the beer around before sitting on the floor next to her brother. To see him like that, no one would ever think the man came from such privilege.

"Somebody's in love," Taylor whispered into her ear.

"Be quiet." Eden ducked her head, laughing. "And so what if I am?"

"I say good for you. Wish I could find a man that fine."

The doorbell rang.

"Would you get that, Taylor? I need to take the wings out," Eden asked.

"Got it." Taylor wiped her hands on a dishtowel as she went to see who was at the door. She pulled it opened and looked right into a pair of mesmerizing green eyes. "What are you doing here?" She tried to ignore the tiny flutters in her stomach.

Stone smiled into Taylor's surprised face. "I was invited." He admired the tight jeans and sweatshirt she wore. No one at the squad had seen her wearing anything other than slacks and a blazer. He wished she had let her hair down today.

"You were? I didn't know you knew my sister." Taylor remained blocking the door. Her eyes slid down his great physique. The man made her crave things she had no right thinking about. *But Lord, the man is good looking.* His long legs were encased in a pair of well-worn jeans that displayed his bowlegs. She cursed under her breath because a pair of bowlegs was her weakness.

"Actually I met your sister at the gala."

"And she just invited you over for a family get-together?" Taylor asked, wishing she had worn her hair down today. *Damn Eden for not telling me Stone would be here.*

The Politics of Love

"Who's at the door?" Eden asked, coming up behind her sister. "Stone, welcome, come on in," Eden greeted her new guest. She turned to her sister as the man crossed the threshold. "No shop talk today, you two."

"We don't have anything to talk about," Taylor muttered under her breath as she made a beeline to the kitchen.

Eden stared at her sister, then glanced at Stone and noticed he too, watched Taylor. He stood with a smile on his face. She got the very distinct impression something was going on between the two of them. "Come on back. Everyone is gathered around the television. I apologize for not having a wall-size plasma."

Stone laughed. "I don't have one either, so whatever you have is good enough for me. I'm just grateful for the invitation."

"You're always welcome here," she said loud enough for Taylor to hear as she escorted Stone into the living room.

Chase approached his friend and quickly made introductions. The bell rang again. "I'll get it. It's probably David."

Eden returned to the kitchen. Taylor and Skye were busy refilling trays and refreshing drinks. "I've got a secret," Eden taunted her sisters.

Skye, always eager to know a secret, rushed to her side. "What is it? Who is about?" Her eyes danced with excitement.

"Our sister has a crush on someone."

"That is such a juvenile expression," Taylor hissed. She popped the lid on a can of peanuts dramatically.

"You're right. How about *the hots* for someone?" Eden wiggled her brows.

Taylor shrugged, but remained quiet.

"Will you just tell me who?" Skye demanded. Her young face beamed with excitement. Her eyes bounced from one to the other. "Who is that?" Her eyes zeroed in on the new arrival.

Taylor and Eden glanced into the living room as Chase and David walked in.

"That's Principal Daniels." Eden turned back, looking at her younger sister. She noticed the way Skye's eyes followed the man's every move. "You have got to be kidding. That's my boss."

"So? He's kinda cute," Skye said shyly.

Taylor laughed. "I know someone else who has *the hots*."

The three women laughed conspiratorially. They moved around the kitchen in hushed conversation, while four pair of eyes watched and admired them.

Mrs. Warner couldn't be more proud of her daughters. They were beautiful on the outside, but even more beautiful on the inside where it mattered. They were intelligent and independent women who spoke their minds. Each were different; however, complemented and supported the other. And when they were like this, she was reminded of their days as children before life became complicated.

Slightly jealous, Chase watched Eden interacting with her sisters. They seemed to be having a wonderful time whispering amongst themselves. Their giggles hinted of love and a bond that despite what problems they may have with each other would always hold them together. They were each unique, despite the strong resemblance to one another. Of course in his eyes, Eden was the most beautiful of the three sisters. A smile tugged at his lips as she leaned against the island, then remembering their lovemaking last night, moved quickly to the opposite cabinet. He met her eyes as she looked over at him and winked.

Stone couldn't believe he was actually spending the day with Taylor's family. This was the perfect time to get her to notice him as a man and not a federal agent. She looked feminine and vulnerable as she laughed with her sisters. The hard-nose attitude she wore around the squadron was gone. She appeared approachable. And when she removed the band holding her hair in her trademark ponytail, his breath hitched. Detective Taylor Warner was a knockout.

David had never met Eden's younger sister. He knew her name was Skye, and she was a law school student; however, no one had told him how stunning she was. She, too, was tall for a woman, but only maybe an inch taller than him. But she stood out nonetheless.

Her sense of style was trendy and sexy. She wore a pair of those dangerously low jeans that were popular now. And the short, tight shirt she wore with them exposed the sparkling stud piercing her navel and the butterfly tattoo in the bend of her back. His mouth went dry simply thinking about what else might be pierced or tattooed.

The sisters came over to the living room to join the others. Eden sat on the floor beside Chase. Taylor deposited the kitchen chair she carried near Stone, while Skye sat beside David on the sofa. One by one, they made eye contact and sighed with satisfaction because they were exactly where they wanted to be.

The game would go down as one of the best in years. The energy level in the room rose and fell with each crucial play. Adding to the excitement was the fact half the room cheered for one team, while the other half cheered for the other. The sisters knew their football as well as their brother, and got into the heckling. By the time the first game ended, everyone was ready to partake in the abundance of food Eden had prepared.

"Man, that was a good game," Victor commented while loading his plate with football favorites before the next game.

"Yeah, and that hit on the quarterback was wicked," Chase added. He tossed Victor a beer.

"What about that pass into traffic?" David said, impressed. He moved over to the table to enjoy his meal.

"Can you believe that guy caught the ball and hung on to it?" Stone asked, joining David at the table.

"But the best team won, fellows," Adam taunted Victor and Stone, who had supported the loser.

"Speaking of loser," Stone added. "What is it with Camden Nelson and his ridiculous allegation against you?"

Chase glanced over at Victor and Adam. He carried his plate to the table and waited for the men to sit down. He glanced in the direction of the dining room where the women were eating and lowered his voice. "Owen hurled the insult at Eden the night of the gala."

"What?" David and Stone parroted.

"Chase told me about it at Christmas," Adam informed the men. "And it seems my partner was using my daughter to get close to me."

"We were like family," Victor responded.

Adam nodded, thinking about how he had hurt his daughter when he thought she had broken the engagement to Owen. "As my wife put it to me, we are not family, and Owen discovered Thursday when we notified him we were severing our partnership."

"That will mean a great deal to Eden," Chase told Adam. "The allegations bother her, but she knows how I feel about her."

"The allegations sound like those of a desperate candidate," David contributed.

Chase shook his head. "Don't believe that for a moment. Camden and I are the front-runners, and as the election gets closer, he'll pull out every trick he knows." Chase drank from his beer. Depositing the bottle, he added. "I just don't want Eden caught in the middle."

"I appreciate that, Chase, but you better believe Camden is going to keep bringing up the issue," Adam commented.

"As much as I hate saying this," Victor sighed, "people are asking the question." He looked directly at Chase.

"Damn it, why can't Eden and I simply be happy together?" Chase slammed his fist onto the table. "Shouldn't they be focused on the issues?"

"Of course they should be, and I'm sure they're educating themselves as well," Adam responded.

"But Camden's tactic is working," Chase acknowledged.

Chapter Thirteen

Eden showed off her Valentine gift from Chase. The diamond heart pendant sparkled in the lighting. She and her sisters were spending this Saturday with their mother. They had started their day with breakfast at Belle's. Eden had wanted her mother to meet Chase's grandmother. The two women had gotten along fabulously. From there, the girls had taken their mother for a little tender loving care at the day spa. A little shopping was next, and to round off the day, the four Warner women were sharing a quiet dinner together.

The Vineyard was a new Italian restaurant in Hilton that was receiving great reviews. The abundance of flowers and greenery befitted the theme. The wrought iron tables resembled furnishings found in an elegant garden. The base of the tables and chairs sported a twisting vine. The lighting in the room was soft, and the aroma of the food heavenly. The women were having a wonderful time together.

"It's beautiful, Eden," Skye praised the gift from Eden's left. Taylor sat to Eden's right and their mother directly across from her.

"Chase has good taste," Taylor added.

"He certainly does," Eunice Warner said with a wink at her daughter.

Eden blushed. She and Chase were doing exceedingly well as a couple. They didn't see each other as much as they would have liked, but when they did, it was quality time.

Eden looked at Taylor. "How's the gorgeous Stone Patrick?"

Taylor rolled her eyes. "How would I know? I just work with the guy." She moved the food around on her plate.

"Oh, please," Eden responded. "I saw the way the two of you were looking at each other."

"Hey, if you don't want him, I'll take him," Skye threatened. She looked at her sister and laughed.

"I don't think so and besides, we all know you've got your eye on *Principal Daniels*," Taylor teased her younger sister.

Mrs. Warner perked up. "I missed something. When did this happen?" She looked at her youngest.

Eden laughed. "Little Miss Skye was checking out David on New Year's Day."

"Interesting," Eunice commented, enjoying this time with her daughters. They all led such busy lives. She was also pleased to see the change in Eden. She and Adam were working through their issues and the girls were actually spending more time together than before. Eden had stopped sitting on the sidelines of the family and was now an active member once more.

"How are you holding up with this election?" Taylor asked, concerned. "Camden and Owen aren't letting this race issue drop."

Eden sighed, heavily. She was exhausted from the need to defend her relationship with Chase. "It's easier to divide than debate the issues. Chase's platform is the best for the city. It's clear and doable. The financial figures are outlined down to the last dime. I just wish people would focus on that."

Taylor covered her sister's hand. "I admire you both."

"Thanks," Eden whispered with a smile. She glanced around the restaurant and noticed a woman wearing a Nelson campaign button staring at her. She gave a friendly smile before focusing back on their table. She excused herself to the ladies' room. Having taken care of her needs, she was washing her hands when the woman who had been staring entered the room.

"How can you allow yourself to be used? Chase Mathews is with you to divide the votes," she spewed her venom.

Eden quickly dried her hands and headed for the door. "I'm sorry you feel that way."

"Owen said the two of you used to be a couple."

Eden looked closely at the woman, realizing she wasn't the average campaign worker. "Now I see where this is coming from."

The women grew angrier. "You're with Mathews to stick it to Owen for dumping you."

"Look, it's obvious you're involved with Owen. I don't want him."

"Oh, I guess you're too good for a black man now," her voice rose. "Well don't get too comfortable." The woman strutted out of the restroom, throwing the door open wide.

Eden leaned against the vanity, getting control of her emotions. Her mind was turning over the woman's parting shot when Taylor game barreling in.

"Hey, what's going on in here? You've been gone a while." Taylor studied her sister's face. She sensed something was wrong.

Eden glanced at the door. "Did you see the woman who walked out of here?"

"Yeah, I did. She appeared to be in a hurry."

"I think she's involved with Owen."

Taylor stood in front of Eden. "What did she say to you?"

"First she repeated what Owen and his father have been telling everyone who will listen. Then as a parting shot, she told me not to get too comfortable."

Taylor tilted her head in thought. "You mean as in with Chase?" Her mind was processing the conversation like a cop. "She knows something."

"I think so too, and whatever it is … will come between Chase and me," Eden said softly. Her mind raced, and she didn't like the direction it was going. Her eyes flew to Taylor.

"Oh, Eden, you don't think …"

"I do and I've got to go." Eden rushed from the restroom. She grabbed her purse from the table, not taking the time to explain. She knew Taylor would take care of it.

Chase sat at his desk, flipping though his calendar while speaking on the phone. "The twentieth is good. Nine o'clock is perfect. I'll see you then." He scribbled down the appointment, and then hung up the telephone. Stanley came rushing into the office at that very moment. He slammed the door to the office behind him.

"Perfect timing. That was Kate Hall, the Executive Director of the Hilton Chamber of Commerce. She has invited me to address the Chamber on the twentieth."

"Don't get overjoyed about it. What's in this folder could blow us out of the water." Stanley waved a brown folder. "There are reporters camped outside, and the news is running the story," Stanley said, dropping the folder in front of him.

"What's this, and where did you get it?" Chase asked as he opened the folder. Several newspaper clippings were inside. He sifted through the stack until he came to one with a photograph of Eden. He looked at Stanley bewildered. "What's all this?"

"Read it for yourself."

"Why don't you tell me, since you're in possession of the information," Chase barked. He knew he wasn't going to like what he heard.

Stanley loosened his tie. He sat on the sofa and slid to the edge of the cushion. "I received this information from a reporter friend. It appears Eden isn't the woman you believe her to be."

Chase glared across the desk to where Stanley sat. "What the hell does that mean?" He glanced back at the photograph of a younger Eden and read the headline. *Candidate Confesses to Affair with Employee.* His gut knotted just thinking about Eden with another man.

"Your girlfriend obviously has a thing for politicians. While in college, she worked for this city councilman. She filed sexual harassment charges against him right before the election."

"I don't believe it."

"Read it for yourself," Stanley told him. "Anyway, a scandal followed and the guy was forced to admit he and Eden had an affair.

He charged that Eden wanted him to leave his wife for her, but when he refused, she claimed sexual harassment."

Chase began reading the clippings. He didn't know what to think. There didn't appear to be another woman to support her claim. This couldn't be happening?

"This isn't the woman I love."

Stanley's head came up on hearing those words. "You're in love with Eden?" This was getting worse.

"I have been for several weeks. This can't be right. There has to be more to this story." He pushed away from the desk to walk around the room.

"Your polling numbers have taken a slight drop since Camden's allegations, and now this."

"I don't give a damn about the election," Chase roared with anger. Eden should have told him about this. She had to know how this could affect his campaign.

"Chase, do you believe Eden could be working with Camden?"

"What?" He stared at Stanley bewildered.

"Think about it. If she pulls a similar stunt right before the election next month, your campaign is tanked."

"She wouldn't do that. Besides, everyone knows we're seeing each other, so sexual harassment wouldn't work. God, I can't believe I just said that. Eden had to have been telling the truth." He rubbed his neck, feeling the tension.

"There are several allegations she could use against you. She's gotten close to you, and I'm sure she knows quite a bit that can be made to appear scandalizing. Think man. It's right there in black-and-white, and you want to ignore it. Well I won't. You and I have invested a great deal of time on this election, and you had best wake up now, and see the woman for what she is."

"What are you suggesting that Eden is a mole working with Camden to ruin my campaign? You honestly want me to believe she doesn't love me, and all this time has been an act?" Chase shook his head with disbelief.

"It's possible. I saw her with Owen at the gala. They appeared chummy."

"Then you need to get your prescription checked, because they were anything but chummy. I heard that conversation and Owen was hurling insults. You're wrong about her."

"For your sake I should hope so."

Eden approached the milling reporters outside of campaign headquarters with trepidation, but she had done nothing wrong and wouldn't hide in shame. She raised her head and walked calmly toward the building. She ignored the reporter's insulting questions, her mind focused on getting to Chase. As she entered the building, all eyes were upon her. She headed straight for Chase's office. She had to tell him the truth before things got out of hand. Raised voices could be heard on the other side as she knocked on the closed door before walking in. Both men glared at her as she came fully into the room and closed the door behind her. Her heart thumped heavily against her ribs with fear, because she knew she was too late.

"We need to talk."

Chase stared at Eden without responding. She looked incredible in a pair of black leather pants and gold sweater. He grew angry with himself for falling under her spell. He needed answers. Walking over to his desk, he picked up the file and carried it to where she stood. He held it in front of her. "Tell me about this."

Eden's hands visibly shook as she took the folder from him. She flipped it open and stared at her worst nightmare. "How did you get this?"

"I'm asking the questions, and I asked you to tell me about it," Chase's voice escalated with anger.

"I will if you'll stop screaming at me. It's not what you think."

"You're stalling. God, Eden, did you have an affair with this guy?"

"No." Eden shook her head vehemently. "I worked for Andrew."

"We know that, Miss Warner," Stanley snapped from behind her. "You also slept with the man, and then when he wouldn't leave his wife for your tawdry affair, you decided to tank his election bid."

"You're wrong," Eden responded to the charge. "I didn't have

The Politics of Love

an affair with Andrew." She looked back at Chase.

"Stanley believes you're working with Camden to bring down my election," Chase told her, not believing he had repeated the accusation.

Eden felt numb. She stared at Chase in shock. "You can't possibly believe that. You know what happened between us. Don't let Stanley put ideas into your head."

He wanted to cave in and wrap her in his arms, but he needed answers. "You have to admit, something like this would blow me right out of the water."

"Maybe so, but I wouldn't hurt you." Eden stared directly into his eyes. "And I didn't have an affair with Andrew. But you know what? You've already made up your mind about me, so I'll leave." She turned to walk out the office.

"No, you don't," Chase said, grabbing her by the arm. "I deserve the truth."

"And I deserve your *trust*," Eden shouted back. "What about all the lies written about you being a womanizer? I trusted you, with my heart and with my body."

Chase flinched as though slapped. He released her and watched as she fled the office. She was right. She had given him the benefit of the doubt, and in his heart, he knew the type of woman Eden was. This was all wrong.

"Don't allow her to turn this around on you, Chase," Stanley shouted from behind him. "It's written in black-and-white. I say let's go out there to the reporters and sever all ties with the woman."

"Not a chance," Chase shouted as he left the office in search of Eden. He did trust her and had to tell her so. As he made it to the door, flashbulbs went off. The reporters began throwing questions at him. It had grown dark, and the cameras flashing in front of him hindered his eye sight. He pushed his way toward the side parking lot in search of Eden when he saw another band of reporters, circling around her.

"Eden, wait," he tried to shout above the questions being directed at him. They were insulting and too intimately personal to

142

be answered. He kept his eyes focused on Eden as he fought his way through the crowd of reporters. At the corner of the parking lot, he suddenly saw her go down.

She had stepped on one of the reporter's foot and missed a step. The momentum and jostling of the reporters carried her forward, causing her to lose her balance. She struck her head on the curb as flashbulbs suddenly went off. She struggled to regain her footing, but felt disoriented. A pair of strong hands reached out to steady her.

"I've got you, baby," Chase whispered, helping her up. Blood ran down the side of her face from a gash to the head. He removed his handkerchief and pressed it to the wound. "I need to get you to a hospital. Get out of the way," he bellowed to the reporters.

"Police coming through," Taylor ordered with badge in hand. She had followed Eden over after telling her mother and sister about the incident in the restroom. She had known Eden would be coming here. She spotted her sister covered in blood. Her anger flared as she shot a menacing gaze in Chase's direction.

Chase spotted Taylor and knew how bad it looked. He didn't bother to explain. He needed to get Eden away from the press and to the hospital. "Get us out of here," he yelled to the woman.

Going into cop mode, Taylor quickly took control of the situation and ordered Chase to place Eden in her vehicle. She opened the back door for him as he helped Eden get in. She was surprised when he climbed into the back seat with her sister. Not having the time to question his actions, she climbed behind the wheel and turned on the sirens. She notified dispatch of her location as she sped off to the hospital.

❦

"Tell me what happened," Taylor demanded of Chase. They waited for Eden to be seen by a physician. She glared up at him, angrily. Hands on hips, she was ready to defend Eden to the end.

Chase wiped his hands on a paper towel. Eden's blood had

covered his hands and stained his shirt and slacks. "The reporters were circling her, and she must have lost her footing. I just saw her go down. When I reached her, she was a little disoriented and bleeding profusely from a gash to the head."

"Why weren't you with her when she fell?"

Chase stared down into Taylor's face, knowing how a criminal must feel when she was interrogating him. Her eyes took on this empty, dark stare that was impossible to read. "Eden ran out of my office upset, and I was chasing behind her."

"You believed the lies about her, didn't you?" Taylor stared at him accusingly. "My sister is no tramp. If you don't know that, then you don't deserve her."

"I was confused, Taylor. Stanley had just shoved these newspaper clippings under my nose and I needed answers."

"I hope Eden told you to go to hell."

"She did better than that. She shamed me." Chase fell into a chair while they waited. When he saw Eden go down, his heart had nearly stopped, and what they had been discussing earlier was no longer important. "I love your sister, and I do trust her. I made a mistake tonight, Taylor."

"A big one, unfortunately." She looked over at Chase and felt sorry for him. She could see he was obviously in love with Eden. "Have you told her how you feel?"

"In actions and other ways, but no I haven't said the words. I'm afraid she'll think it is too soon."

Taylor chuckled. "You obviously haven't heard the story of our parents' courtship."

"No I haven't. Wasn't it a long one?"

"My parents were married two months after meeting."

Chase's head whipped around. "You're kidding? I can't see Adam Warner being so hasty. He's known for being slow and methodical in court."

"Yeah, but with his heart, he recognized his mate right away." Taylor glanced up as her family came storming into the hospital. She and Chase both stood up.

"Those vultures are swarming all over the place," Victor informed them. He, like his father, was dressed for the gym, indicating their prior location.

"How's my baby?" Mrs. Warner asked. She was visibly shaken, and stood, clinging to Skye for strength.

"She's with the doctor now," Chase told her. He stood with his hands shoved in his pockets.

Mrs. Warner looked him up and down, noticing his exhausted features. The man was suffering.

Adam Warner wasn't sure Chase was suffering enough. "What the hell happened? Did you believe those lies about my daughter?" The man bellowed each word. He and Victor had caught the breaking news at the juice bar. They had left immediately.

"Of course he didn't, Dad," Taylor answered for Chase. She believed he loved Eden. She prayed she wasn't making a mistake.

Chase could have kissed Taylor, because the last thing he wanted to do was tangle with Adam Warner. He could only pray that Eden forgave him as easily for being stupid.

"Good," Adam sighed with relief. "This is Camden and Owen's doing."

"I agree," Taylor commented. She quickly informed them of Eden's encounter with the woman in the restroom and her parting shot. "Eden and I put two and two together, and she knew what was coming. She took off headed to see you." Taylor looked at Chase.

"I knew it," Adam said with confidence. "The allegation against you and Eden's relationship wasn't as effective as Camden had hoped. As it stands today, you and he would be in a runoff. Hilton is a growing city. The populace is getting younger and more educated due to your software business and the other technological companies moving in."

Chase nodded. "Bottom line, people are more tolerant."

Adam shook his head in agreement. "So, he gave the press a scandal about my daughter, as a way of striking back at me for asking Owen to leave the firm."

"I can't believe I never saw this side of Owen," Victor

commented.

"You did, son. In the courtroom everyday."

"I guess you're right, but now he has crossed the line."

"Damn straight, and just as soon as I know Eden is going to be all right, he and I are going to have a talk," Chase promised. Anger was etched into his worried face.

Eunice Warner knew how Chase felt because at that very moment, she could kick both Owen and Camden's behinds. She laid a comforting hand on his arm. "You take that anger and focus it onto the campaign. You stand tall, above the dirty politics, and sell your ideas to the public. I guarantee you you'll win. And that will be the best revenge."

Chase studied Mrs. Warner's face, seeing Eden in it. He smiled and reached out, drawing her into an embrace. "You're right. Thanks for keeping me from slipping into the mud with the Nelsons."

"My daughter cares about you," Eunice said, meeting Chase's eyes. "Be there for her."

"I have no intentions of going anywhere."

Chapter Fourteen

Take it easy," Chase whispered as he assisted Eden into bed. She had agreed they needed to talk and therefore had come home with him. The press had been out front near the drive, awaiting their arrival. Instead of parking in his usual place out front, he had driven around to the back and entered the house through a rear entrance.

He handed Eden a pain pill and glass of water. The head wound had required ten stitches. A small white bandage covered the injured area. Taking the glass from her, he perched on the side of the bed, feeling thankful to have this opportunity to clear the air. He had feared she wouldn't want to see him.

"I owe you an apology."

Eden studied Chase's eyes, seeing all the hurt and self-loathing he felt. She knew she held some responsibility for their current situation and therefore reached out, taking his hand.

"There's no need to apologize. In your shoes, I probably would have doubted you as well."

He shook his head. "No you wouldn't. Even knowing the rumors about me, you still gave me a chance." He squeezed her hand with affection.

"I should have told you about the councilman, but I honestly didn't think it mattered."

Chase looked at her sharply. "You could have told me *why* you were so uncomfortable with the press."

"You're right, I could have." She looked regretful and glanced around his room. She remembered their first time together. "How much did you read?" She looked back at him.

"Enough, but I want to hear what happened from you."

She nodded. "I worked for City Councilman Andrew

The Politics of Love

Chapman. He was making a bid for re-election at the time of my hiring. Anyway, I had been there for maybe three weeks when he started coming out of his office for small talk. You know, like asking advice about gifts for his wife. It appeared to be innocent."

"What changed?" Chase kicked off his shoes and eased into bed beside her.

"He began touching me. If I was working at the computer, he would stand behind me and massage my neck. At first I didn't say anything, but would find a reason to move. It made me uncomfortable." She looked over, meeting his eyes. "Then he went to caressing my arm while paying me a compliment. I asked him politely to stop, explaining how inappropriate and uncomfortable his behavior made me feel."

"What was his response?" He laced his fingers through hers.

"He assured me I was misinterpreting his actions. The touching stopped, but he then began making comments. He would compliment what I was wearing. He actually told me one evening that he had dreamed about me and *my long legs*." Eden glared at Chase in disgust.

"I just bet he did," Chase muttered, knowing exactly what the guy had been thinking.

"I reported him to the president of the city council, and he promised to speak with him. For a while, everything returned to normal."

"Just long enough for you to relax," Chase guessed correctly. "Were you the only person working in the office?"

"No. Another woman worked full-time for him. Our hours would overlap, and then I would be alone with him from four to seven."

"Did you mention his behavior to her?"

"Yes I did, and she told me it was just his way. I personally believe she liked the attention. I went to the council president once more, and this time the man tells me that Andrew informed him we were having an affair."

"You became the villain."

"Right. I thought about quitting, but then I thought, why should I quit? Why shouldn't he be held accountable for his behavior?" She looked at Chase for understanding.

"He should have been and you were right to file formal charges."

"I thought so, but then the press got wind of the story and began printing his version."

"His version made for better reading."

She leaned against his chest. "I guess, because they weren't interested in discovering the truth. I was labeled a vindictive co-ed, while he played the role of a remorseful husband. His polling numbers began to decline. He was finally forced to resign."

"Was the truth ever revealed?" Chase asked, pulling her back into his arms.

"Two former employees came forward afterward. A small write up appeared in the middle of the newspaper, but no one ever saw it."

"Eden, did you tell your family what was going on?"

"Not right away. My dad was already upset with me, and now I had gotten myself involved in a scandal. I was determined to handle it myself. But then it became more than I could manage alone." She looked at him. "My dad came to my rescue. He was instrumental in getting the women to come forward."

"I'm sorry you had to go through that." He kissed her head tenderly.

She reached out, caressing his face. "I think for the sake of your campaign, you and I should take a break." It hurt just thinking about not being with him.

"Not a chance," Chase fired back. "I love you, Eden, and I'm not letting you out of my sight."

She was speechless. Chase had finally said the words. "I love you, too. That's why I don't want to ruin the election for you."

Chase grabbed Eden's chin, tilting her face up. "You are more important than this election. Now, I'm not pulling out, and I'm not denying my love for you." He scrambled off the bed to reach the telephone on the dresser.

"Who are you calling?"

"Your father."

Eden lay on the sofa under a blanket while Chase, her father, and brother plotted. She never would have imagined seeing such a sight, but it made her heart happy, nonetheless. Chase made her happy as well. He loved her and trusted her.

"I want to know who leaked that information on Eden. If either Owen or his father did, I want the proof," Chase told the men.

"I'm already ahead of you," Adam informed his daughter's boyfriend. He hadn't been very pleased when he learned of Eden's involvement with the candidate, but since getting to know the man, had come to respect him. "I have a top-notch private investigator who works for me. He'll get to the bottom of it."

"Where did Stanley get that folder with all the newspaper clippings?" Eden interrupted, asking Chase.

"He said a reporter friend."

"I'll have him checked out as well," Adam assured them.

"I want to hold a press conference tomorrow."

Three pair of eyes swung in Eden's direction. "You aren't serious?" Victor spoke up. "Eden, they will crucify you."

"I need to do this. I allowed the press to write what they wanted before, but not this time. I'm fighting back. They want a story, and I'll give it to them." She sat straight and determined.

"That's my girl," Adam said with pride. "Take the fight to them."

Chase watched father and daughter, realizing they were more alike than they realized. He smiled privately, knowing neither would see the similarity. He returned to Eden's side. "Are you sure about this? I don't want you to do this on my behalf. We'll find another way to turn the tide."

Eden placed a hand on his thigh. "This is the only way. I can do this."

Chase studied Eden's determined expression. He wouldn't be talking her out of this anytime soon. "Okay, I'll call Alison and have her set it up for noon tomorrow."

"Thanks," she said and yawned. She leaned back on the sofa while the men discussed strategy.

Chase closed the door behind Adam and Victor Warner. They had proven to be of great help in redirecting his campaign. He returned to the den and stood there, watching Eden. The pain medication had finally set in, and she slept like a baby. But as he scooped her into his arms to carry her to bed, the feel of her soft womanly curves reminded him she was no child. She was all woman and his.

The next morning, Eden chose her outfit carefully. Chase had driven her back to her home after coordinating the press conference with Alison. Standing in the mirror looking at her reflection, she felt strong and confident in the gray suit. Professional-looking in color, but feminine as well in the detailing, she wore a soft pink shell underneath. She ran a comb through her hair and turned to leave the bathroom, when she spotted Chase watching her. He leaned against the doorjamb in the bedroom.

"So what do you think?" She held her arms out from her body.

His eyes slowly traveled down her body before returning to her face. He pushed away from the frame and met her in the middle of the floor. He noticed she had combed her hair slightly forward onto her forehead to conceal the bandage. "You look beautiful."

"Thanks."

"I love you, Eden. I want you to always remember that." He covered her mouth with his. He kissed her with a desperation brought on by almost losing her last evening. While his tongue mated with hers, his hand held her firmly against him, as he tried to imprint the feel of his body onto hers.

Eden tore her mouth away. "Stop. Chase, stop," she said again, but a little more forceful.

Coming back to his senses, Chase released her. He blew out a breath as he looked at her.

"Want to talk about it?" Eden asked.

Chase laughed with embarrassment. He had allowed his emotions to control his actions. He shook his head as he sat on the edge of the bed. "It just hit me pretty hard. I came so very close to throwing away what we have over a lie. It shook me to the core, Eden. It frightened me."

She was humbled by his sincerity. She sat down on the bed beside him. "I was scared last night as well. When I left your office, I didn't see any way back, but we're together." She took his strong hand and laced her fingers through his. "Do you remember the politics of love?"

Chase laughed. "Yeah, I do. How corny was that?"

"No, it was the most beautiful declaration I've ever heard. You spoke about promising to be there when it seemed as though the entire world had gone crazy. Well, last night I felt the world had gone crazy. I needed you, and you were there. I love you, Chase. I've never felt this depth of emotion for any man. And just for the record, I've only been with one other man. The relationship was short-lived and more a mistake than memorable."

Chase nodded with understanding. "I still hate to think about some man touching you. But, I am glad to know Owen didn't, and that this guy didn't make an impression."

"Only one man's name is imprinted on my heart, and it's spelled, C-H-A-S-E."

"You keep talking sweet like that, and we're going to miss our own press conference," he told her before kissing her passionately.

Chase led Eden into campaign headquarters through the rear entrance. The noise level was high and filled with anticipation. The Warner family was with them and looked ready to do battle with anyone who threatened Eden. They spotted Belle and Chase's parents as they stepped from his office. The gang was all there.

Stanley met them at the door. "Why didn't you let me know about this?" he directed the question to Chase. "May I speak to you alone?"

"We don't have time for that," Chase said dismissively. He continued to walk with Eden beside him, and located Alison.

"Is everything ready?"

"Yes, sir, and I have to say it's the right move." She beamed up at Chase with pride.

Stanley glared at the women. "When did you become the campaign manager?"

"She isn't," Chase answered on her behalf. "She's my spokesperson, and as such, she speaks for me." He turned to Eden, blocking out everyone else. "Are you ready?"

"Yes. Let's do it."

He gave her a quick kiss. "For luck."

Eden smiled. "Let's hope I don't need it."

The reporters grew silent as both families walked out before them. Chase gave a brief speech in support of Eden, and then turned the microphone over to her.

"First off, I would like to say that your reporting of the Chapman incident was incomplete. The job of a reporter is to discover the truth, not repeat what someone else has written. None of you did that, therefore I'll tell you the truth."

Chase stood in awe of the woman. She had politely, though firmly taken the reporters to task for their poor job of reporting the story. She used her teacher voice, the one that held the student's undivided attention in class. Glancing around the room, he could see it had the same effect on reporters, because they were enthralled. She set the timeline of events and in a matter-of-fact manner, supplied the answers to the who, what, when, where, and why questions. She provided the reporters with the name of the point-of-contact in the city council office who would be in possession of her formal complaint, and the findings uncovered by a private detective. She took a few questions when finished.

"Who do you believe leaked this information?" a reporter asked.

"Why don't you tell me, since you were waiting outside the building last evening when I arrived." She remembered him shouting an obscene question.

The reporter looked truly embarrassed. "You know I can't do that, ma'am."

Eden smiled politely. "Yes, I do. And I can't go around speculating without proof. My goal today was to set the record straight so the voters could make an informed decision two weeks from now. The last thing I am going to say is this. Chase Mathews is a respectable man who cares deeply about this city. The success of his business in Hilton is testament to his business talents. His plan for this city has been spelled out clearly, and excludes no one. I ask that the citizens do their own thinking and vote for the best candidate."

"Miss Warner, are there wedding bells in the future?" a female reporter asked.

Eden smiled shyly. She turned slightly to look at Chase, who winked. Facing the reporters once more, she answered. "I guess we'll have to wait and see, won't we?" She stepped back from the microphone. She felt it had gone well.

Alison took over and quickly managed to clear the building of reporters. The families were shown to the conference room, out of sight of the large front windows. Eden and Chase joined them.

"So, how did I do?" she asked, the minute they were behind closed doors.

"Sweetheart, I think the wrong person is running for office," Chase told her. He wrapped his arms around her for a big embrace. "I am so proud of you. You are one hell of a woman." He released her to plant a quick kiss on her lips.

"Chase is right," Alison agreed. "We need you out there campaigning as well. You have a timely platform to show your strength."

"Baby, you had those reporters eating right out of your hand," Adam said proudly. "You would have made one heck of an attorney."

"Adam," Eunice reprimanded.

"Daddy," Eden responded, and laughed. "The limelight is not for me. I like being in my classroom with my students."

"There's nothing wrong with that, baby," Adam said and meant it. Eden had made him very proud today.

"Young lady, you and my son make quite a team. I haven't had this much fun in quite a while. Maybe I'll come down here more often, if that's all right with you son?" Edward looked to Chase.

"Sounds like a good idea, Dad."

Stanley hated to admit that Eden had done an excellent job. He still didn't believe she was good for Chase's political career, but for the moment, they were still in the race. He forced a smile on his face as he joined in on the congratulatory celebration.

"Eden," Stanley said drawing everyone's attention. "You were excellent today. I believe you've turned the situation around. We're lucky to have you on our side." He gave what was meant to be a smile.

"Thank you for the kind words." Eden studied the man's eyes for any sign of deceit. He appeared sincere, but her instincts told her not to let her guard down. "I hope it helps with the voters."

Chase didn't know what to make of the exchange. Maybe he was just a concerned campaign manager looking out for his well being. For now, he would play it as normal as possible, but if the detective uncovered evidence that he was involved in hurting Eden, then all bets were off. The man would have to be dealt with by him.

Chapter Fifteen

I was very proud of you today," Chase told Eden as they lay in the den. The crackling of the fireplace was like music in the quiet of the room.

"I'm proud of me, too," Eden replied. She caressed his face lovingly. "I hope it helps your campaign."

Chase rolled placing her beneath him. "Will you stop feeling guilty? Just think if it hadn't been for the campaign, you and I never would have met."

Eden placed her arms around him. "I can't imagine my life without you."

"Nor can I. Can you believe both our families came to support us?"

"That's a good sign, don't you think?" She kissed the hollow of his throat.

Chase groaned with longing. "Why don't we take this to the bedroom?"

"Lead the way."

The telephone rang. Chase and Eden looked at each other and groaned.

"Get it," Eden whispered. She slid from under him and began removing her clothing.

Chase didn't budge. He was enjoying the show. The telephone rang again, just as Eden's shirt hit the floor.

"You better answer that. It could be important." The bra hit the floor next.

"What you're doing is far more important." Chase licked his lips as she opened the button on her slacks.

The telephone rang a third time.

"Don't you want to take that?" Eden peeled the slacks off to stand before him in white lace.

"I want to take you to bed." He rose from the sofa. The answering machine picked up on the fourth ring.

"Chase, this is David. I really need to speak …"

Chase rushed to the telephone. "David, sorry I was busy."

"Hey, buddy. I was hoping to find Eden at your place. I've tried her home …"

"She's here."

"Oh. Look, you can have her call me back, if I'm interrupting."

Chase laughed. "She's right here." He beckoned Eden forward with a finger, while his eyes devoured her body.

Eden reached for her shirt to cover herself at the same time Chase did. "Give that to me," she demanded.

"Not a chance," he mouthed back, handing her the telephone.

With no choice, Eden grabbed the telephone, and glared at Chase. "Hello."

He drew Eden down to straddle his hips. His fingers skimmed down the column of her spine to disappear into the lace panty. He felt her tremble in his arms and smiled.

"Sure. Of course I understand," Eden whispered. She shoved hard against Chase's chest. "Who'll replace me?" Tears tracked down her face.

"What's going on?" Chase asked, concerned. He grabbed the telephone from Eden. "David, what the hell is going on?"

"I'm sorry to have to do this."

"Do what? Just tell me," Chase demanded. He watched Eden gather her clothing and get dressed. She was crying.

"Some of the parents have contacted the superintendent with their concern about Eden being at the school."

"Did they believe those lies about her?" He stood, pacing the floor. He watched as Eden fled the room.

"They're afraid the children are being distracted by the press camped across the street from the school. It's a safety issue as well when they jump into their cars to follow Eden," David explained.

"So what do they want?" He leaned against the mantle,

massaging his temple.

"The superintendent has placed Eden on administrative leave for the remainder of the year."

Chase's heart sank. He knew Eden was taking the news hard. "This isn't right, David. She isn't responsible for the press."

"Don't you think I know that? But my responsibility is to the children first. Look, tell Eden I'm really sorry."

"Yeah, sure."

"She can come by after school and pick up her things."

"I'll tell her." Chase disconnected from the call and tossed the telephone onto the sofa. It seemed every time they turned around, they were being hit by something else. He turned the lights off and went in search of Eden. He found her curled on the bed sobbing. Kicking off his shoes, he joined her in bed, fitting himself against her body.

"I'm so sorry, baby." Chase wrapped his arms around her.

"It's not your fault any more than it's mine." She turned in his arms to face him. "It's best for the children I know, but it hurts. I worry about them. The boys are doing so much better with their reading."

He caressed her back. "Maybe you could make a suggestion for the replacement."

"They've already made a selection. David wouldn't tell me who."

"This is my campaign, but you're the one taking the beating." Chase wiped away her tears. "I don't want to be mayor this badly. I'm going to pull out of the race."

Eden pushed his hands away. "You'll do no such thing. Hilton needs you, Chase."

"And I need you."

"I'm here. I'll be okay."

"I'm afraid all this will come between us."

"Nothing and no one can come between us that we don't allow. We can't allow them to win. Promise me you'll stay in the race," she demanded.

Chase shook his head with uncertainty. "All right. I'll stay in the race."

They lay in the quiet for several minutes, doing no more than holding each other. Chase thought of the office he had wanted from childhood and realized that dreams changed. He wanted the woman lying beside him more than he had ever wanted anything. This campaign was getting ugly, and the only person getting hurt seemed to be Eden. She made him happy. She made him believe in himself and in his vision for the city. As he held her, a new vision emerged. One with the two of them growing old together. He kissed her head, mindful of the bandage. His blood boiled with anger all over again, just thinking about her tears.

Eden thought about her students completing the school year without her. What would they be told of her absence? Would they think she abandoned them? She prayed they wouldn't. And what was she suppose to do with her time? Maybe she would apply to work at one of those learning centers. She could always volunteer at campaign headquarters, but did she really want to be around Stanley?

It appeared the decision was removed from her hands as Alison called her down to headquarters the next day. She dressed quickly and prepared to drive through the line of reporters waiting out in the street. She didn't think she would ever get used to such close scrutiny. All she wanted was to teach and to be with the man she loved. A dreamy expression spread across her face as she thought of Chase. He had actually considered pulling out of the election because of her. Of course she couldn't allow him to do that, but just knowing he loved her enough to consider dropping out was humbling.

She arrived at headquarters a little after nine and was quickly greeted by Alison, who led her into Chase's office. He and Stanley sat waiting for her.

"Hi, baby," Chase said, rising to plant a quick kiss on her lips.

"Why am I here?" she asked the moment they parted. She looked from Chase to Alison.

"This is so wonderful. The Mothers of Hilton have requested you to speak at their luncheon tomorrow," Alison told her with excitement.

"What?" Eden couldn't believe the news.

"They were so impressed with your news conference they are launching a new campaign against sexual harassment and would like you to be their spokesperson." Alison was practically jumping up and down with excitement. "And they're not the only ones calling. The local junior college would like you to speak there as well. As of right now, if you're willing of course, you'll be the guest speaker at five separate events."

Chase watched Eden closely. He knew how she felt about public attention, but watching how she handled herself yesterday in front of the press, left no doubt in his mind she could do it.

The news was overwhelming. She needed a moment to process it all. Yesterday had been about helping Chase and setting the record straight. She wasn't a public speaker. She was a teacher who belonged in the classroom. But that had all come to a halt last evening.

"I know you don't necessarily like being in the limelight," Chase said, gaining her attention. He rubbed her arms affectionately. "But, you were really amazing yesterday. You were poised and gracious, while being direct and informative. You had those reporters eating right out of your hands. I think this will be good for you, and will go a long way in healing an old wound."

Eden sighed, deep in thought. She placed a hand on his chest, appreciating his confidence in her ability. She had to admit she was honored by the invitations. Maybe she could do this. "I guess it's not like I have anything else to do."

Chase smiled. He could see the light returning to her brown eyes. "You can do this."

She could. Eden met his eyes. A smile spread across her face at the possibility. "You're right, I can. Thanks for giving me a pep talk."

"Anytime, sweetheart." Chase placed a kiss on her cheek.

"Schedule me and get the particulars," Eden said to Alison.

The woman nodded. "I'll notify the press of your speaking engagements. I've also taken the liberty of setting up an office for you."

Eden looked to Chase. "I don't need an office."

"We think you do. You'll be speaking more and making appearances, it only makes sense to make a place for you here."

Stanley suddenly stood to join them. He adjusted his glasses on his nose as he looked up at her. "You must accept the fact, Miss Warner; you are now a part of this campaign. The women of Hilton are interested in your story. It's also the perfect opportunity to spread Chase's message and the focus of his campaign."

Eden couldn't agree more. Although as she looked at Chase, she could tell he wasn't comfortable with her representing the campaign. "Will you both excuse us?" Eden waited for Stanley and Alison to close the door. "I know what you're thinking," she said, turning back to him.

"Then you know it will appear as though there's some truth to Owen's claim. I love you, and I respect the woman you are. I want people to hear the message you have to give about the effects of sexual harassment."

"They will, but they also won't be able to separate the fact that you and I are a couple. We can't ignore the possibility of questions. I am the woman in your life. I should possess a certain insight into the man." She smiled at him.

"Do you?" Chase pulled her into his arms.

"Most certainly, I know you like to be touched ..." she whispered the words into his ear.

"What a mouth on you, woman?" Chase laughed, swatting her backside. "You won't be telling those secrets I hope?"

"Not a chance. Some other woman may try to steal you away."

"There's only one woman for me." Chase lowered his mouth to hers. He encouraged her to open under him as his tongue slipped inside. It had been a while since they had been intimate, and it didn't take much to arouse him. He held Eden's head as he took control of the kiss. God, he couldn't get enough of her. He tore his mouth away. His body was heavy and aching with the need to love her.

"I need you."

"I know." Eden ran a hand across the bulge in his slacks. "But not here."

"Come on," he said teasing her. "Haven't you ever wanted to make love on a desktop?" He ran his hand across the wooden surface. His eyes traveled up and down her body in a suggestive manner.

Eden giggled. She backed her way to the door. "I can't say I have."

"Liar. You're thinking about it now." Chase stalked her. "You're wondering how the desk will feel on your backside."

"You're crazy."

"About you." Chase kept coming. "Will the wood be cool and hard, or will it heat up and become slippery." He trapped her against the door. His body touched hers in all the right places. "The thought of where to brace your hands entered your thoughts." He raised her hand above her head.

"Chase?" Eden was being turned on.

"We'll continue this later." Chase released her and suddenly stepped back.

Eden's eyes opened wide. "What was that?" She raked a hand through her hair.

Chase smiled sexily at her. "A preview of what's to come tonight." He pressed a kiss to her lips.

"You're going to pay for that," Eden said as she opened the door and slipped out.

"I sure hope so." He watched her go with a smile.

Chase greeted Eden at the door with a kiss. "Follow me please," he said, taking her by the hand.

"Not that I'm complaining about the kiss, but what are you up to?" She followed behind him. She was led to the small bathroom toward the rear of the house. She stopped outside the door and faced him. "What's going on?"

"You'll find a box. Put on what's inside and meet me at the patio doors." He waited for her to enter the room, and then pulled the door closed behind him. He hurried back down the hall and out to the patio area. He quickly shed his clothing and waited for her to join him. He looked over his handiwork, liking what he saw. Everything was in place for the perfect evening.

Eden spotted the beautifully wrapped box resting on the vanity countertop. The pink floral wrapping was almost too pretty to be torn. However, childlike when it came to surprises, she lit into the box like a kid on Christmas morning. Removing the lid, she pulled back the white tissue paper to reveal her surprise. She picked up the teal bikini top and bottoms. *Now why would he want me to put this on?*

Chase waited by the door for Eden. It had been quite a while since the two of them had spent quality time together, but tonight he was making up for it. Private security guards had been hired to keep the press away from the property. He heard the sound of bare feet against the hardwood floor. Looking in the direction of the footsteps, his heart kicked into overdrive at the sight of her in the bikini. Something about a woman in a little bikini did things to a man. "This way, beautiful lady." Chase wrapped a white terry cloth robe around her.

A cool breeze greeted her as she stepped onto the patio. She clutched the robe together to ward off the chill. As she did, she caught sight of tiny white twinkling lights illuminating the pergola and screen of shrubbery. A haze of steam billowed from the bubbling hot tub sheltered beneath. Trays laden with cheese, crackers, and fruit sat on a small serving cart. Chocolate-covered strawberries were also included. Someone had gone to an extreme amount of effort.

"This is wonderful. I can't believe you did all this." The

thoughtfulness that went into planning such an evening settled deep within her heart. Her eyes reflected the emotions.

"I'm glad you like it," he told her, caressing her cheek. "We've been so involved with the election we've neglected our relationship. I don't want to do that, because that's when couples begin to take each other for granted and drift apart." He peeled away the robe, tossing it on the back of a chair.

"I don't want that to happen with us either. So you did all this for us?" Eden accepted his hand as she stepped into the heated water.

"Yes, I did." He slipped into the water and sat down beside her. "I needed to add the romance back to this relationship."

Eden smiled with delight. "Well you've certainly done that."

He passed her a glass of wine. "Tonight I just want to hold you and snuggle under the stars."

"Sounds like the perfect way to end the day." Eden accepted the glass of wine and leaned back into Chase's waiting arms. She closed her eyes, taking pleasure in the night sounds around them. She sat that way for several minutes, enjoying the solitude and safety of his arms.

"Are you falling asleep on me?"

A smile spread across her face. Turning toward him, she opened her eyes. "Not a chance, but this is wonderful."

He kissed her temple and laughed. "It is pretty great." He caressed his chin against her hair. "How are you holding up today?"

"You mean the children."

"Yeah, I know how extremely difficult it is for you not to be in the classroom."

"It was torturous. I kept thinking about the boys and wondering if my substitute would adhere to their additional hour of reading. They have made such progress since their time with you, and I would hate to see them stall because I'm not there. However, working on my speech for tomorrow with the Mothers of Hilton helped to distract me."

"How so?" He pressed a kiss into her hair.

"I want to do more tomorrow than retell my story. I want to be able to provide valuable information about sexual harassment that will help both men and women. So I searched the web for statistics and contacted some organizations that assist victims and provide educational services on the subject to corporations. I was able to pick up some brochures on the subject to hand out afterward."

"Couldn't resist the opportunity to impart a little wisdom, could you?" He chuckled when she elbowed him in the side.

"Guilty as charged." Eden rolled her eyes and laughed as well.

"In all seriousness, I'm very proud of you and the way you have handled the mud slinging."

"Thank you." Eden sipped her wine. "Mmm… that's really good. Any feedback on the press conference?"

Chase reached for his glass of wine and took a sip. He returned it to the table, settling back with her in his arms. "All indications are positive. Everywhere I went today, people talked about you, and how courageous you were to reveal such a personal matter."

"I really had no choice, and I needed to set the record straight. I also hope being candid will help your campaign. For a man who didn't want me, Owen and his father sure are spending a great deal of time tearing me down."

Chase removed the glass from her hand. He placed it on the table beside his, and then turned to face her. "I can hear the pain in your voice."

Eden looked at him, shaking her head. "I don't have feelings for Owen."

"I know, but it hurts when someone we cared about shows us just how little we really mattered to them."

She met his eyes, sensing a real understanding of her emotions that could only come from being hurt as well.

"Know this one thing. Whether I win this election or not, I'm still a winner because I have you in my life."

"Thank you." Eden caressed his cheek. "Are you nervous?"

"About the election?" He looked at her and shrugged. "A little, I guess. I want to win because I believe I'm the best man for the job, but if it doesn't happen, then I return to my company."

"You'll be able to do that with no regrets?" Her eyes conveyed her real question.

"Come here, baby," Chase crooned, low and sexy. He picked her up to straddle his thighs. "I do not regret falling in love with you. And, I am not Owen. I'm not letting you get away from me.

"I know."

"I don't think you understand the depth of my feelings for you. I've never felt what I feel for you with *any* other woman." His eyes were dark and penetrating, demanding that she really grasp the meaning of his words.

"A girl could lose her head when you talk sweet like that."

"I'd much prefer your heart." He leaned forward, placing a kiss over her left breast.

She was in love with the man, and each day her love grew stronger. Eden's heart responded with a thunderous pounding inside her chest. "What are you telling me?"

"I'm telling you that in the very near future, we're going to have a conversation about the rest of our lives."

"Are we?" She blushed happily.

"Yes, we are," he repeated. "But for now I'd rather express my feelings in this manner." His mouth claimed hers in a scorching kiss that mimicked the pulsing rhythm of the blood surging to his groin. Wet, open-mouthed kisses intent on heightening her desire, stole her breath away. His hands found the ties of her bikini and released them one by one. The garment fell into the churning water to float away. His hands came up to cup her breasts, rolling the dark hard nipples between his thumbs and index fingers. Eden quivered on his lap. The small trimmers stimulated where they were connected. She clutched his shoulders to anchor herself against the wave of pleasure coursing through her body. And then, Chase's hands fell to her hips as he began a back and forth slide against his rigid length. The motion set off fireworks inside her head. She fell against him, breathless and warm with desire.

Chase held Eden against his body while the trimmers eased. He pushed her hair away from her face so that he could look at her. Flushed, and with wet tendrils of hair sticking to her face and neck, she was beautiful. She had become everything to him.

"I need you," he rasped out with an urgency brought about by the depth of his emotions. His hands peeled the small panties from her body. He tossed them over the side without thought. Then with Eden's assistance, he removed his trunks. They too went over the side of the tub. He fumbled behind him on the table and located the foil square. Quickly sheathing himself, he eased Eden down onto him, gritting his teeth with every inch that her body accepted. They stared into each other eyes as they began to move. The tempo was slow and easy, like the music playing softly around them.

Eden gasped every time he surged inside of her. Warm and slick with the heated mist rising from the water, she rode each stroke, giving just as much as she was receiving. Then Chase leaned forward and drew her breast into his mouth. His teeth nipped and pulled. The sensation sent shockwaves through her system. She threw her head back, savoring the slow ride.

But Chase had other ideas and began picking up the pace. Water splashed around them as their movements became frenzied, each stroke more pleasurable than the last, and each cry of pleasure more desperate than the last. Then with one final slide, he pushed them over the edge as their cries of rapture were absorbed by the gurgling sound of the water surrounding them.

They made love off and on throughout the evening before retiring to his bedroom. A fire danced in the fireplace, providing their only light in the room. Chase lay curled around Eden as they laughed and whispered quietly into the night.

"Where do you want to be in five years?" Chase asked from behind her.

Was this a trick question, or a sincere one? Either way the answer came from her heart. "With you and our children down the hall." She held her breath for his response.

"So you do want children?"

"You sound surprised."

"Not really, considering what you do for a living, but ..."

"But what?" She waited for him to explain.

"I wasn't sure you would want them with me."

She turned in his arms to face him. "Why wouldn't I want children with you?"

"Stone is biracial, black and white."

"I didn't know."

"He considers himself a black man. But he once told me his father had suggested to his mother that they not have children, because to be black in America was difficult enough."

"And being of two worlds is even more so," Eden finished the words she had heard and read before.

"That's it." He looked at her, waiting for her feelings on the thought.

"I believe the world has changed, but that's not to say children of mixed heritages don't run into prejudice, because I know they do. However, I believe children experience so many types of prejudice, that race is just one more. And with the love of their parents teaching them self-worth, they get through it as strong individuals."

"It's all about self-worth for most children, isn't it?"

"Yes."

"So how many are we talking?"

"Six." Eden looked him square in the eyes.

"Six, as in five plus one?"

"Or three plus three," she said, smiling. She detected a little anxiousness in his eyes.

"Are you serious?" A definite hint of concern sounded in his voice.

"No." She burst out laughing.

"Whew! What a relief. Not that I mind making six babies with you, but I kept envisioning the years of changing dirty diapers."

"You would change diapers?" she asked with awe.

"I plan on being a hands-on father some day. And if you wanted six babies, I would gladly give them to you." His tone was completely serious now.

Eden was surprised. She stared at him. "You would give me six babies?"

"Sweetheart, I would give you the stars and the moon if you asked."

"Wow! Mr. Mathews, you do know what to say." She leaned forward and kissed him, initiating a new round of lovemaking.

Chapter Sixteen

The next day, Eden stood before the Mothers of Hilton retelling her experience with sexual harassment. She imparted valuable statistical information that grounded her speech and drew the audience in. It became clear to those in attendance the problem continued to exist, despite corporate efforts to educate the work force. She reminded them that sexual harassment wasn't only a female issue, but a people issue. She held the women's rapt attention with her soft, commanding, teacher's voice. They hung onto her every word, and when she finally fell silent, the room exploded in an exuberant round of applause.

"I'm open for questions, if there are any out there," Eden said, and saw several hands fly into the air. She smiled and pointed to a woman near the front.

"How do you respond to the allegations levied by the Nelson camp?"

Eden didn't pretend not to understand the question. She looked the woman directly in the eyes as she responded. "Race is an easy diversion from the real issues. Mr. Nelson fails to recognize that today's voters are highly educated and form opinions for themselves. I'm not concerned with his allegations."

She recognized another woman. "Why should we give our vote to Mr. Mathews?"

"You should vote for the man you believe will better serve our city. I will vote for Mr. Mathews because I know he's that man. His heart is good and his mind sharp. His vision for our city will benefit all, instead of the usual few. Compare the records for yourself and decide. That's all Mr. Mathews requests."

"And he's hot," someone screamed out from the back. The room erupted into laughter.

Eden laughed from the platform. "I agree with you."

More questions followed before the chairwoman called an end to the luncheon. But Eden was only getting started, as more requests for her to appear came in. She spent a great deal of time revamping her speech and conducting research. However, with each appearance, more questions were levied at her about the campaign and the man in her life. A positive sign that the voters weren't interested in Nelson's negative campaigning.

Chase was also quite busy as Election Day neared. He addressed the Chamber of Commerce on the twentieth and received their endorsement. Wherever he was invited, he spoke. He, too, was receiving positive feedback from each stop as the questions about the allegations lessened. People were asking questions that would affect the future of the city. He had picked up several more endorsements within the city and appeared to be doing well in the polling numbers. It would definitely be a race between him and Camden Nelson.

The first Tuesday of March, Chase returned to campaign headquarters after casting his ballot early that morning. Stanley and Alison had both accompanied him to the polls. He shook a few hands on the way in and out, then went to Belle's for breakfast. As usual, his grandmother had been supportive. Eden had phoned as he was getting dressed this morning to send her love and offer him good luck. She would be down later after casting her own ballot.

He continued on into the building with Stanley on one side of him issuing orders to their staff, and Alison on the other, reminding him about the press' arrival later that day. People were actively working the telephones. Others were carrying out flyers and buttons to encourage people to vote. His nerves were a little frazzled as all he wanted was a quiet moment alone. He excused himself to his office and closed the door behind him. He removed his jacket, hanging it on the coat tree, and then loosened his tie. Settling behind his desk, he realized this was it. Either he would be mayor by the end of the day or he wouldn't. He reclined his head against the back of his chair just as a knock on his door interrupted the peace he was seeking.

"Come in." He didn't bother to get up or right his clothing. But as the door opened and his father walked in, he bolted into an upright position. "Dad? Is everything all right?"

"Of course it is," Edward Mathews said as he closed the door behind him.

Chase took in his father's office attire of khaki slacks and a navy blue jacket. "What's going on?" He rose from his chair to greet him. The men exchanged handshakes, moving further into the space. Chase slid his hands into his pockets as he made himself comfortable.

Edward looked at his son, exasperated. "I wanted to come down and offer support on your big day."

Chase didn't quite know what to say. He had always thought of his father as too consumed by his construction business to care what went on in his children's lives. Sure, he had come down for Eden's press conference, but that had been upon request. This was completely different. "Really?"

"Look, son, I know you and I haven't been close, but I'm very proud of you."

"Thank you for telling me." Chase sat on the edge of his desk. He watched as his father walked around his office aimlessly. "What is it, Dad?"

Edward stopped pacing and turned back toward his son. He looked into his blue eyes, so like his mother's, and remembered the first time he had held him. "I've always been jealous of your relationship with Belle and Ruben. You're my only son, and I wanted us to have that closeness."

"You were never around," Chase told him honestly.

Edward nodded. "I thought there would always be time. I was building our future, but then I turned around one day and you were a man. You didn't need me any more."

"I'll always need you."

"Will you?" Edward asked, hope brimming in his eyes. "It's not too late for us to build a relationship?"

"No, it's not too late. Right now I could really use my father's support."

"Well I'm here as long as you want me." Edward settled on the sofa. "You'll make an excellent mayor of this city."

"I think so, but will the voters? There's so much I want to see happen in Hilton."

"You'll get to make them happen." Edward meant every word. He kept up with his son's business dealings and some of his more private endeavors. He knew Chase was a good man with the skill and vision to see Hilton into the future. "Are you happy, son?" Edward wanted to know. He had watched Chase and Eden on the two occasions he had been around them, but this was a conversation between father and son.

Chase glanced at his father, knowing what he was asking. "I'm very happy. Eden makes me happy."

Edward studied his son's expression. "She's the one, isn't she?" He chuckled when his son smiled brightly. "I know your mother can be a little reserved, but she puts a smile on my face as well."

"I know. I've seen the way you look at her," Chase teased his father.

"So tell me about Eden."

"She's the best thing ever to happen to me. She's loving and compassionate. Her students adore her. The day she was attacked by an abusive father, her first thought was of her students. She was battered and bruised, yet she told me to take care of the children."

"She wanted to protect them from the violence."

"And she protects them from embarrassment when they show up to school without supplies or a coat. She goes to her magic cabinet and produces whatever they need."

"She sounds like an incredible woman."

"She is and she's all mine." Chase looked at his father with pride. "Despite the outcome of the election, Eden and I *will* have a future together."

"I'm happy for you, son. Have you told her about Tammy?"

Agitated, Chase glared at his father and pushed away from the desk. He didn't want to deal with this issue today. "No. I'm hoping there will be no reason to ever tell her."

Edward shook his head with disapproval. "You're risking a lot. She's bound to hear about it from your mother or sisters. Don't you think it would be best if she heard about her from you?"

"Maybe you're right. But how will she be able to forgive me for what I've done?" He looked out of the window. He didn't like the idea of a threat hanging over their lives.

"If she truly loves you, she'll forgive you. But she may not forgive you for hiding something this important from her."

The two talked for several more minutes before Chase was called away. Eden arrived during that time. Learning Chase was out; she decided to wait in his office. She heard the television as she neared the door. Sticking her head in, she spotted Mr. Mathews reclined in Chase's chair. She started to duck out, when Mr. Mathews called her back in.

"Please, join me." Edward waved her forward. "Chase is with that Crystal, being interviewed for the noon day news."

"That's just great," Eden mumbled under her breath. She hung up her coat and took a seat on the sofa to watch the interview.

"My wife doesn't care for her either. She says the woman is too ambitious and will use anyone to further her position."

Eden laughed. "You weren't supposed to hear that."

"It'll be our little secret." He smiled at the young woman. "My son tells me you're an excellent teacher."

"I love what I do."

"Me too, although I'm afraid I've allowed it to take over my life. By the time I realized what had happened, my children were adults."

"Take it from me. It's never too late to reconnect with your children. My father and I haven't been close over the years, but we're working through that, and it's really wonderful getting to know him again."

"That's what I'm trying to do with my son now."

"You will. Chase loves you."

They talked a few minutes more, getting better acquainted, then sat back watching the interview. Chase was charismatic as ever as he projected the image of a winner. He used the moment to reiterate his campaign platform. The camera switched to Camden at his local polling station. He had just cast his ballot and was now before the cameras.

"Ask yourself what is the school board hiding behind the heading of administrative leave," Camden said. "If this woman has done nothing wrong, why dismiss her? I tell you, there's more to this story and that couple than the public knows. And I won't stop until I expose them for the frauds they are. So when you vote today, cast your ballot for a truthful man who will take this city into the future."

Edward glanced across the room at Eden. "Are you all right?" He pointed toward the television. "That guy won't let up."

"No, he won't." Eden rose from the sofa. She went over to the window, looking out. "My father removed his son, Owen, from his firm a short while ago. I believe tearing my character down is Mr. Nelson's way of striking back at my father. But Chase and I just want to be left to our lives. We love each other."

"I know already. My son told me how happy he is."

"He did?" She looked at him.

"Yes he did."

"He's pretty wonderful himself. He's kind and generous, despite the money. Not to mention extremely smart and just what this city needs to move forward. He deserves to win. If he doesn't ..."

"He will still love you," Edward assured her. He saw what his son did when he looked at the woman. "Know that he loves you and no other."

Eden nodded, but found the remark odd. "If you'll excuse me, I'm going to step out onto the floor and see if I can give them a hand."

Edward watched her go. He liked her and knew she was good for his son. But despite Chase's wishing for his problem to go away, he knew secrets had a way of coming out when you least expected them.

The Politics of Love

Both families gathered at campaign headquarters to await election returns. An assortment of food and drinks had been ordered to feed supporters and family alike. Chase was currently speaking with the press in his office, while Eden waited on the floor with family and supporters. She was as nervous as could be. This was Chase's dream, and she prayed it would be fulfilled.

"I think you're more nervous than Chase," Taylor said, coming up behind her. She had watched her sister fidget and pace the area twice.

"This is so important to him. And he is so deserving of it. He's done things for this city that people know nothing about."

"He'll win. Trust me on this," she said with a wink. She glanced at the front door once more.

"Are you looking for someone?"

"No, just looking." She tried to look casual. "It's just the cop in me checking out my surroundings."

Eden laughed as she hugged her sister. "You are so looking for a certain man."

Taylor blushed. "So what if I am?" She was tired of fighting her attraction.

"I think it's great. So what's going on with you two?"

Taylor snagged a bottle of water from the nearby bar. She unscrewed the cap and took a long drink. She looked at her sister and shrugged. "Nothing is going on. I guess he got tired of my putting him off."

"Why did you?" Eden took her sister's hand. "I know you're attracted to the man."

"Because guys always want me to quit my job, just because they can't handle what I do for a living. And cops are the worst."

"Stone impressed me as a strong man. I think he might surprise you."

"Who might surprise who?" Chase asked, joining them. He pressed a kissed to Eden's cheek. Excitement danced in his eyes.

The women stared at each other smiling. "Nothing. How did it go with the reporters?" Eden changed the subject quickly. She could feel his enthusiasm.

Chase looked from one to the other. He knew the sisters were keeping secrets. "Okay, ladies, I get the message."

"First returns are coming in," Stanley said, gaining everyone's attention.

The room fell silent as several televisions around the area, each on a different area channel, began posting the returns. With ten percent of the polls counted, Chase and Owen were virtually tied. After the news break, the channels returned to regular programming and conversation continued. But as the news breaks progressed and the local stations stayed on to the end, the two candidates went back and forth in the lead. Eden stood beside Chase, chewing on her bottom lip with nervousness. He appeared to be calm and taking everything in stride, only she knew how important this election was to him. While he, Stanley, and Alison put their heads together, she slipped out of the room. She needed some place quiet to hide out. Chase's empty office was the ideal location.

She entered the office and closed the door. She didn't bother with the lights. Taking a seat behind his desk, she leaned back in the chair and closed her eyes. So much was hanging on these last few minutes. What if he didn't win? Could he put the election behind him and be happy with her? She hoped so. She knew he loved her, but sometimes disappointments could eat away at a relationship.

She sat there remembering the night they'd discussed children. They had agreed upon two initially, with the possibility for more. Chase had told her he wanted to be an involved father. He wanted to know what was going on in his children's lives. He wanted them to know they were loved. In that moment, she really understood what he had missed out on while growing up. But his parents were with him tonight. Obviously, from her earlier conversation with his father, the two were making an attempt to develop a bond.

The door to the office suddenly opened. Chase stood there watching Eden sitting in the dark. He had noticed she appeared a little nervous tonight. He closed the door as he walked over to the desk to join her.

"Hiding out?" he asked, as he perched on the desk beside her. He reached out, taking her hand.

"I just need a little quiet time." She forced a smile.

"I'd say you're extremely nervous."

Eden smirked because he was right. "I don't know how you're remaining so calm. Everything you've ever dreamed comes down to this, and you appear absolutely at peace with it."

"Sweetheart, I either win or lose. Either way, the sun will come up in the morning." He kissed her palm.

"I'm afraid being with me may cost you the election," she whispered the words, ashamed to be admitting her fear. "I'm also afraid the disappointment of not winning could eat away at our relationship."

"Eden." Chase pulled her into his arms. He gave her a good hard shake. "You put that thought right out of your head. I love you, and winning or losing the election isn't going to change that. And you will not be the reason I lost. It will be because I didn't get my message out there where it needed to be."

"I love you, Chase." She wrapped her arms around him, drawing on his strength. She would be strong for him as well. Stepping back, she presented a fortified image. "Let's go. We don't want to miss the next returns."

They left the office and returned to the floor in time for the final announcement. With the fourth candidate receiving two percent of the votes and Rogers taking fourteen percent, Owen and Chase split the remaining votes right down the middle. A runoff election set for June would be required to determine the next mayor of Hilton. Chase was quickly hustled off to speak with the press. Stanley and Alison followed behind him.

Adam Warner's cell phone went off as Chase began addressing the public. He ducked into the conference room. "Warner," he answered in his usual style. He listened as the private detective filled him in on the case. The man was well worth the money, because he had uncovered the source behind the leak to the press. As Adam listened to the detective, he grew angrier by the moment. "There will be a bonus for you. I'll be in touch," he ended the call. He returned his cell phone to his jacket pocket and joined the others on the floor. The mood was excited and geared for a fight. And so was he. He waited patiently for the press conference to end. He signaled for Chase, Edward, and Victor to join him in the conference room.

"What's going on, Dad?" Victor asked as he stood beside his father.

"The detective just contacted me with his findings."

"Did he discover who was responsible for leaking that information to the press?" Chase asked anxiously.

"He did, but I don't believe you're going to like it." The men fell silent as Adam filled them in on the details. By the time he concluded reciting the detective's findings; Chase was spitting fire and swearing to do bodily harm.

The door to the conference room opened. Eden spotted Chase and read his mood. Something was extremely wrong. The man looked ready to do battle. He charged across the room in her direction. She quickly searched her brain for a reason that he would be angry with her. But as he drew closer, then went past, she sighed with relief, knowing she wasn't his target. She spun around to see who was. All eyes followed his angry footsteps.

"Chase, what's the matter?" Stanley asked, sitting with Alison. They had been discussing strategy for the next phase of the campaign.

"I believe Alison can answer that," Chase said cryptically. He was unaware of the room going suddenly quiet behind him. His blue eyes were glacier as they bore into the woman he had considered a friend.

Alison rose from her chair. "I don't know what you're talking about."

"Enough with the lying. A private investigator uncovered your betrayal."

Eden rushed to Chase's side. She couldn't believe what she was hearing. "Are you saying Alison is the one who contacted the press with that story about me?" She looked first at Chase, then Alison.

"Tell her what you did, and then explain to me why. All this time I was sure Owen or possibly Stanley had a hand in this. You were quite clever."

Alison knew there was no way of talking herself out of this situation. Squaring her shoulders, she told Chase the truth. "Guilty as charged. I wanted to show you I was just as valuable to this campaign as Stanley. The scandal afforded me the opportunity to work my magic with the press, to turn a negative into a positive. And I did that. Putting Eden on the speaking circuit, giving her a platform to promote, distracted the public from Nelson's nasty racial allegation. The voters got to see her as a strong educated woman, and partner for their mayor."

"But at Eden's expense. That incident was a private matter. Then you didn't bother to tell the entire story."

"Don't you see by not exposing the complete story, Eden was able to do that? She demonstrated her strength and courage. And what did I really hurt?" she asked, not grasping the depth of her betrayal.

"You hurt Eden. You exposed something painful and personal. You also caused angry words to be exchanged between us, and for that I will never forgive you." Chase shook with anger.

Eden approached Alison. Her face was filled with hurt and disappointment. "I thought we were friends. You were always so nice to me. Why use me to advance your career?"

"Chase loves you. I knew if I could turn things around for you he would look favorably in my direction. I meant you no harm. You have to know that."

"But you did hurt me. You made me relive a painful time of my life in public. You caused the man I love to doubt me." Eden glared at the woman. She could feel her control over her emotions slipping. "Tell me this. How did you find out about the harassment charge?"

"Actually, I overheard a conversation between Owen and his father at the gala. He was angry about a confrontation with you and Chase. He threatened to expose your secret."

"So you what, hired a private investigator to dig into my past?"

Eden was shaking with rage.

"Yes, I did, and the woman that confronted you in the restroom."

"You deliberately lead me to believe Mr. Nelson or Owen was behind this."

"Right again."

"Is that all you have to say for betraying us? What more could you have wanted from us? You had all our trust," Eden's voice rose with her mounting fury.

"I'm sorry. So sorry, but I only wished to show you all what I could do," Alison whimpered. The ramifications of her actions were only now registering. "Please understand I meant no harm. But I knew Stanley had plans of taking Chase to the Governor's mansion and then on to the White House. Those plans didn't include me. Stanley wanted all the glory for himself, so I wanted to secure a place on the team for me." She searched the room, looking for a friendly face, but found none. She turned to Stanley, who stood off to the left. Surely, he would understand her reason for doing what she did. He was ruthless and as devious as they came. She went to him, grabbing his arm. "Tell them you understand. That it's something you would have done."

Stanley looked at the poor girl with disappointment in his eyes. She had such potential. "You should clean out your desk. In an election, a candidate has to be able to trust the people around him. We can no longer do that with you."

"Chase, please forgive me," Alison wailed.

"You should pack your things and go." Chase turned, taking Eden by the hand and heading back to his office.

But Alison didn't go quietly. She kicked over chairs and threw things from the desks as she hurled threats. "You'll be sorry. I promise you. You'll never win without me." Stanley led the screaming woman away as the mood in the building turned solemn. Alison was well loved. Her betrayal was a serious blow to the staff's morale and the campaign in general. Instead of enjoying the fact that they were still in the fight, they collectively began cleaning the area in preparation for the next leg of the campaign.

The Politics of Love

The couple said their goodbyes to their families. Chase and Stanley gathered their supporters and gave them a pep talk. They expressed their gratitude for their dedication to the campaign. Chase personally let it be known that each one of them were a valuable asset. Before calling it an evening, he reminded all that tomorrow was a new day and they had an election to win. Stanley and Chase returned to his office where Eden waited. They needed to appoint someone into Alison's position.

"We could move the assistant into her slot," Chase suggested.

"No," Stanley answered, shaking his head. "The man is too young and inexperienced. I fear what he might say if pushed by the press." He looked over at Eden who sat on the sofa listening. He had a thought, but couldn't believe he was actually thinking it. However, she had demonstrated she could hold her own with the press.

"Ms. Warner could do it."

Eden nearly fell from the sofa. Surely he wasn't suggesting she take over Alison's duties.

"Before you say no, please hear me out," Stanley said, holding up a hand. "I know you have no experience, but you can do this. You handled the press beautifully at the press conference. You didn't allow them to place words into your mouth. You're articulate, and the rest I can teach you."

"You would do that, considering how you feel about Chase and I being together?" Eden looked him directly in the eyes.

Stanley flinched. He wasn't use to people standing up to him and certainly not a woman. "Nothing personal, but I would be against any woman who I felt was a distraction or a hindrance to this campaign. And yes, I did feel that way. However, you've convinced me you can be so much more."

Eden had to admire the man's honesty. She looked over at Chase while considering the offer. "I need you to be honest with me and tell me how you feel about this."

Chase smiled at her from where he stood. "I think it's perfect. Say yes."

Taking a deep breath, Eden looked back at Stanley. "Yes. I'll do

182

it, but I'm counting on you to help me."

"Thank you."

Stanley gave Eden a crash course in the duties of the spokesperson while Chase waited in his office. He was still upset over the Alison development. He took his chair, trying to decide where he had gone wrong. Had he said or done something to indicate she wasn't appreciated? He sure hoped not, because he truly had valued her superior skills, as well as her friendship. Exhausted, he leaned back in his chair and closed his eyes. When he had decided to run, he had never considered this type of setback. But he felt confident in Eden's ability and slowly began to relax. The telephone rang several minutes later, disturbing his peace. He automatically picked up on the second ring.

"Hello?"

"I love you."

Chase sat upright. "Tammy?" he whispered, as a knot formed in the pit of his stomach.

Silence.

"Don't call here again," he grated out into the telephone before slamming it back into its cradle.

"Who was that?"

Chase glanced up quickly. He looked at the telephone, then back at Eden. He hadn't heard her come into the office. "Wrong number," he lied. "Are you ready to go?"

Eden looked at Chase closely. He appeared nervous and a little disconcerted. She was sure he was lying, but why? "Past ready, actually. It's been a long night." She pulled on her leather gloves and adjusted the collar to her coat.

"Well, let's get you tucked into bed." Chase rose from the chair and took her hand. He snagged his coat on the way out, feeling like he was on borrowed time.

Chapter Seventeen

Chase entered the Hilton Police Department early the next morning on his way to campaign headquarters. He only had a few minutes before he was due to meet Eden and Stanley. He was on a mission, and only one person could help him. He took the elevator to the detective's offices on the third floor. As he approached the door, it swung open, and the person he had come to see stood staring at him.

"Chase? What are you doing here?" Taylor asked, surprised to see her sister's boyfriend.

"I need to speak with you about a personal matter, if you have time."

"Sure, we can talk in my office." Taylor turned around and escorted Chase to her corner of the room. She closed the door behind him. "Have a seat. Can I offer you something to drink?"

"No. I won't be long."

"All right then, so what can I do for you?" She sat in the chair across from him.

"Can you keep a secret?" He locked gazes with Taylor. She reminded him so much of Eden that he almost changed his mind.

Taylor leaned back in her chair and folded her arms across her chest. "That depends on what you are about to tell me, and whether my sister will be hurt by it."

"Fair enough."

Returning to headquarters sometime after ten the next morning, Chase was immediately overtaken by the energy in the room. Volunteers were everywhere. The majority of the faces he knew, but there were quite a few new ones he didn't recognize. The telephones were being worked with military precision, while an assembly line of campaign mail outs was running smoothly. He gave a warm greeting to all as he went in search of Eden and Stanley. But first, he made a stop by his office and deposited his coat and briefcase. He quickly checked the stack of messages on his desk. One in particular caught his attention. The name written in Eden's handwriting nearly stopped his heart. Stuffing the slip into his pocket, he left his office and went in search of her. He located her in the office set up by Alison. She was busy on the telephone, arranging for a news conference at one that day. When she spotted him, her eyes lit with excitement and love.

Chase felt his heart squeeze tightly in his chest. He hadn't been expecting this all those months ago when he had accepted David's invitation to speak at his school. Eden had come out of nowhere and blindsided him. And right when his life was damn near perfect, it teetered on blowing up in his face.

"Earth to Chase," Eden said, waving her hand in front of him. She had disconnected from her call and turned, filling him in on her conversation, only to discover him lost in thought. "Hey, are you all right?"

"I'm sorry." Chase pushed the dark clouds away. "My mind was wandering." He reached down and pulled her into his arms. He held her tightly, never wanting to let go. "I love you?" he said thick with emotion. He pulled back, looking deeply into her eyes. He swept his left hand over her hair. "God, I love you." He lowered his mouth to hers and kissed her slow and tenderly.

Eden pushed against his chest. "Stop," she ordered, while dodging another kiss. She giggled girlishly as he showered her face with kisses. "I've got big news about the campaign."

"It'll keep." He returned for another kiss before being pushed away again. "All right, I'll behave." Chase smiled at Eden. She practically vibrated with excitement. He backed against the desk and sat down. "What's this news?"

"Rogers called this morning to throw his support behind you. I got him to agree to a press conference to make the announcement. The press has been contacted, and the piece will air on the five and six o'clock news. Those new faces out there," she pointed to the front area, "are volunteers from the Rogers' campaign."

Chase was indeed pleased with the news. "Now, if I can win over his voters."

"You will. I have no doubt. Your platform isn't that dissimilar from his. He pushed for an increase in the number of police officers. Community safety is important to the voters. But your educational plan, early and adult, can address that, as well as your goal of bringing higher paying technical jobs to the area. Those two elements are key to community safety."

"I couldn't have said it better," Stanley commented from the doorway. He actually smiled as he entered the room. He pushed his glasses up on his nose. "Eden is right. Education and higher paying jobs help to promote community safety. You play those things up, and this election is yours."

Two weeks later, the proof of Rogers' endorsement was finally materializing. The latest polling numbers had Chase well ahead of Nelson. He had received further endorsements from the business leaders who had supported Rogers. Momentum at headquarters was strong and full steam ahead. New commercials were hitting the airwaves, as well as a new round of speaking engagements. Chase enjoyed having Eden at headquarters. Working side-by-side reminded him of their time together in the classroom. She was truly an amazing woman. Not once, since her forced administrative leave, had she complained or faulted him. She had learned a new job and jumped in to help his campaign. She had recently agreed to tutor two of her former students in the evening. He loved sitting in the living room watching her with the children. Her face and eyes lit up every time the students grasped a concept. He would sit there and pretend the four of them were a family. He liked the image and couldn't wait to make it a reality.

He found Eden in Stanley's office talking shop. The two had

surprisingly become friends. Stanley had actually apologized to them for his earlier behavior. They had accepted his apology and put the past behind them. As he entered the office, they both looked up.

"Mind if I take my lady out to dinner?" Chase carried his coat and briefcase.

"Not at all. She's put in a full week here and deserves an evening out," Stanley responded with a wink.

"Let me grab my things," Eden replied coolly. She said good-night to Stanley, then walked past Chase. She wondered if he remembered today was her birthday. She had waited all day for a delivery of flowers or something, but nothing had come. He hadn't even said happy birthday. Her family, of course, had called early that morning with their birthday wishes, but it just wasn't the same as from the man in your life. Perhaps over dinner he would wish her a happy birthday, but then again, he had so much going on with the campaign he had simply forgotten.

Well, to ensure she held Chase's complete attention tonight, she wore another Allure creation. Surveying her appearance in the mirror, she liked what she saw. Flirtatious and daring, the dress guaranteed the man would notice.

Chase couldn't take his eyes off of her, nor could he think past the hard-on pressing up against his zipper as he caught sight of Eden in the open door. The woman was a temptress dressed in black. The little black dress she wore was a definite invitation to sex. The corset-like bodice with strings begging to be released, pushed her full breasts mouthwatering high. They were delicious brown swells, daring him to touch them.

"Where the hell did you get that dress?" The question came out harsh and offensive.

"You don't like it?" Eden ran her hands down the bodice to rest on her hips.

"Ah, it's great, but it's pretty cold outside. Wouldn't want you to catch something." His eyes were glued to the rise and fall of her breasts.

Eden shrugged. She almost felt sorry for the man. "I have my coat." She turned and walked to the far chair where her things lay. She wanted Chase's attention completely on her for the evening, so she gave him a good look at what he had. The skirt of the dress wasn't tight, but it definitely formed to all the right areas. She heard his intake of breath as she leaned just so to retrieve her gloves. She turned, meeting his eyes and wondered if she had taken this thing a little overboard. He was looking at her with so much desire she began to doubt he would be able to enjoy the evening. "Are you okay?"

"Yeah," he responded, burning with desire. "I just need a little fresh air." Chase joined her by the chair and removed the coat from her hands. He held it while she slipped it on.

Wide-eyed, Eden looked concerned. The thing at the chair had obviously been a little over the top. Poor Chase looked to be having difficulty walking. She grabbed her purse and followed him out.

The drive to the restaurant was quiet. Chase stole glances at his beautiful passenger. He wondered what was on her mind. Did she suspect his secret? He turned into the parking lot of The Vineyard and parked. Running around to her side of the vehicle, he helped her out and escorted her inside. The hostess greeted them and promptly took their coats. She grabbed two menus and escorted them back into an unusually dark room. As the lights suddenly came up, the room erupted into "Surprise!" Sitting at the tables were family and friends.

A rendition of "Happy Birthday" rang out, as Eden stood speechless. She looked at Chase who stood beside her, grinning from ear-to-ear. Tears spilled from her eyes as she thought about her earlier suspicion. "I thought you were so busy with the campaign that you had forgotten," she told him.

Chase looked dumbfounded. "I'll never be that busy, sweetheart."

"I see that. Now I know what all the whispered telephone conversations were about," she said laughing. "God, I feel so foolish."

The room filled with laughter. Chase glanced across the room and locked gazes with Taylor. She looked as guilty as he felt. They had shared several secretive telephone calls. "Happy Birthday, sweetheart."

"Thank you." Eden threw her arms around his neck and hugged him affectionately. She kissed him quickly, and then began accepting hugs and kisses from family and friends as the party got underway. For tonight, the place was theirs. A table in the rear held an assortment of food. The bar to the right was manned by a handsome bartender, shaking and tossing. She was pulled onto the floor by Chase as a slow tune filled the air.

"Have I told you how much I love you," he whispered as he pulled Eden into his arms. They danced slow and close as the ballad played in the background.

"I love you, too. I feel foolish for believing you had forgotten."

"Never doubt my love for you." Chase would have held her closer if that were possible. No other woman had ever felt so right in his arms.

"I don't." she replied softly.

"Shut up and kiss me."

"Gladly." Eden covered his mouth with hers.

The couple took a break from dancing and moved around the room, greeting everyone. They finally stopped to speak with Taylor and Stone who, unfortunately, stood discussing a case.

"I can't believe you two. This is a party. You're supposed to be having fun," Eden told them.

"You're right, sis, so let's hit the line." Taylor pointed to the line forming for the electric slide.

"Chase?" Eden asked.

"Oh, no, baby. I'll watch," he said the words low and intimate. His eyes held hers.

Eden smiled, flirtatiously. "I'll make sure to give you something to see." She wiggled her hips as she strutted off to the dance floor with her sister.

Chase and Stone took up position by the bar where they

ordered two beers. Chase watched the dance floor with great interest as Eden fell into step with the others. She moved her hips to the rhythm of the music, adding a little something extra as she turned with the line. Chase watched transfixed as the seductive little black dress made her movements that much more sensual. He was already in a state of semi-arousal from her earlier exploits, and now this. His eyes followed the bounce of her hips as he groaned. The woman was definitely going to pay for taunting him.

"I know what you mean," Stone commented from beside him. His eyes were glued to Taylor bopping to the music beside Eden. She was so unlike the woman he dealt with everyday on the job. Tonight she was seductive in a little red dress. The fluttery hem was flirtatious and sexy as it moved with the rhythm of her body. And those trademark Warner legs looked incredible in sheer hose.

Chase glanced over at his friend and realized who held his attention. He was glad to know he wasn't the only one head over heels in love. "Does she know how you feel about her?"

"I don't think the woman knows I'm alive. Correction, outside of the job that is."

"Why don't you join her?"

Stone laughed. "Why don't you?"

"Oh man, I didn't learn these types of dances."

"Just do like the guy behind Eden and follow her butt," David said as he joined the conversation.

"Is he looking at her butt? Who is he anyway?" Chase asked, focusing on the guy. "Hold my beer."

David accepted the bottle as Chase joined the dancing line. He laughed deeply as his friend squeezed in beside Eden, pushing the other guy out of the way.

"The man must definitely be in love to embarrass himself like that," Stone commented while watching Chase make a fool of himself. He and David slapped each other on the back laughing.

"He is and we're no better. I saw you drooling over Taylor."

Stone leveled a knowing glance on David. "Like you haven't been walking around here panting over that woman." He pointed in the direction of Skye.

David looked at the younger sister, dressed youthfully in another pair of those low jeans. But tonight she wore them with a purple camisole that looked to be worn in the privacy of the bedroom. He felt his nature stir and downed the beer he held. "She's incredible, but she looks so young."

"Have any idea how old she is?"

"No. But I'm sure I'm not her type of guy. I wear suits," David said with a laugh.

"I don't know, buddy," Stone commented, running a hand through his jet-black hair. "I noticed the young lady looking at you on New Year's Day.

That got David's attention. "You think she was interested?"

"I think maybe she was."

"I don't know, Stone."

The two ordered new beers while they watched Chase shake his booty.

Later, everyone gathered around as the cake was brought out. After a wish, Eden blew out the twenty-nine candles. She kissed Chase and thanked him once again for a wonderful surprise. Cake was quickly served while Eden unwrapped her gifts. Her parents gave her a beautiful charm bracelet, which reflected her love of teaching, a bright red apple charm, a colorful book, and ruler. Another charm was of a desk and tiny blackboard. Eden knew this was a special order item, and a lot of love and time had gone into selecting it.

"Thank you both," she said to her parents. She hugged them lovingly.

Eden worked her way through the table of gifts until she had nothing left to open. They were all wonderful and thoughtful. She realized one gift was missing.

"Are you looking for my gift?" Chase asked, smiling at her.

Eden returned his smile. "You have something for me?" Her eyes roamed his body for a sign of a gift.

"I do, but it requires me to get down on one knee."

The room went completely silent as all eyes were focused on the young couple. Everyone held their breath as the two stared into each other's eyes.

"Chase?" Eden glanced into the faces of their family and friends. "You don't have to get down," she said with a shaky voice. Her hands stroked down her thighs with nervous energy. *Is he actually doing what I think?*

"Girl, will you be quiet and let that man get down on his knee," Taylor spoke up.

Everyone laughed as Eden looked embarrassed. She chewed on her bottom lip nervously as Chase took her hand and dropped down on one knee. His eyes met and held hers as he removed a little black velvet box from his pocket.

"You entered my world when I least expected it," he began. "But once I looked into your eyes, there was no other woman for me. I love you, Eden Warner, and would be honored if you would agree to be my wife."

Tears streamed down Eden's cheek, while a tiny smile fluttered around her mouth. "Yes. I'll marry you," she answered, wrapping her arms around his neck as he rose. "I love you so much."

"Not half as much as I love you." Chase held Eden close to his heart. After a while, he planted a kiss on her lips, and then got down to removing the four carat diamond engagement ring from the box. He shoved the empty container back into his pocket. Taking Eden's left hand, he slipped the engagement ring onto her finger. He brought her hand to his lips and kissed it. "I love you," he whispered, then led his fiancée back onto the dance floor.

Chase and Eden moved slowly to the music, whispering sweetly to each other. A few kisses were exchanged, and then Chase executed a series of spins around the room that put a broad smile on his face. Eden laughed joyously. She seemed to float across the floor in his arms. Their giddiness was infectious to all who saw them. Eventually, others joined them on the dance floor, and shared in their love.

"May I have this dance?" Stone dared to ask Taylor who stood watching her sister and future brother-in-law. She appeared to be dreamy-eyed and longing. Stone had felt now was the best opportunity he would ever have to get the woman in his arms.

Taylor glanced into his handsome golden brown face. "I'd love to." She followed Stone onto the dance floor and slipped into his arms. Her heart thumped heavily against her ribs as they danced. His movements were smooth and sure as he, too, threw in a couple of turns. Taylor looked into his green eyes and smiled. She was enjoying herself.

Stone couldn't believe he was finally holding Taylor Warner in his arms. He wasn't sure how long the weak moment would last, so he made the most of the moment by placing his head beside hers, allowing the music to carry them away.

David looked on as his friends held the women of their dreams within their arms on the dance floor. He glanced at the younger Warner and discovered her soft brown eyes focused on him. Maybe Stone had been right. He took the plunge and invited Skye to dance. Her acceptance put a wide toothy grin on his face as he led her around the room. She too danced beautifully. Maybe a chance for future Warner engagements would occur.

Victor Warner stood near the bar, watching his sisters on the dance floor. Eden looked truly happy as she danced in the arms of the man she loved. Taylor also appeared to be enjoying herself with Stone. Even Skye was having a good time with the very straight-laced Principal Daniels. Finally, the girls had found some deserving men to share their lives. But as he stood there watching new love grow, he was reminded of what he had lost. He had been engaged to a wonderful woman two years ago, but lost her to a drunk driver. He had dated since her death, but found no one who spurred a deeper interest.

"Are you all right son?" Eunice Warner asked. She had been watching her son and knew the signs of longing.

"I will be, Mom."

"There's a woman out there for you."

"I'm sure there is, but tonight is Eden's night." He wrapped an arm around his mother's neck. "She sure seems happy."

"I believe they will be as you will one day."

"Well, let's concentrate on getting these lovebirds married first."

"Thank you for a birthday I'll never forget," Eden said to Chase as he drove her home. She held her left hand up to catch the streetlight as they passed. "My ring is gorgeous." She smiled over at him.

"I'm glad you like it." Chase glanced over at her. She was practically glowing. "Do you have a date in mind?" He turned at the next corner.

"I think we should wait until after the election. I want your attention focused completely on it." She reached over, caressing his neck.

Chase sighed with contentment. "The minute the winner is named, I want a date from you."

"You sound as though the date is more important than the election." Eden continued to caress his neck.

Chase captured her hand and brought it to his lips. He looked over at her. "You're more important to me than the election. I can't wait to begin our life together." He pulled into her driveway. He unfastened his seatbelt and went around to assist her out of the car. They both grabbed a large shopping bag containing birthday gifts. Chase followed Eden inside her home and ran the gifts upstairs to her bedroom. He flipped on the lights and stared at the queen-size bed, wishing for the day they would share one bed, under one roof. He turned to leave and found Eden watching him.

"Very soon we'll share the same bed."

"That's what I want as well." She held out her hand to him. "I tell you what. I'll begin making those wedding plans I can, and after the election, we can finalize things."

Chase took her hand and followed her back down stairs. "You do that, because by the time I'm sworn into office, I want you to be my wife," he told her at the front door.

"Have I told you how much I love you?" She brushed a kiss across his lips.

"Yes you have, but how about showing me." Chase held the back of her head as he deepened the kiss. They stood in the foyer wrapped in each other's arms. When they finally whispered goodnight, they were both overheated and in need of a cold shower.

"I'll see you tomorrow."

"Drive carefully," Eden said as he climbed into his car. She waited until he was at the corner before turning out the lights downstairs and returning to her bedroom. She removed her clothes as she headed to the bathroom to run her bath. She slipped into the berry-scented water, admiring her beautiful engagement ring—the symbol of Chase's love. She giggled, remembering her earlier suspicion. She had actually thought he had forgotten. She lay in the quiet of the room, dreaming of their future together.

Life with Chase was good. Better than good to be specific. They enjoyed family and friends. They took great pleasure in their time together, curled on the sofa. They had recently begun cooking together, which sometimes led to making out. And at campaign headquarters, they worked well together. In bed they were downright combustible.

She left the bathroom and climbed into bed. As she settled under the covers, the trill of the telephone pierced the silence. She reached for it and rolled over on her back, expecting to hear Chase's voice. What she received instead was silence, as the person on the other end never said a word, before slamming down the telephone in her ear. She dismissed the call as a teenage prank and turned out the lights.

Chapter Eighteen

The pair rejoiced in their love over the next few months. The newspapers had announced the engagement with bold headlines. And although the couple had agreed to finalize their wedding plans after the election, neither could resist behaving like a newly engaged couple. They selected a June date and decided upon the place for the reception. The wedding would definitely be held at the Warner's family church with Reverend Carter officiating.

The bride-to-be traveled with a library of bridal magazines and wedding etiquette books. She possessed clippings of the bouquets she wanted and found pictures of the cake and invitations as well. She and her sisters along with their mother had gone dress shopping for the bridesmaids. They had narrowed the choice down to two. However, no choice would be made when it came to the bridal gown. Eden knew exactly what she wanted. She had located the boutique that carried the dress and taken her mother with her to see it. Trying on the store sample of her dream dress had caused her mother to cry. The moment had been special, as mother and daughter reminisced about when she was a child, and then looked to the future, when she would one day be a mother herself. The dress was everything Eden had dreamed for her wedding day. Now all she had to do was try to wait patiently for a dress to be made specifically to her body measurements.

The groom-to-be occupied his spare time with the honeymoon plans. In the evening, he could be found reading through several travel brochures and guides. Surprisingly, he was deriving more pleasure from planning their trip than the election. He guessed that was because he loved Eden, and she loved a good surprise. It also had a great deal to do with the state of the campaign. The campaign had turned nasty, filled with horrible, distasteful allegations. He wanted their honeymoon destination to be something spectacular that would erase the ugliness of the election from their minds. He wanted it to be someplace neither of them had visited before, because discovering the wonder of the land together would only add to the experience. He knew wherever they spent their honeymoon; it would definitely have to be warm and sunny. He wanted Eden in as little as possible. He remembered the night in the hot tub under the stars and that skimpy bikini she'd worn. *That's it*, he thought with a laugh. Select a destination where swimming in the buff was legal.

"What has you laughing to yourself?" Eden asked from the floor where she sat. Chase sat at her desk chair, surfing on the web. She knew he was searching for the perfect honeymoon destination.

"Don't you dare try to sneak a peek at the monitor." Chase turned the screen so only he could see.

Eden laughed. "You didn't answer my question."

"I was thinking about one of those nudist retreats for our honeymoon." His eyes shined with humor.

"Ha, ha. There is no way in heck you'll catch me running around strangers butt-naked."

"I've seen you butt-naked, and what a butt." He wiggled his brows suggestively.

Eden rolled her eyes, blushing. "Yours isn't bad either, but you better not be showing it to anyone but me."

Chase laughed as he slid from the chair to join her on the floor. He crawled over to where she sat and covered her mouth with his. "A little possessive, aren't we?" he teased when they parted. He was looking deeply into her eyes. A taunting smile danced around his lips.

"Only where you're concerned. I don't like to share."

"Neither do I, sweetheart. I wouldn't dare take you to a nudist resort. I don't want any other man looking at your butt." He kissed her once more, while reaching for the bridal magazine Eden was looking at. He tore his mouth away from hers at the same time he tore the magazine from Eden's hands. He waved it in the air. "Look what I have." He flipped through the pages. "Which gown have you selected?"

"Give that back to me," Eden yelled, reaching for the magazine. She swatted his arm when she couldn't reach it.

"What do I get in exchange for it?" He continued to hold it out of reach.

"I'll give up one piece of clothing for the magazine." She saw Chase's eyes light up with interest.

"One piece? Well, darling, that doesn't take much thought," he said, eyeing the long T-shirt she wore. "Deal."

"The magazine first." Eden held out her hand. "Thank you," she said, accepting it. She tossed the magazine onto the desk. "One piece."

Chase smiled with male satisfaction. "Give up the bottoms."

"Are you sure that's what you want?" Her smile was seductive.

"Take them off," he repeated.

"Okay."

Eden took two steps back, then reached under the long T-shirt and removed a pair of running shorts. She threw them in Chase's face, and took off running. She could hear him coming behind her.

"You little tease. You knew I was talking about the panties."

"You said bottoms," Eden screamed as he followed her into the bedroom.

"You'll pay for deceiving me." Chase fell on top of her.

After a heavy dose of fooling around in the bedroom, Eden finally walked Chase to the front door. May had finally arrived and they were gearing up for the final push toward Election Day. Their time together would take a backseat to the campaign, so tonight had been special.

"In a couple more weeks, the election will be over, and you and I will be married," Chase said, caressing her face. "I can hardly wait to come home to you each evening."

Eden liked the image. "It will be nice, but you'll probably be too busy for your wife."

"Never," he said, right before pulling her into his arms for a goodnight kiss. "I'll see you in the morning."

"Drive carefully." Eden watched until he got into the car before securing the door. She returned to the den and picked up the room. As she turned out the lamp on the desk, the sound of the telephone Ringing broke the quiet of the house. She hesitated before answering. The prank calls were becoming more regular. She decided to ignore it and allow the answering machine to pick up. On the fourth ring, she waited for a message to be left, but what she heard was the telephone slamming down once again.

Eden set the security alarm and ran upstairs to her bedroom. She hadn't mentioned the hang-ups to Chase because she didn't want to distract him from the election. However, the calls were increasing, and she was becoming frightened. She feared the calls might be racially motivated. She hated jumping to that conclusion, but she really couldn't think of another reason why someone would be targeting her. She decided the time had come to discuss the matter with Taylor. She would know how to proceed. In bed, she tried to clear her thoughts of some sicko out there fixated on her. She drifted to sleep only to be awakened by the telephone. She listened for a message, but like before, none was left. The calls continued off and on until the wee hours of the morning when she finally unplugged the telephone from the wall. However, by this time her nerves were strung tight and she was too spooked to go back to sleep. She sat awake in bed until the first light of dawn.

Eden slowly came awake as the chiming of the doorbell persisted. Her head ached as she got her bearing. She reached for the robe draped across the side chair and headed downstairs. Checking the peephole, she spotted Chase and unlocked the door. She ran a hand over her hair self-consciously.

"Were we meeting for breakfast?" she asked, stepping back from the door.

"Breakfast?" Chase looked at her closely. She appeared hung over, but he knew that wasn't the case. They had only shared a couple glasses of wine at dinner. "Sweetheart, it's after noon."

"It is?" Eden ran to the clock in the kitchen.

"I was concerned about you when I couldn't reach you on the telephone, and you didn't show up this morning." Chase followed her into the kitchen and began making coffee. "You want something to eat?"

She shook her head no as she settled into a chair. "I unplugged the telephone last night."

"Why?" he asked before she could explain.

"Prank phone calls. I've been receiving them quite regularly here lately. The last one came around three in the morning. I couldn't sleep after that."

Chase's head came up and his heart beat with fear. He stared at Eden while she spoke, reading in between the lines. He squatted down beside her chair. "Why didn't you tell me you have been receiving harassing phone calls? And why didn't you call me to let me know this was happening and that you were frightened? How long is regularly?" he demanded to know. He held his breath, waiting for her response.

"Two, three times a night, over the last week. Before that a few times over the last couple of months. It's probably some kids having a good laugh at my expense." She touched his shoulder. "I didn't want to bother you. I'm being foolish. I scared myself, that's all."

"No you're not. Has anything happened around here that seems suspicious?" His mind raced with questions. He felt his past converging on his present and future.

Eden could tell Chase was concerned for her safety. Maybe his thoughts were along the same lines as hers. But he shouldn't be thinking about her problem with an election to win. "Let it go. It's probably nothing." She kissed his cheek. "I'm going to grab a shower. Could you toast a bagel for me?"

"Sure." Chase watched Eden leave the kitchen. He sagged

against the kitchen counter, thinking. Was he jumping to conclusions? He didn't believe so. *His* telephone calls had stopped coming, and so he had thought he had dodged a bullet. But now he knew where the woman's energy was focused. He pulled out his cell phone and dialed.

"It's me. I need to see you later today." Chase carried on a hushed conversation while keeping an eye out for Eden. Ending his discussion, he returned his phone to his pocket and went about toasting the bagel. He could do nothing at the moment but pray he was doing the right thing.

Eden returned downstairs dressed casually in black slacks and a yellow blouse. Her hair was pulled back into a ponytail that bounced with her movements. She carried her shoes into the kitchen where Chase waited. She joined him at the table and sat down to slip them on. Taking a bite of bagel that waited on a plate for her, she rose and walked over to the cabinet, removing a travel mug. She quickly filled it with coffee, cream, and sugar. Retracing her steps, she placed a kiss on Chase's lips.

"Love you," she said as she reached for her bagel and announced she was ready to leave.

Chase smiled back at her. "I love you, too, baby."

They left her place and drove directly to headquarters. While Eden ate her bagel and discussed their upcoming wedding, Chase kept a vigilant eye out for anything suspicious. They entered the building a short time later. Eden was immediately cornered by two of the volunteers, and led away to clear up an issue. He took the opportunity to look out the front window, checking left, then right. People passed by the window in both directions. No one appeared to be taking particular interest in the building, and no one's face caught his attention.

Stanley observed Chase's unusual behavior with interest. He joined him at the large window. "What's going on? You seem a little jumpy."

Chase glanced back over his shoulder. Eden was still talking with the staff. He nodded for Stanley to follow him into the office and waited for him to close the door. "I think Tammy is in town," Chase informed his campaign manager. "I stupidly thought she had faded away because I hadn't heard from her." He looked at Stanley with concern. "It appears she turned her attention onto Eden."

"How? When did this happen?" Stanley began pacing the floor nervously. This wasn't good for the campaign.

"The night of the election I received a phone call from her. She said 'I love you.' I told her not to call anymore and let it go. But this morning Eden tells me she has been receiving prank calls off and on for a couple of months. Recently, the calls have increased to the point of frightening her." He glanced at the door, thinking about her sleepless nights.

"Last night," he continued, "she was so disturbed by the phone calls she unplugged her telephone from the wall. The last call came around three this morning. You should see how exhausted she looks."

"You told me you contacted Tammy's parents, and a judge had ordered her to stay away." Stanley swore under his breath. "This just can't be happening when we're so close to winning. The polling numbers are on our side. The public is disgusted with Camden's dirty politics, his racial allegations, and now the innuendo of impropriety regarding Eden's administrative leave. We've got the numbers to beat him. We have to put an end to the nastiness—now."

"I don't give a damn about the campaign, or Camden. I'm worried about Eden's safety. It's obvious therapy hasn't helped her. Who knows what she's capable of doing?" Chase stormed across the room and collapsed onto the sofa. He hung his head in his hands while wishing he could turn back the hands of time.

"Let's try to keep this quiet. The last thing we want is for Camden to get wind of this and take the focus off his IRS probe. Hire that private investigator who uncovered Alison's betrayal. With any luck, he can locate the woman and send her back to the sanitarium." He paced the room while working the various angles.

Chase shook his head in disagreement. "I'm tired of keeping quiet. I'm going to tell Eden what's really going on before she gets hurt. And just so you know, I've asked Eden's sister, Taylor, for help in locating her. I do know Tammy's parents are unaware that she's back in Hilton."

"The police can't keep a secret," Stanley bellowed, angrily. "You're throwing away the election." He paced for a few minutes, before turning around. "Or, we could go to the press with this ourselves," he said as an idea took shape. "Make the announcement. Seek the public's help and garner their sympathy." Stanley was definitely liking the idea.

Chase could see the advantage, but owed it to the parents to keep it out of the press. "I can't do that. Her parents are good people and highly respected in the community. I'd like to keep it out of the press if at all possible."

"Okay then, so what's the plan until Taylor can track this woman down?"

Rising from the sofa, Chase knew what had to be done. He ran a hand through his hair, weighing the difficult decision. "I'm going to take Eden away for a few days while Taylor steps up the search. While we are away, I'm going to tell Eden the truth about her caller and pray she forgives me for keeping her in the dark."

Stanley could see Chase was deeply concerned for Eden's safety, as well as their relationship. "You take care of Eden, and I'll manage things around here. I'll notify the press you're taking a mini-break before the final weeks of the election. With any luck, the matter will be handled without the press getting wind of it."

"I still want to be mayor, Stanley," Chase stated unwavering.

"Hopefully, Camden is busy with the IRS, trying to explain the questionable math on his tax returns to get wind of the situation."

Chase chuckled. "We can hope, but the guy seems to have eyes and ears everywhere. The last thing I need is for Eden to hear about this from someone else. It's my place to tell her, and I will," Chase said to Stanley. "Also, I'm not sure if Tammy's dangerous. She seemed to be teetering on the edge in Savannah, and who knows what she's capable of now."

Stanley knew what Chase was thinking. "You're right of course, but let's try to keep this amongst ourselves. The last thing we want is for Camden to find out and exploit the situation.

"You're absolutely right."

"So where will you go?"

"Gatlinburg. I'm going to take Eden to Stone's mountain cabin. I'll be in touch with you in a few days."

"You go ahead and try not to worry. I'll take care of things here. I'll also check in with Eden's sister to see what she knows."

"Thanks Stanley." Chase shook hands with his manager before leaving the office in search of Eden. He found her at the copier. "Give that to someone else. We're going to the mountains," he told her casually, seeing no need to alarm her before necessary.

Eden looked confused. "Excuse me? Did you just say we were headed to the mountains?"

"I did." He managed a smile, despite feeling like things were closing in on him.

"Just like that." Her eyes sparkled at the prospect of being alone with him in the mountains.

"No appearances are scheduled until the middle of next week. We have the perfect chance to get away." He only wished the trip was for pleasure and not coming clean about his past.

"And Stanley is all right with you taking some time off?" she asked, her tone skeptical. She knew the man liked everyone focused on winning.

"Yes, I am," Stanley answered, coming up behind them. "Now get out of here before I change my mind."

Eden smiled. "We're gone."

❦

Chase swapped his sedan for the black Hummer. He headed out of town with Eden sitting quietly in the passenger seat. She switched on the radio, locating their favorite Atlanta jazz station. The soft music filled the interior of the vehicle as he took the on ramp to the interstate. They discussed their upcoming wedding. And just as they settled back for the drive, the music ceased. The disc jockey announced they were interrupting the Miles Davis tune for a press conference from the Nelson campaign. The hairs on the back of Chase's neck stood up. He quickly reached over, turning the radio off.

Eden glanced at him. "Why did you do that? Aren't you curious to hear what Camden is accusing us of now?" she laughed, turning the radio back on.

"I've called the press here today to bring something to the attention of the voters. While the rumors about my taxes are swarming, no one has been investigating my opponent."

Eden glanced at Chase, giving him a here we go again expression.

"If anyone had invested as much time investigating Mr. Mathews as they have me, they would have discovered my young opponent is the one with the counting problem. The man has one too many fiancées. I'd like to introduce Ms. Tammy Johansen."

A series of expletives flew from Chase's mouth as he slammed his hand against the steering wheel. The time he had been dreading was now. A few more minutes and they would have been out of range of the station, and he would have been allowed to break the news about Tammy on his own. Now he was bracing for the fallout.

Eden jumped in her seat in response to his explosive response. She reached over, stroking his arm in a calming manner. "Camden is just trying to deflect attention from his IRS probe. No one's going to take him seriously." But as the woman stepped to the microphone and Chase clutched the steering wheel with a death grip, Eden grew concerned. She held on to the door handle like a life preserver as the woman identified herself as Tammy Johansen, and began detailing her relationship with Chase.

"Chase and I were introduced by friends two years ago. We dated for a year before becoming engaged. We had the best engagement party. Everyone who was anybody was there. He loves me. We spent a romantic weekend in Savannah, and then I learned of that woman.

He's not in love with her. It's about votes, and I couldn't go along with this lie."

This time Eden turned off the radio. She sat in the silence of the vehicle, absorbing what she had just heard. She looked over at Chase, expecting him to say something. When he didn't, she took the initiative. "Is this press conference the reason for our sudden trip?"

Silence.

"Okay. Look, I'm trying not to panic. I'm thinking logically, but your silence isn't helping the situation."

Chase looked at her. He reached out to touch her cheek. "We'll discuss it at the cabin."

Eden shied away from his hand. "No, let's discuss it now. I've just heard a woman claiming to be your fiancée, and I know you've been to Savannah. But I also know Camden will do just about anything to win this election, so tell me what's going on. Do you know that woman?"

"Yes, I do, but it's not what you think."

"What I think is that you're keeping something extremely important from me. I don't like being kept in the dark."

"Like you did about the harassment case," he reminded her.

Eden nodded. He was right; she had done the same thing. "Yes, and we both know how that turned out. Haven't we learned anything from that mistake?"

"What I have to say is too important to do in the car. I need to be facing you when I tell you what's really going on. I need you to trust me. Can you do that?" His eyes held hers before returning to the highway.

"Okay, but the moment we get to the cabin, you come clean." She was trusting him because he had never given a reason not to, but this second fiancée thing had her unsettled.

Chapter Nineteen

Chase opened the door to the modern log cabin, later that evening. Flipping on the lights, he stepped aside so Eden could enter. He returned to the porch for their luggage. Once inside, he eased the door closed with his elbow and preceded to deposit their luggage in the bedroom, but thought better of it. After he told Eden about Tammy, she may not want to share the room with him. He sat the luggage outside the bedroom door then headed in the direction of the kitchen. He opened the refrigerator, followed by the cabinets, finding they were both well stocked.

"Do you want something to eat?"

"I want to know what's going on, and now." She walked across the room. She scrubbed her hands nervously along her thighs, slipping back into her old habit.

"You're partially right about my reason for bringing you here," he began, and sat down on one of the oversized green leather chairs. He raised his eyes to hers. "I brought you here first so Taylor could do some investigating, and ..."

"Taylor? What does my sister have to do with any of this?" Eden moved in closer and sat on the sofa. She listened intently to his every word.

"I asked Taylor to locate Tammy."

"Whoa! You asked my sister to help you find this woman?" Eden shook her head with confusion. It made no sense. "Start at the beginning and don't leave anything out."

Chase nodded as he launched into his story. "I met Tammy through a friend of the family about five years ago. We began dating and I actually thought she was the one."

Eden cringed at the thought, and then realized she was being foolish. After all, he was a handsome man who'd had a life before her. She admired his lean physique in the worn pair of jeans. He seldom wore them and each time he did, he looked years younger, and undeniably sexy. The blue-and-white striped shirt he wore was a gift from her. She had purchased the shirt because it brought out the blueness of his eyes.

"We came from the same background, knew a lot of the same people, and had traveled extensively. Everyone expected us to get married." He looked at her. "I thought we would have a good life together."

"So what happened?"

He would have preferred to be talking about the life he wanted with her, but the sooner he got the truth out into the open, the sooner he could deal with the fallout.

"What I thought was love turned out to be nothing but an act. She wanted the money and the lifestyle. I arrived at her parents' home one day without her knowing, and overheard her talking and laughing with friends. She was telling them about her plan to get me to marry her. How she had convinced me she was in love with me. They all laughed and said things about men being so gullible. She told them about the wedding arrangements she had waiting for the moment I popped the question."

"What?" Eden couldn't believe what she was hearing.

"Tammy didn't love me, nor care about me. She laughed and told her friends about intimate moments we'd shared and how she had me under her spell. I heard her say she would make sure to get pregnant on the honeymoon, to secure herself a cut of my fortune. Seems her parents had cut off her funds because of her extravagant spending."

"But she said she was your fiancée, which means that at some point you got past the hurt and asked her to marry you."

He shook his head sadly. He hated to have to tell her the rest of this ugly saga. "I was devastated and hurt." He looked at her. "I concocted this plan to seek revenge and teach her a lesson. I proposed and sat back while she planned this elaborate engagement party. Then, in front of those same friends who had laughed at me,

I informed her I knew about her little scheme, and that I had no intention of marrying her."

"Oh, Chase, you didn't?" She watched as he hung his head in shame. She knew he wasn't proud of himself.

"She shattered, Eden. Right before all our eyes, she had a break-down. She tried to convince me she loved me, that we loved each other. Her friends tried to tell her the relationship was over and to walk away, but after a while I realized something was extremely wrong. She slipped into this imaginary world she had created. She's back there now."

"My God, the engagement is all in her head." Eden looked at Chase. She honestly felt sorry for this Tammy.

His eyes held remorse. "I never meant to harm her, Eden. You have to believe me."

"I do, Chase." Eden scooted down the sofa, and reached out touching his arm. "Taylor knows about this?"

"Yes. When the phone calls started, I became concerned because she was back in Hilton. I didn't know she was calling you, and when I learned of this, I became alarmed for your safety."

Things were falling into place for her. "The prank phone calls I received, were all from Tammy?"

"I think so."

"Is she dangerous?"

"Initially she wasn't. But, I believe things are escalating."

"I can't believe you told my sister without telling me. Why didn't you?" Eden demanded.

Chase scratched his head, with shame. "It's not a pretty story to tell, and definitely not to the woman you love. You're always going on about how I'm a good man. Well, I wasn't a good man that night and will forever be ashamed of my actions."

She turned over his words. Obviously, he was disappointed in himself. "What about the trip to Savannah that Tammy mentioned?"

Chase looked down at his arm where her hand still rested. He covered it with his other hand. "In preparation for the campaign and hopefully the position of mayor, I visited several mayors around the state to educate myself. While in Savannah, Tammy showed up at my hotel door one morning as though nothing had ever happened. In her mind, we were still this happily engaged couple. I tried to make her remember the present, but she grew extremely angry and agitated. She ran away, swearing obscenities. I phoned her parents about her behavior, and they were definitely surprised by her actions. They told me after leaving the sanitarium three years before; Tammy was able to lead a normal life in another city with the assistance of medication. They feared she'd stopped taking her prescriptions."

"So she has retreated back into her own little world?"

"Yes. I realized right away she must have followed me to Savannah. But for months I saw no sign of her being in town. I thought her parents had located her and gotten her back on the medication. When Taylor contacted the Johansens after I received a call from Tammy, they said they were unaware she had returned to Hilton. They have someone looking for her." He reached into his pocket and removed his cell phone. "We should probably call Taylor to learn the latest on Tammy, and you can talk to her to confirm my story."

Eden took the telephone without hesitation. She desperately wanted to hear the woman was in custody. "I don't need my sister to confirm your story. I believe you, but I would like to know the latest information."

Chase made sandwiches while Eden talked to her sister. He was thankful she had believed him, because he couldn't imagine his life without her. He heard the telephone call end and turned toward the entrance as she walked in. She still held the cell phone. Her eyes met his as she moved toward him. His heart beat rapidly with anticipation.

"Taylor asked that I tell you she and Stanley have met with the press. The record has been set straight. Tammy is now with her parents and will be receiving her medication."

"That's good. I hope she sticks to them this time." He watched and waited for her to address their personal situation. When he could take the silence no longer, he approached the subject. "What about us? Are we going to be all right?"

Eden leaned against the counter. If they were going to have a future together, there had to be complete honesty. "We can't build a future by keeping secrets from each other. We have to trust the other person to understand our mistakes and not to judge."

"I agree."

"I need to know one last thing." She met and held his gaze. "Why did you pursue a relationship with me? We didn't share similar lives, or the same friends, so what was the attraction?"

"I pursued you because you appealed to the man inside of me. I pursued you because my heart recognized you as my other half. I pursued you because I couldn't think of the future without you in my life." He was now standing directly in front of her. "I love you, Eden, and want to marry you."

Eden moved into Chase's arms and sighed when they closed around her. "I love you, too."

"And what about being my wife?"

She laughed against his chest. "Yes, I'll be your wife, but if you ever keep anything from me again, you'll answer to me." She swatted his backside.

"I never knew you were into spankings," Chase said close to her ear. He felt extremely blessed to have her in his arms.

"Oh, be quiet and kiss me."

"Gladly." Chase lowered his mouth to hers and sighed. The feel of her lips beneath his was like coming home. He had been afraid of losing her. He swept his tongue into the warm interior of her mouth, stroking and feasting off her honeyed sweetness. His hands slid down her back while his mouth ignited the flames of desire. He held her firmly against him and allowed her to feel what having her in his arms was doing to his body.

Eden pushed against Chase's chest. He was moving a little too fast for her. She was still processing the fact that he had been planning a future with someone else. And what about the stalking? "I can't. Not tonight."

"What?" Chase asked, releasing her. He looked rejected. "You no longer want me?"

She shook her head as she placed her hand on his chest. "You have no idea how badly I want you, but my emotions are a little jumbled. I need to come to terms with the fact that you were planning a future with another woman." She looked at him, hoping he understood.

Chase covered the hand on his chest. Looking directly at her, he nodded. "Know that I have never loved any woman the way I love you. I hope we can get past this and back to the life we were making together."

"Just give me tonight."

"Precious, you can have all the time you need. I'm not going anywhere." He kissed her quickly. "I've made sandwiches, and you need to eat."

"I am hungry," she admitted. She allowed him to lead her to the table. Taking the chair that he pulled out for her, she held onto his hand as he started to walk away. "I love you, Chase." She needed for him to know that. "And just for the record, I still think you're a wonderful man."

After a casual meal of sandwiches and another hour of talking, Chase went to bed. Eden, after a shower, sat wrapped in her robe in the living room, looking out of the large window onto the majestic mountain range lit by the moonlight. How beautiful, she thought as she glanced around the large room that served as living room, kitchen, and dining room. A large stone hearth was the focal point of the room, but competed with the spectacular view out the large window.

She rose from the sofa, realizing what she wanted most out of life was in the next room. Okay, so she hadn't been the only woman he'd loved. She was the woman in his life now, and the one he wanted to marry. They had both made mistakes; however, one mistake she didn't intend to make was letting that man in the other room get away.

She eased into bed beside Chase. She scooted closer and wrapped an arm around him. A kiss was placed on his shoulder as she settled in. Chase rolled over, facing her. His fingers trailed over her face while his eyes conveyed all the love in his heart.

"Will you hold me?"

"Come here, baby," Chase said as he opened his arms to her. She too was nude and so nothing was between them, as their hearts beat against each other. He didn't need to make love with her to express his love. Just knowing she had come to bed nude, trusting him to be a man of his word, spoke volumes. He held her for several minutes before they both finally gave in to sleep.

The next morning Chase stood under the shower, which had a window view of the mountain range below. An unusual feature for a shower, but in this rustic, private setting, it added to the experience of mountain living. The stall door was opened as Eden stepped in. She smiled at him as she walked into the spray of the dual showerheads. She picked up the bar of soap and built up a lather. Her hands moved over her flesh while he watched. His breath hitched as her fingers glided over her breasts and around the dark nipples. Licking his parched lips, he watched as a hand swept lower over her body, raising suds. His body instantly responded to her actions. He ached for her, but was determined to honor her request for time.

Eden's eyes roamed over his body, paying particular interest to that part of him, demanding her attention. "Are you going to stand there with that thing pointing at me, or are you going to help me rinse the soap off?"

"Are you sure about this? I don't want you doing something that your heart isn't into. I'm a patient man."

Her eyes raked over his lean, muscular, and wet body. Even with his dark hair slicked back and wet, Chase Mathews was the best looking man she knew. "But I'm not a patient woman." She reached into the soap dish and retrieved the condom she had deposited there, waving it at him. "I want you."

"Then you're about to have me, darling," Chase crooned as he pulled her into his arms. He hadn't noticed the condom, but was pleased not to be forced to spoil the moment. His tongue eased into her mouth at the same time he entered her body. He held her against the stone shower wall, with her legs wrapped tightly around his waist, and thrust in and out of her. Their lovemaking was fiery and desperate. Their insatiable passion became a cornucopia of pleasure as they moved from the shower to the bedroom. By the time they climaxed for the last time, noon had come and gone, and both were starving for nourishment.

Eden lay beneath Chase's gasping body. Her hands caressed his back and lower. She laughed when the muscles of his hips tightened in her hands. "Easy big fellow. I couldn't take another round without food first."

He smiled down on her. "It might be months before my body replenishes itself."

"I hope not, because after the election, we're getting married, and I'll be expecting you to be in top form for the honeymoon."

Chase rolled, taking Eden with him. He lay on his back looking up at her. "I can't wait for that day."

The barking of Eden's cell phone pierced the air. They looked at each other, groaning. It suddenly stopped ringing, and then rang again. They looked at each other, both sensing something was extremely wrong. Eden jumped up and raced into the living room. She located her cell phone on the kitchen table. Checking the screen, she flipped it open and hit speakerphone.

"Taylor, what's wrong?"

Chapter Twenty

Tammy slipped away from her parents," Taylor said, "and her current whereabouts are unknown. When they located her in a hotel in Atlanta, they found the room trashed, the furniture slashed and torn and the wood gouged and kicked in. But get this. The police found four Teddy bears, neatly arranged on the bed. Her and Chase's name were stamped on the T-shirts of two of the bears. The other two possessed a boy's name and a girl's."

"She's created a family," Eden whispered, suddenly frightened.

"This woman is potentially dangerous. I want you two to stay where you are and be extra careful."

Chase took the phone back. "Taylor, this is Chase. We should be safe here. Tammy doesn't know Stone or about this cabin. And, I won't allow anything to happen to your sister."

"I want you both to be careful," Taylor told him. "The entire state is looking for Tammy. With any luck, she'll be located before you return."

"Keep us informed."

"I will and take care of my sister."

Chase had every intention of keeping Eden safe, but the mood was lost as reality returned with full force. They showered quickly, ate a late breakfast and around two o'clock, Chase suggested a walk along one of the trails behind the cabin. Eden was all for it. After learning of Tammy's make-believe family and that she may be potentially dangerous, she was starting to feel caged in. Fresh air was just what she needed to help relax her and clear her mind. So hand-in-hand, the couple hit the trail that wound through the picturesque forest. The smell of evergreen and wildflowers scented the air. Small creatures scurried about in front of them, adding to the music of the forest.

After two hours of walking, they came to a clearing that ended in a sharp cliff overlooking a small stream. The location was beautiful. They decided to rest and eat their snacks before turning back. But it was also a little dangerous if one stood too close to the edge of the cliff. No railing or natural rock cropping would prevent a potentially deadly fall. However, Eden had no intention of getting too close to the edge. She shook off her backpack and removed the sandwiches and snacks that she carried. Chase removed a small blanket and spread it in the middle of the grassy spot where the sun poked through the canopy of trees. The air was a little cool now that they had stopped walking. The sun would help to warm them. He removed two bottles of water from his backpack and handed one to Eden.

"I was thinking that maybe we could locate a piece of property and build a house up here," Chase told her.

"If you're elected, we'll need an escape from the city."

"So, you think we should build up here?"

"Yeah, I do. The views around here are breathtaking."

"When we get back to the cabin, let's go into town and do a little shopping."

"Sounds wonderful. I hear there are some unique finds in the shops."

"Well eat up, so that we can get to it," Chase ordered as he took his last bite. He downed the remaining of his water, then stood and walked toward the edge of the cliff. "The view down below is spectacular."

"I'll take your word for it." Eden remained where she sat.

"Come on, you have to see this. You can see a few deer at the stream."

"Chase, I am not leaving this spot unless it's to retrace our steps. That ledge makes me nervous."

"What do you think is going to happen?" He turned looking at her. They'd had a wonderful day walking the trail. They'd also talked more about the Tammy situation. Eden had helped to ease his guilt over a bad decision. She pointed out that everyone made mistakes, but without them, people wouldn't learn valuable life lessons. She was pretty wonderful. "Baby, I'll hold your hand."

"Who's going to hold your hand?" Eden shook her head adamantly. "The view is fine from here."

Chase returned to the blanket. "Are you afraid of heights?" His voice held surprise.

"Will you love me less if I say yes?"

A small smile formed on his lips. "Of course not, but the only way to get over a fear is to confront it."

"That's a lie. I flew to Texas once for a funeral of a family member, and I was still scared to death. The flight cured nothing, confirming my decision to stay safely on the ground."

Chase roared with laughter. He had never heard Eden speak this way. She was always so positive and upbeat, always encouraging others to do. "Fear of flying is a different type of fear."

"Planes fly high in the air, and I don't like being high in the sky. This ledge is beautiful from here, but over where I can see just how high above the forest floor we are, it isn't beautiful, but terrifying. I can enjoy the beauty of the mountains with no problem from here. It's the visible drop offs that cause me problems."

"Let me help to confront your fear." He held out his hand to her. "I promise not to let you fall."

Eden continued to shake her head no, until she realized he wasn't going to let her succumb any longer to her fear. "All right," she said finally relenting. "But, if I fall and kill myself, I'm coming back for you."

Chase laughed at the absurdity of the statement. "You do that, sweetheart, now come on and enjoy the view."

She placed her hand in his, and they slowly walked to the edge of the ledge. The sound of the water below taunted her as she took her first peep over the side. She immediately pulled back. Gathering her wits about her, she leaned forward once again, this time listening to Chase's voice as he pointed out some deer down below, as well as a log home with horses in a coral. She had to admit it was a beautiful sight. Before long, she was really appreciating the view. But a noise behind them caught her attention. She glanced back over her shoulder but didn't see anything.

"Did you hear that?" she asked Chase.

"No, what was it?"

"I don't know. I guess I'm a little jumpy." Shaking off, yet another fear, she looked once again over the side of the ledge.

Snap.

This time they both turned around as they realized something or someone was behind them. The sight of their intruder staring back at them caused their blood to run cold. Eden gripped Chase's arm, realizing they had nowhere to run. The ledge was behind them and their only escape was directly behind the intruder.

"Don't make any sudden movements," Chase warned Eden.

"What are we going to do?"

"Try to remain calm. If we panic, she'll panic, and we don't want that."

Their intruder stood there for several minutes without moving. Her dark eyes watched them as though sensing their fear. She taunted them. She suddenly moved slowly to the right, and then stopped. She stood in the middle of their blanket and once again leveled her dark eyes on them.

Eden's grip tightened on Chase's arm. They waited to see what the intruder would do next.

Suddenly, the dark eyes seemed to grow darker as the intruder raised her weapon in their direction.

"Oh, no!" Eden screamed as the intruder took aim.

Chase pushed Eden out of the line of fire at the very moment their intruder fired her weapon. He took the full blast in the chest, and then watched as the intruder ran back into the forest.

Eden howled with laughter while covering her nose. "Oh, my God, you stink!"

"That's what happens when someone screams and scares the hell out of a skunk," Chase roared back. He immediately began removing his clothing. Thankfully, he was wearing heavy jeans and a long sleeve shirt. The odor was like nothing he had ever smelled before. Removing his personal effects from the pockets, he left the clothing right where they fell.

Eden removed her over shirt and handed it to Chase. "You can tie it around your waist. I would hate for you to scare off any more animals." She continued to giggle as they marched back toward the cabin. Small animals ran in the opposite direction as they approached. The sight of Chase in boxers and hiking boots was enough to send her into another round of laughter.

When they reached the cabin, Chase went around the back to the outside shower. Eden had wondered why anyone would have such a thing, but under the circumstances, it became clear it was used to avoid tracking muck and grime back into the cabin. In this case, it would be skunk.

"I need you to go inside and locate the hydrogen peroxide, baking soda, and liquid detergent," Chase told her. "Oh, and something to mix it in." He stripped out of the remainder of his clothing and stood under the spray of the shower.

"What are you going to do?"

"The mixture will help to counteract the chemical element of the skunk. Now go before I decide to come out there and kiss you."

"I'm gone."

Eden heard Chase chuckle behind her. She entered the cabin and ran into the bathroom, searching for peroxide finding it under the vanity. The kitchen was next. Grabbing what she needed, she returned to the bathroom for a washcloth and towel. Letting herself out the bedroom door, which opened near the outside shower, she followed Chase's instructions for mixing the ingredients.

After an hour of scrubbing and mixing, he finally emerged from the shower, smelling like a man again. His skin was slightly red from all the scrubbing, but other than that, he was back to his old self. He returned inside to find Eden at the stove cooking. He inhaled the aroma of smothered steak and onions. His gut rumbled with hunger.

"Now will you kiss me?" He wrapped his arms around her waist.

Eden turned in his arms to face him. "Gladly." She pressed her mouth to his.

Chase pushed Eden away and began sniffing the air. His eyes twinkled with mischief. "You know, you could use a little of that concoction yourself."

"You skunk. Are you telling me I stink?" Her eyes were wide and dancing with laughter. She punched him playfully in the chest.

"Is that anyway to treat the man who took a direct spray from a skunk for you?" He pressed kisses along her neck. She had never smelled sweeter.

Eden laughed as she wrapped her arms around his neck. "How did you know how to get rid of the scent?"

"I remembered my grandfather mixing it up to clean one his hunting dogs. I guess it stuck."

"Thank goodness you remembered it, because I didn't have a clue what to do." They shared a laugh. "I had a good time today, despite the skunk."

"So did I. But, unfortunately, after tomorrow, I should probably return to do damage control. I'm hoping Tammy will have been located by then."

The next day, they strolled the streets of Gatlinburg. They mostly window-shopped, but Eden managed to find a few unique items for the home they would share together. They agreed she would move into his home. Chase had informed her that her name would be added to the property as joint owner. She hadn't expected the gesture, since it was family property. Her heart and mind was now set on turning it into their home. The place where they would one day raise a family together.

Chapter Twenty-One

C hase and Eden returned to Hilton around one in the afternoon. After dropping off their luggage at their respective homes, they drove straight to campaign headquarters. Chase had phoned ahead and asked Taylor to meet them. He needed to know the latest on Tammy. Stanley would provide the information on the state of his campaign. They entered the office and were greeted by the volunteers. Stanley met them on the floor and informed them that Taylor waited in Chase's office.

"Thanks for meeting me, Taylor," Chase said as he entered.

"Not a problem. I'm glad to see you both are well." She accepted her sister's hug. "You look pretty cheery," she whispered under her breath to Eden.

"We'll talk later."

The sisters smiled at each other. Eden took a seat on the sofa while Taylor had the floor.

"This is the latest photograph of Tammy," Taylor said, handing the five-by-seven to her sister.

Eden stared down into the porcelain white face of the woman Chase had once considered himself in love. Blonde hair and blue eyes, she was the epitome of white America's concept of beauty. She looked at Chase, envisioning the two of them together. No doubt they would have made a beautiful couple. But, damn it, Chase was hers and Tammy Johansen would just have to get over it. She gave the photograph to Chase and watched as he glanced down at the image. Something resembling guilt washed over his face, then disappeared just as suddenly. She watched as he gave the picture to Stanley, and then listened as her sister began speaking.

"Tammy Johansen is still out there. In what mental state we aren't sure. A report was filed of someone lurking around your home." She looked at her sister. "But by the time we arrived on scene, the person was gone. Unfortunately, Hilton PD doesn't have the manpower to sit on an empty house."

"Did a neighbor get a description? Could they tell who the intruder was?" Eden asked, frightened.

"No they couldn't. All they saw was a shadowy figure in the darkness. Mr. Denny's German Shepard alerted him to the fact someone was in your yard."

"Eden, you'll be staying at my place until Tammy is located," Chase told her in a tone that didn't invite a rebuttal.

"Good idea," Taylor agreed. "In these types of cases, it's best to be safe. You never know what is going to set someone off."

"Do we know why she stopped taking her medication?" Chase asked.

"The standard answer, according to her parents, is that Tammy didn't like the way the medications made her feel. But with any luck, we'll locate her without anyone being harmed, including her."

"How did Mr. Nelson find out about Tammy? Is there any chance he's helping to hide her?" Eden asked.

"Evidently, Alison knew about Tammy, and when she signed on to the Nelson campaign, she informed him about her. We questioned him about Tammy's whereabouts, but he swears he doesn't know where she is. I believe him. With the IRS hot on his trail, and now this public outing that has turned into a lie, his reputation has taken a serious hit. He fired Alison. Then in traditional Nelson style, he tried to blame everything on her."

Stanley jumped into the conversation on that note. "The polling numbers are in our favor, but Nelson is playing the sympathy card by trying to connect us with Alison."

"What?" Chase asked, dumbfounded. "I didn't even know Alison knew about Tammy.

"Neither did I. Obviously, the young woman did a great deal of eavesdropping, but nonetheless, he's claiming Alison was a plant by us to discredit him."

"He can't be serious?" Eden interjected. "To think our parents

222

considered him a family friend."

"Dad considered him a friend. Mom never liked the man."

Eden looked at her sister with surprise. "And how would you know?"

"I read people, observe their body language, and listen to what they say."

"The makings of a good cop," Chase added.

They talked for several minutes more before Taylor announced she had to head back to the station. Eden walked her sister out.

"So the mountains were that good?" Taylor said low and teasing. She looked at the blushing smile on her sister's face.

"After some pretty heated words were exchanged, we got down to making up." Eden winked at Taylor. "Oh, and then Chase got sprayed by a skunk."

"A skunk?"

Eden doubled over laughing. She quickly told her sister about their adventure. Chase heard the laughter and knew what the women were discussing. He cut a quick path toward the door.

"Are you two having a good laugh at my expense?"

Taylor looked at Chase and tried to sober. "We're laughing with you."

"Sure you are. I thought I was being chivalrous when I stood there and took the blast." He glared at Eden.

"You're right of course. You were gallant, and I shouldn't be laughing."

"You're both crazy," Taylor commented. She actually envied their love. "I'll see you both later."

Eden wrapped her arms around Chase's neck. "You were wonderful on the trail."

"Oh shut up and kiss me."

"All right you two, we have an election to win," Stanley said, coming up behind them.

They returned to Chase's office, where Stanley discussed the plan of attack leading into the election. Eden was given instructions to contact the press and alert them to Chase's return to Hilton. She was also told to schedule a meeting with the press, so that Chase could discuss his involvement with Tammy in person. As for Chase, Stanley gave him a schedule of upcoming appearances: the most important being a debate with Nelson at the local community college on Monday. Stanley had drafted some of the staff to assist him with prepping Chase for the debate. Now all they needed was for Tammy to be located and returned to her parents.

Hilton Community College Auditorium was a hub of activity. All of Hilton appeared to have turned out for the mayoral debates. Both candidates waited in the wings to be announced. A panel from local television and radio would ask the first hour of questions, and then a select few from the audience would be given an opportunity to ask questions the remaining hour. The Mathews were present as well as the Warners. Eden and Stanley sat on the front row nervously. No matter how one practiced, you never knew how a person would respond to the real thing. Nor did you know what questions would be asked.

The candidates were finally announced with an equal amount of applause for both candidates. The men were each given a set time to make their opening remarks to the public before the questions began. Camden had won the toss backstage and would be going first. He outlined his agenda of commercial development and affordable housing, both seemingly reasonable goals. He only forgot to mention that the condominiums he supported under the heading of affordable housing were more businesses than homes, and the majority of Hilton's citizens couldn't afford to live in them. He also elected to forget that in order to build the condominiums, rezoning of current residential neighborhoods would have to be changed. This act alone would stick high-rise complexes in the heart of family-based neighborhoods. Instead of looking out at trees, people would be looking up at steel and glass towers.

Chase followed with his agenda of education and the increase in technological jobs. He spoke of his partnership with the local business community to get more funding for teachers into the classroom and aides to assist them. He drew the connection between better education, higher salaries, and the decrease of crime, which leads to a stable home environment. He cited programs utilized in other Georgia cities that had been proven to work. The time came for the panel to start asking the tough questions.

Both men handled themselves quite well. The debate heated up when the public began asking the questions. Integrity, unity, and ethics questions had Camden struggling hard to defend his public displays of hostility toward the Mathews camp. But in true Nelson style, he managed to pull his backside out of the fire. Chase tackled each question head on. He was poised and unruffled as he answered each question clearly and with an honesty that resonated throughout the room. Despite the verbal barbs hurled by the opposition, Chase maintained the high ground and stuck to the issues.

Eden sat in the audience, extremely proud of her guy. He had proven himself worthy of being mayor, despite his age and his privileged background. Tonight the people got to see the man she knew and loved.

The days after the debate were a whirlwind of appearances and speaking engagements. Eden and Chase felt like ships passing in the night rather than a couple on the verge of marriage. She was up early coordinating his next appearance and making sure the press was there to cover it, while Chase was out late making the rounds and trying to garner votes. Both looked forward to tomorrow and getting back to a semblance of normalcy. However, Eden knew that when, not if, Chase won the election, normal was about to change.

Chase awakened to the smell of breakfast. Opening his eyes, he was surprised to see Eden standing by the bed with a tray in hand.

He smiled at her as he pushed into a sitting position.

"What's all this?"

"Breakfast for the new mayor."

He chuckled as he threw back the covers and walked into the bathroom. "I'm not the mayor yet, honey."

"Oh, but you will be by the end of the day." Eden placed the tray in the middle of the bed, then sat on the edge and waited for his return. "Haven't you been reading the newspapers? The polls indicate the public loves you."

"The public can be fickle," he said, returning to the bedroom after brushing his teeth and washing his face. He leaned over, giving Eden a kiss. Climbing back into bed, he reached for the cup of coffee on the tray. "It's going to be a long day. Have you eaten this morning?"

"Yes I have, now you should eat." She rose from the bed and began dressing.

Chase ate his breakfast while enjoying the view of Eden standing in lace undergarments. He could hardly wait for her to become his wife. But first things first. Today he had to win the election. As she stepped into her navy skirt and pulled on a sleeveless white shell, he sighed in protest.

"Come back to bed."

Eden looked at him and laughed. "Absolutely not. I have to cast my ballot for that sexy young candidate everyone's talking about." She stepped into her shoes and retrieved her purse. Going back to the bed, she leaned down, kissing him. "I love you," she whispered.

"I love you, too, and thanks for supporting my campaign. I know it cost you the job you love."

"Concentrate on the election." She smiled as she straightened to full height. "I'll see you later.

Eden arrived at her neighborhood polling place a little after it opened to a crowd of reporters. She left her vehicle and was immediately set upon. Microphones and cameras were thrust in her face as questions were hurled. Being as polite as possible, she pushed her way into the building. After depositing her ballot, she was met by area supporters of Chase's campaign. All wished him success. She finally left the building to return to her car and once again was forced to walk through the gauntlet of reporters.

"Ms. Warner, who did you vote for mayor?" a reporter yelled above the crowd. The question received a round of laughter.

"Gentleman, now you know a person's vote is private," she said jokingly. Over the months of working with the campaign, she had grown quite comfortable in their midst and was adept in charming them. "I expect to see each one of you tonight at headquarters." She reached her car and unlocked the door to get in.

"Who's going to win tonight?" another reporter screamed in her direction.

"The public will decide guys." She flashed a gracious smile.

On the other side of town, the scene was much the same as Chase and his family arrived at their local polling site. Cameras followed him inside and right to the curtain of the voting booth. When the curtain was opened a short time later, the cameras went along as he fed the ballot into the counting machine. Chase left the building and was met by supporters wanting to shake his hand. He then crisscrossed the city for last minute speeches. He ended his day by appearing on the evening news. Once the red light on the camera faded, the campaigning was officially over. The race for the mayor's office rested in the hands of the voters.

Chase returned to headquarters and received an enthusiastic round of applause. Family, friends, and volunteers had come to lend their support while they waited for the results to come in. Once again, food and drinks were supplied. The entire place was decorated in a sea of red, white, and blue. Each of the local networks had cameras set up off to the right of the podium that would either be used for an acceptance speech or a conciliatory speech.

He was met by his father and Adam Warner, who both shook his hand and wished him luck. His mother greeted him with a hug and whispered she had never been more proud of him. Eunice Warner followed with a hug of her own, saying he was definitely the best man running. Then his grandmother, whose blue eyes shimmered with pride, wrapped her arms around him and rocked back and forth. She told him in a voice only meant for his ears, that he had done his grandfather proud. Eden brought up the rear and kissed him with all the love she felt in her heart. Caressing his face, she expressed her love and her pride in the manner in which he had conducted his campaign. By the time he had received and absorbed the love around him, Chase was overwhelmed to the point of being speechless. When he was able to talk past the lump in his throat, he spoke to the gathering.

"I would like to thank each and every one of you who has believed in me and my dream for this wonderful city. And to my family, both Mathews and Warners, your love and dedication have been my strength through the ups and downs of this campaign. Thanks for being there for me."

After another round of applause, people began to meander off. Chase reached out and pulled Eden into his arms, whispering low and intimately, "I'll thank you later."

"I'll hold you to that. Now go mingle."

She stood alone, observing the room crowded with well-wishers, all hoping to be associated with a winner. People moved in and out of milling circles all evening while waiting for the results. Chase stopped by as many of them as possible, personally thanking each one for joining him on such an important night. Then, at seven o'clock, the polls officially closed and thirty minutes later the results began coming in. The music stopped as the first results were revealed. With ten percent of the ballots counted, Camden Nelson was leading the race. The room collectively groaned, but it was too early to get concerned. The music started back as people began to socialize once more. Eden tried to smile and carry on small talk, but her heart just wasn't into socializing. By the end of the night, Chase would either be the new mayor of Hilton, or he would be returning to his company. She hated to think about the latter. He had poured his heart and soul into this election, and he deserved to win.

But as the next results came in and Camden was still in the lead, Eden became concerned. Was this to be a pattern of things to come? Did the public not care about ethics and fair play? She scooted off to her small office to await the next update. Her nerves had started to fray around the edges and she began to doubt her ability to be a politician's wife. The waiting to see if the public saw and respected the man she loved was unbearable.

"Stop borrowing trouble," Adam Warner said to his daughter as he stuck his head in. "Your young fellow is going to win."

Eden smiled at her father and hugged him. "From your lips to God's ears."

"You have to have faith in the system, baby." He held his daughter's hands, something he hadn't done since she was a little girl visiting his office. Once again, he was reminded of what he had missed, and what he would have missed if Eunice hadn't stepped in. "Come on back out here with your dad. You can't allow the press to think you're worried."

Eden nodded because he was right. "Okay, let's go. The best man is going to win tonight."

Chase spotted Eden with her father. The two had made their peace and found their way back to each other. He looked at his own father standing beside him and acknowledged that even if he were to lose tonight, he had ultimately been the big winner. He and his father were finally building that father and son relationship he had always wanted, and he had found the love of his life in Eden.

He glanced around the room of people, drawing on their energy. He had fought a good race and fought it the way he wanted. Despite the ugliness and the betrayal, he had managed to maintain his dignity. And as the next result came in, he saw the fruit of his labor as he surged ahead into the lead. This unexplainable feeling descended upon him as he felt confident of a win. But in one of the larger voting districts he and Camden split the ballots, yet he maintained a small lead. Eden returned to his side as though sensing the change in his mood. She didn't ask questions, only slid her hand into his and believed.

Taylor slowly crisscrossed the room. Always the cop, she was especially concerned tonight because the crowd was so thick. It would be easy for trouble to hide in the midst of bodies. As she came to a clearing on the left side of the room, Stone stepped into her path. Her heart beat with excitement. He had returned to the FBI building in Atlanta after assisting in clearing a case. The absence made her realize just how much she had come to care about him and missed having him around. But a new case, of the likes of which she prayed never to see again, had drawn him back to the department. Looking into his green eyes, she didn't try to hide her pleasure at seeing him.

"I was wondering if you were going to show tonight," she said.

"Good evening, Taylor, how are you?" Stone allowed his eyes to drink in her beauty. She looked especially wonderful tonight. She had left the slacks and jacket at home for the stunning little black dress she wore. The only question he had was where she was hiding her weapon? He trailed his eyes slowly down her body, thinking of the only place it could be, and groaned. He sure wouldn't mind being a cold piece of steel right about now.

"Just peachy, and you?" She hadn't missed the direction of his eyes.

"Better, now that I've seen you." He flashed a white smile that sent her tummy into somersaults. "Any sign of the Johansen woman?"

"No. All leads have dried up. It's possible she's left town."

"But you and I both know she probably hasn't"

"Right. But looking at those two ..." She nodded in Eden and Chase's direction. "They're so happy and in love, I hate to rain on their parade."

"Well don't," he whispered, slipping his arm around her waist. "You and I will be their eyes and ears this evening."

Taylor looked over at him. Stone Patrick was a good man, and from here on out, she wasn't going to fight what she was feeling. "I'd like that."

Around the buffet table, Skye tried to pretend not to notice David. She hoped he would make his way to say hello. She had thought of him since their last time together, but although he appeared interested, something was holding the man back. She turned in her stilettos and decided to take matters into her own hands.

David saw Skye advance in his direction with determination blazing in her eyes. The short little skirt she wore drew attention to her beautiful long legs. The woman was a firecracker, and he had the feeling once he gave in to what he was feeling, she would set his night on fire.

"Is there a reason you're ignoring me?" Skye asked, feeling bold and daring.

"No man could possibly ignore you," David said honestly.

Skye wasn't expecting that and turned just as suddenly, leaving him to watch her go. David's laughter could be heard behind her.

By nine o'clock, all local networks were staying on until the new mayor had been named. Eden stood with her arm wrapped around Chase's waist as the next results came up on the screen. For a while, the lead was too close to breathe. Then, as the ten o'clock hour approached, the tide changed. The numbers were beginning to stack up on Chase's side of the board. A roar went into the area, as all could smell a victory. With only one large district left to be counted, Eden was confident the voters would select Chase as their new mayor. Her heart beat with excitement. After all of her doubts and the mud slung by Camden, it appeared that the people of Hilton had proven her wrong and demonstrated that the only issues that mattered were a man's character and his ability to lead the city.

"The final ballots are in," the evening news anchor announced. "And it appears the people of Hilton have elected Chase Mathews as the new mayor of our city." The final ballot numbers flashed on the screen and the margin had grown substantially. The room erupted into cheers of joy and celebration. Chase pulled Eden into his arms and kissed her with excitement. His baby blues blazed with success and a sense of accomplishment. The charismatic, Mathews smile was in place and beaming with joy.

Celebratory balloons, streamers, and confetti began raining down on the exuberant crowd. There were people chanting his name, while others jumped and danced, others chose to link their hands and raise them in victory. Champagne was distributed throughout the room as Stanley made the first toast to the new mayor. Right afterward, a telephone call from Camden Nelson came through. Chase excused himself from the crowd to accept the customary conciliatory phone call. He wove his fingers through Eden's as he brought her along with him. After all the hell she had been through during the campaign, she deserved to be there with him when he accepted Camden's call. And in the vacant office down the hall a lone figure dropped down from the hiding place in the ceiling.

Chapter Twenty-Two

"Mr. Nelson, you fought a hard race, but I hope we can put everything behind us and work together to move Hilton forward," Chase said, extending an olive branch. His opponent had been humble in his conciliatory remarks, and now was the time to move forward. Chase finished up his conversation, and then turned to Eden who beamed with pride beside him.

"Having you believe in my dream has meant more to me than you'll ever know."

"I was honored to be a part of it. I'm so proud of you," she told him.

The two stood arm-in-arm smiling with happiness before returning to the party. As Chase opened the door and stepped back into the main room, the noise level grew with excitement and anticipation. The sea of bodies continued to grow as the celebration got officially underway. Balloons were being batted around in the air, while streamers hung from the ceiling, and confetti continued to rain down in a fine mist. The family was being corralled up front around the podium for Chase's acceptance speech. The energy in the room was contagious, and Chase looked infected with it. He smiled, and pumped a fist in the air as the crowd began chanting his name. The local network reporters stationed in the room captured the excitement for the city to witness. As he prepared to make his acceptance speech, all rushed for a good viewing spot.

Eden stood behind Chase, observing the enthusiasm in the room. People jostled for positions to see and be seen by the newly elected mayor. The networks' lights were bright, nearly blinding everyone in their path. She was so happy for Chase. His childhood dream had finally materialized. But as he took to the microphone, she tried to see down the road into their future. His new position would be demanding, not only of him but her as well. As his wife, she too would be called upon to serve the community, but she was ready. Her family was already well-known and quite active. The only difference this time would be that she was the mayor's wife. She glanced out over the crowd as Chase began to speak. A sudden movement of bodies caught her attention.

"This is truly one of the best moments in my life," Chase opened his speech. "To the citizens of Hilton, I'd like to say thank you for your votes of confidence in my ability to lead this fine city. You have embraced my message and endorsed the direction I want to move our city. You have also embraced Eden and I as a couple, and that in itself says so much about our great city." A grumbling of voices broke into his train of thought. He glanced into the crowd to see a surge of bodies down front. Dismissing the movement, he returned to his speech.

"To Mr. Nelson, I wish him the very best. To my talented campaign staff, led by the best manager ever, Stanley Elliot, you promised a win and you delivered. To my family behind me," he waved his hand to include the Warners, also around the podium, "I couldn't have done this without your love and support. To the volunteers who got out there knocking on doors and handing out buttons and flyers, you all will forever be a part of my family. To the wonderful friends who have come to celebrate with us, I thank you. Last but definitely not least." He turned toward Eden.

"She has a gun!" someone in the crowd screamed.

Taylor and Stone immediately sprang to action, removing their weapons and taking aim. They had deliberately positioned themselves on opposite ends of the stage. They now zeroed in on their target with dyed-brown hair. Security in the room controlled the crowd as they fled to the exit door to escape the potential danger inside. But as the woman continued to wave her weapon, it became clear who her target was.

Eden sucked in a breath as the muzzle of the gun stared her in the face. The beautiful blue eyes she remembered smiling in the picture were now cold and empty as they focused on her. She felt Chase's hand clutching her arm while they waited for the woman to make a move. Foolishly, Eden was aware of the cameras off to the side still filming. Her thoughts were of her students out there who would hear of her death on the morning news. But as the woman slowly walked closer, her thoughts returned to the present.

"Tell them who I am," the woman demanded of Chase. "And take your hand off that woman," she screamed out of control.

"Calm down, Tammy," Chase spoke quietly and with a calm voice. "I know you don't want to hurt anyone."

"No, of course not," she replied. "But everyone is saying I'm ill. That I'm crazy and need medication," she continued to ramble. "But I'm not." Her blue eyes looked to him for confirmation.

Chase slowly positioned himself in front of Eden. "No, you're not crazy," he stated the words loudly in support. "But someone could get hurt by that gun."

Tammy looked at him, weighing his words, and then looked at Eden just to his right. "I don't want to hurt anyone, but she has to go. She's telling everyone you're in love with her. And that's not true," she yelled angrily, while waving the gun.

Chase held out a hand to her and took another slide over in front of Eden. He had never wanted her short and petite as he did at that very moment. Her height nearly matched his, which made her difficult to shield. "She lies," he managed to say. "You know who I love." His voice dropped to an intimate whisper.

"I told them that, but they say I'm imagining it." She moved toward Chase, still pointing the gun in his and Eden's direction.

"Chase." Taylor warned from the side, but he waved her off. She took a quick glance at Stone, who also looked extremely concerned by the close range that the two now stood.

"It doesn't matter what they say. Do you remember the night I asked you to marry me?"

Tammy smiled dreamily as she heard their song playing in her head. "We danced all night." She began to sway from side to side.

"I want to dance again, Tammy. Will you dance with me?" Chase bowed before her as he had done that night. He held his hand out to her.

Tammy looked around the room, but didn't see the cameras filming or the police with their weapons drawn. She was back at the country club where he had proposed. But the sight of Eden brought her back to the future. She waved the gun once more. "You're trying to trick me. You're protecting her," she bellowed as though coming apart at the seams. "I should shoot you both," she said with an eerie steeliness to her voice.

Chase heard Eden gasp behind him and saw Taylor and Stone tighten their grips on their weapons. Tonight was to be a celebration, and he couldn't allow it to be tainted by death. Nor could he allow a woman whom he had loved and held a responsibility for her illness, be harmed. He moved further toward Tammy. They were almost within arm's reach of each other.

Taylor swore under her breath, as she could no longer take a clean shot at the woman. Stone was also hampered by Chase being in his line of fire. When this was over, he was going to be giving his friend one good butt whipping.

Eden was thinking the same thing if they survived. However, a part of her loved him even more because he was trying to spare a life. But in the process, he was giving her a heart attack, as she waited for Tammy's next move.

"If you kill her, then you and I have no future together. I don't want that. I want to visit all those places we talked about. Do you remember some of them?" He prayed rewinding to the past would be successful again.

Tammy giggled, startling everyone. "You were going to teach me how to ski, but I broke my leg trying to stand on them." She laughed, recalling the disbelief on his face when she informed him she thought her leg was broken. "You said I could break something simply by breathing."

Chase began to laugh as well. He remembered the time she spoke of. "As I recall, you broke your leg, a finger, and chipped a tooth on a bottle, all within a matter of weeks."

Tammy laughed even harder and lowered her gun. By the time she realized what she had done; Chase was on her wrestling for the gun. It hit the floor and landed between them. They both dove, but Chase managed to kick the gun away. He wrapped his arms around Tammy and hung on while she cursed, clawed, and kicked at him, before breaking down crying. Chase held her while she cried, then positioned his body between her and the camera. "Can you please turn those off?" he asked, only now remembering they were there.

His request was immediately complied with, as they all knew they had captured a powerful moment.

Chase held Tammy in his arms as he helped her from the floor, and then led her back to his office.

Eden nearly fainted with relief. The crisis was over and no one had been hurt. Stone had secured the weapon, while Taylor placed a call to the Johansens. Tammy would have to be taken down to police headquarters and processed. Eventually, because of her history of mental illness, she would probably be placed back in the sanitarium for further treatment. They all hoped she got the help she so desperately needed.

After the building had been cleared of the police, family, supporters, and reporters, Eden and Chase sat quietly alone. The elation he had experienced over winning the election had paled in comparison to his victory of saving a life. The citizens of Hilton got to see firsthand that they had indeed chosen the best man to lead their city.

As Chase stood waiting to take the oath of office on the steps of City Hall, he was keenly aware of the woman beside him. He had made good on his promise to thank her privately after the election, and two weeks later, she had become his wife. He recalled how beautiful she had looked when she walked down the aisle to join him in matrimony, and now knowing that she carried the fruit of their love beneath her heart, she was absolutely stunning. On this occasion, he was reminded of the politics of love. He had spoken the words to Eden to convince her of his love and dedication. However, they took on a greater meaning as they weathered through a nasty election and the threat of harm. But it was Eden who exemplified each line of the declaration.

Later that night in the privacy of their bedroom, he waited patiently for his wife. He liked saying that. He also liked having her permanently under the same roof. After the wedding, they had quickly merged their furnishings to create a home that reflected both their tastes. He had presented Eden with papers to the house, making her an equal owner. The act had caused her to cry because she knew what the house meant to him. Now, as he waited for her to join him, he thought of the life they would make together. She was headed back to the classroom in the fall, and then in early spring, they would welcome their child.

Eden walked into the bedroom and discovered Chase deep in thought. She stood there, watching him for several minutes. So much had happened in a short span of time, but through it all, their love shined through. Now she carried his child and couldn't be happier. The day she had told him of her pregnancy, the man had held her and cried with joy. She struck a pose in the doorway.

"Oh, Mr. Mayor, I have a little something for you," she purred sexily as she stood in a red sheer nighty with thong.

Very little, Chase thought as he devoured the image of his wife. He licked his lips as his eyes traveled from her red painted toenails to the simmering thong taunting him. "Well, come over here and give it to me." He held out a hand to her.

Eden strutted over to the bed, taking his hand. "Mr. Mayor, I love it when you take charge."

"Sweetheart, I haven't been in charge since the day you confronted me. You, Eden Mathews, have used weapons to steal my heart that I've never been up against before."

Eden wrapped her arms around Chase's neck and allowed him to lower her to the bed. Looking up at him, she whispered, "Haven't you heard that all is fair in the politics of love?"

Group Discussion Questions:

1. Eden was opposed to politicians using the public schools, and the children in particular to make campaign announcements. What are your feelings on the subject?

2. Do you believe it's possible for a Caucasian candidate married to an African American to be elected mayor in your city? How would you vote? Would race be a determining fact in how you cast your ballot?

3. Eden and Chase have a conversation about having children. Do you think biracial children face greater social challenges than other children? Place yourself in the role of the parent when your biracial child comes to you with issues of not fitting in. How do you handle the situation?

4. Both Eden and Chase are dealing with the dynamics of their families. Which family closely resembles yours? Did a parent influence your career choice? Explain.

5. How would you handle being the victim of sexual harassment on the job? Would you be strong enough to press charges against the person? Have you witnessed sexual harassment on the job and what was your response?

6. Was there a special teacher in your life and how did he/she influence you?

7. Which character did you find the most interesting and why?

About the Author

Giselle Carmichael was born into a military family. Now married to a career military man, she has lived from coast to coast, and several places in-between. Two years of living in England afforded her the opportunity to travel extensively throughout Europe. Her experiences as a military spouse have given her a perspective on love and relationships that is reflected in her writing. A finalist in the 2005 Gayle Wilson Award of Excellence Contest with *Lace*, her works include *Magnolia Sunset, Life Goes On*, a novella, and *I'll Be Your Shelter*. A native of Birmingham, Alabama she now calls the Hurricane Katrina-battered city of Biloxi home.

Giselle loves to hear from her fans. Visit her at www.gisellecarmichael.com.